THE SNOW ANGEL

THE SNOW ANGEL

ANKI EDVINSSON Translated by Paul Norlen

THOMAS & MERCER

Text copyright © 2021 by Anki Edvinsson by agreement with Grand Agency
Translation copyright (English edition) © 2023 by Paul Norlen
All rights reserved.

Previously published as *Snöängeln* by Norstedts in Sweden in 2022. Translated from Swedish by Paul Norlen. First published in English by Thomas & Mercer in collaboration with Amazon Crossing in 2023.

www.apub.com

Amazon, the Amazon logo, and Thomas & Mercer are trademarks of Amazon.com, Inc., or its affiliates.

ISBN-13: 9781662515989
eISBN: 9781662515972

Cover adaptation by kid-ethic
Cover image: © olaser / Getty Images; © Vadim Zakharishchev
© happykanppy / Shutterstock

Printed in the United States of America

Death is not the greatest loss in life. The greatest loss is what dies inside us while we live.

—*Norman Cousins*

1

Anton stared at the front tyre of his bike as it cut through the snow on the uphill climb, getting caught in rough furrows before lurching forward a moment later. His hands were damp and he could barely feel them gripping the handlebars. His heart was pounding hard in his chest. He gulped down the cold air with an open mouth, every breath aching in his lungs. He could feel the hill's steep incline in his legs, but he made it to the top where he could rest a little, watching his shadow in the dull glow of the streetlights. Far off and below him was the bridge.

Anton had to squint to see through the snowfall. The cold and wind stung his cheeks. In his imagination he'd always pictured that it would be summer when he did this – a late evening when everyone else was sitting in the grass getting drunk or swimming. He didn't know why. Now it was January, a Sunday evening. But it was time. The right time. Life would soon be over. His head was clear, and nothing mattered more than the bridge he was now rolling out on to. Anton had decided to liberate himself a long time ago but other things had got in the way. It was only when he woke up this morning that he knew. For some reason, the choice to jump was also clear. The bridge on the West Beltway had just been completed and it was the only one in the area that was high enough. Survival was not an option.

Now was the time.

Without a doubt.

The cramping started in his chest and spread throughout his body. He could not remember a single day when he experienced anything other than the anxiety that made his adrenaline surge. Usually it made him restless, every muscle in his body craving movement. Hands, arms, jaw, legs . . . But sometimes it was so intense that he had to lie down on the floor and let it work itself out. Or take tramadol or benzos. His chapped skin stung constantly, as if someone had dipped him in acid. Even so he showered several times a day; sometimes he cried because it simply hurt so much.

Now it was just him, the bicycle and the whiteness whirling around in the air. The further out on the bridge he went, the more the wind took hold.

Mum didn't understand a thing, Dad was a fucking wimp, and no one would ever get what he was going through. He'd thought about that as he'd left home, how Mum and Dad would react. The shock they would get.

Anton squeezed the handbrake and let one foot touch the ground. He wiggled his toes but couldn't feel them. Got off the bike and let go of it. He would be free of all this shit.

He looked out over the bridge. Grasped the railing. Dark was all around. The wind rushed past his ears, rustling his hair. He brought his hand to the inside pocket of his jacket. Took out the pills and with a quick movement threw them into the darkness. They no longer helped. They fluttered down from the bridge like butterflies in the wind. Nothing could help him now.

Anton had cycled across the bridges in Umeå many times and searched. Even if he hadn't been ready, there was consolation in planning. Feeling that he was coming closer to an end. Even when he was eight years old, he'd started wondering which bridge would be high enough. A kid at his school had jumped from the Kolbäck Bridge but failed. Still alive. Anton would not fail. He was prepared. He wondered whether Frida would miss him – cry and be absent from school.

He took firmer hold of the railing, raised his body up and swung one leg over, followed by the other. Left tracks in the snow that had settled like soft down over the steel. His nerves relaxed. The closer he came to his goal, the calmer he felt.

His butt touched the cold railing, melting the snow and soaking into his underwear. He was not afraid of losing his balance. He was going down anyway. When he was sitting steady he let his legs hang free. The height made his stomach contract. It was higher than he'd imagined, completely silent all around.

Anton took out his phone. The screen flashed. Frida. This time she wouldn't stop him. He threw the phone out into the air.

His eyes met mostly darkness; he didn't hear anything from the water below. Anton didn't know if it had frozen over completely, whether he would die by ice or water.

A car approached. Anton saw it in the corner of his eye. Didn't look at it. He didn't want to see anything else now.

He wondered whether it would be scary to fall down. To see death come closer, second by second. Would he be able to close his eyes? The thought made him hesitate a little. He didn't want to see but simply fall. Not feel. Anton waited until the car had driven past, then turned his body around. His back to the precipice, he arced into the darkness.

2

Charlotte was behind the steering wheel.

'Here it is! Turn left,' Anja said firmly, pointing with her whole arm so her mother wouldn't miss the exit.

Charlotte obeyed her daughter and turned on to the narrow street. Anja was spending the weekend with her in Umeå and they had come to The Island to view a property. Charlotte worked as a detective inspector at the Major Crimes unit and was used to taking orders, but not from her daughter.

Anja looked at her phone and let the navigation app guide them.

'We go straight ahead two hundred metres.'

Charlotte looked at her and smiled; she loved having Anja in Umeå. Anja had talked about moving here, changing schools and leaving her dad in Stockholm, but Charlotte hadn't dared hope too much. Anja was like Albanian currency – up and down a lot. But then she was seventeen years old, so that was natural.

To their right were snow-covered fields that had been developed with red Västerbotten estate homes, classically framed with white corners. To the left was the Ume River in winter garb and white wooden houses with private docks. It was five o'clock on Sunday evening and it was already dark. Charlotte suffered with the short days, when the sun went down at two thirty, but the snow was like a natural sparkling lamp and the whole city was lit up. The first winter she lived there she terrorized her friends in Stockholm with snow pictures. She'd stopped doing that now.

'Here, number six,' said Anja, and Charlotte slowed down, noting that the car had just warmed up nicely when it was time to turn it off. The instrument panel showed that it was twenty-one degrees Celsius below freezing outside.

Charlotte immediately recognized the house from the property website. It was their fourth viewing and she had high hopes because it was on The Island – an island in the middle of the Ume River, in the middle of town, with its own dock and a striking vista. Everyone in the police station talked about The Island, that it was Umeå's most unique place to live – and the most expensive. Some three hundred people lived here and Charlotte wanted to be one of them. The best thing about the house was that it was possible to move in immediately. The owners were no longer living there and wanted to be rid of the expense. She could sell the apartment in the city centre later.

'Seriously, Mum, this looks good,' said Anja, winding her checked scarf an extra turn around her neck.

Charlotte let her gaze linger on her daughter. The Burberry colours really suited her.

'We've been disappointed before, so we'll have to see what it looks like in there,' she replied, bringing her hand to the door handle.

Anja offered a demonstrative sigh.

'Maybe the psychologist you go to ought to teach you to think a little more positively,' she said, getting out of the car. Charlotte followed.

'You know why I'm in therapy now,' she answered, taking a few quick steps to catch up with her daughter. 'It's not as simple as becoming more positive. It's about things I've experienced, both at work and privately, that are hard to process.'

'Sure, I know, but—'

'Not now,' Charlotte interrupted, extending her hand to the estate agent who was coming over to them from the entrance. 'Hello, my name is Charlotte von Klint and this is my daughter Anja.' She gripped the man's hand firmly.

'Welcome,' the agent said with a limp handshake. 'You two are our last viewing for today so there's no hurry.'

'How many have been here?'

The estate agent was smartly dressed in a green shirt that was barely visible under an even greener sweater.

'There are three people who are extremely interested and two who are going to think about it. It's not that often that this type of property is available on The Island.'

Anja took the lead into the house, her long hair hanging down her back, curling at the tips.

'Have you received any offers yet?' Charlotte asked.

'Yes, we have one at 10.5 million. You know, this house is unique. Epic.'

Charlotte looked at him. Wasn't that a rather odd choice of words?

She was an experienced property owner. She had bid on much more expensive homes than this property. The most expensive one was the apartment in Östermalm in Stockholm that now stood empty, but the house in Falsterbo hadn't been cheap either when she and Carl bought it, though she'd been awarded it at the estate division after the divorce. The home she missed the most, and which had stayed in Carl's family's possession, was the castle in Skåne. The calm that prevailed there, the magnificent rose garden and the wide expanses . . . that was the only thing she missed about him. Everything else was nice to escape. Like his constant nagging about how she ruined her life when she'd become a police officer. It took a long time before he stopped introducing her as a medical student after she quit the programme and jumped into the police academy.

She wondered whether the estate agent really had received an offer, or if that was a way to get the merry-go-round started.

'Why are you looking at houses, if I may ask?' the agent said, following Anja into the open kitchen.

'We live three hundred metres from the massacre at Gotthard's, and that's not cool,' Anja said before Charlotte could answer. She glared at her daughter, who was referring to the shooting that took place over a year and a half ago.

'Yes, what happened at that hotel was horrendous,' the estate agent said, leaning against the kitchen counter. He shook his head and looked at Charlotte. She was about to change the subject when he continued talking.

'But aren't you a police officer? I remember you from the newspapers. Is that right?'

Charlotte turned her back to him and faced the large panoramic windows in the living room with a view of the river. The snow-covered dock looked pristine.

'Correct,' she replied. 'Is the dock new?'

'Yes, it was constructed in September of last year. Barely used. Everything is documented.'

He left the kitchen island and came toward her through the living room. When he was standing beside her she detected a scent she thought was Hugo Boss, the same that her colleague Per used.

'What's your theory about all the shootings that are happening in this country nowadays?'

'Do you want to sell a house or talk about crime? You decide,' she said without taking her eyes from the view. 'We can leave.'

The estate agent laughed. 'Oh, no, sorry. The whole city is talking about everything that's happening, so I thought . . . Well . . . Excuse me. Now, let's talk house. Come along and I'll show you the rest of it.'

He jumped back to his sales pitch and Charlotte let him talk about the house without asking any counter-questions. She already knew that she was interested, but wanted to check with Per and his wife first to get their opinion. Anja was somewhere else in the building when Charlotte received a text message.

Mum, I love this house. Let's buy it! Please!

Charlotte smiled to herself. She was happy that Anja hadn't said that in front of the real estate agent at least. Then her negotiating position would have been considerably weaker. She wrote an answer on her phone.

Come on. Time to leave. We can talk more later.

They said goodbye to the man and got in the car. Anja tapped feverishly on her phone. Snapchat. She had stopped texting with her friends long ago – now they just tapped off pictures of whatever, wrote a short message at most and sent.

Charlotte backed out from the car park and searched with her index finger for the button on the underside of the steering wheel that would make the car pleasantly warm. She saw how Anja brought the phone closer to her face. Stared at the display.

'Oh my God . . . What the hell?' she said, snapping a picture of herself.

'What is it?' Charlotte asked, without expecting a response.

'Wait,' Anja replied, her fingers moving quickly over the screen as she wrote.

Charlotte guided the car toward the city and their apartment. It had been snowing heavily during the day and the road was bumpy. They ended up behind a snowplough pushing masses of snow to the side of the road. The snow drifts must have been over a metre high.

They know their snow removal, Charlotte thought. In Stockholm this amount of snow would have created chaos, but here in Umeå everything went on as usual.

Anja placed the phone on her lap and leaned her head against the headrest. Sighed.

'Has something happened?' Charlotte asked.

'Mm. You know my friend here in Umeå – Linn?'

'Yes . . .'

Charlotte tried to sound calm but she felt the worry in her gut at once.

'She knows a guy named Anton, who is really strange. A little suicidal, kind of, and now he's been acting weird. Quit his strange rituals.'

'Who's saying this?' Charlotte asked.

'Linn, she's saying it now on Snapchat.'

'What kind of strange rituals?'

'So, she says that he, like, showers several times a day, refuses to shake hands with people and one time he stopped his bicycle on the sidewalk and got hysterical because a dead bird was lying there. He couldn't go past it because then he would get the bird's germs on him. How weird is that?'

Charlotte looked at her daughter. The conversation was going in a direction that didn't feel good.

'It sounds like he suffers from obsessive compulsive disorder – OCD. That creates compulsive, anxious thoughts.'

Anja shrugged her shoulders. 'Maybe so. Linn says that he takes a lot of drugs, like Frida.'

'Who is Frida?'

'Linn's best friend. I've met her a few times. She's in her first year at the Dragon School. There are a lot of rumours about her.'

'Like what?'

'That she does drugs and such . . .'

Charlotte's gut feeling was right. She passed the snowplough, which sprayed snow over the bonnet and windscreen.

'Those sound like serious rumours,' she said, turning on the windscreen wipers. 'Even more serious if there's truth to them. I'm not comfortable with you socializing with her friends if those rumours are true.'

'Oh my God, knock it off,' said Anja, the glow from her phone lighting up her face.

Charlotte knew very well that drug use was rampant at several schools in town. The detective unit even had personnel in the corridors.

'If they're true, someone has to contact her parents and inform the school.'

'Mum, do you have any idea how many of my friends are depressed and take, like, benzos, trammies, Dolcontin and stuff? You can tell just by looking at them,' Anja replied, as if it were the most obvious thing in the world. She looked out the window.

Charlotte felt like she'd been kicked in the stomach. How could Anja rattle off the names of Schedule II narcotics as if they were various brands of snacks?

Anja held her phone up to Charlotte, who tried to look while driving.

'I can't see when I'm driving.'

They came to a traffic light and a few gentle snowflakes settled on the windscreen. *More snow,* she thought as Anja showed her the display again. It was a picture of a scantily clad young girl.

'Mum, this is Frida. The picture is from her Instagram. I mean, you can see in her eyes that she's, like, high.'

Charlotte looked at the girl with long ash-coloured hair. Her lips were pouted, and she was wearing a bra that did not leave much to the imagination. *A young girl who is testing the boundaries and needs a lot of validation,* Charlotte thought.

'Now you're being harsh, Anja. You don't know what her life is like. Don't judge other girls that way.' The phone in her back pocket started to annoy her. She took it out and placed it between the seats.

'In any case, her parents don't seem to care that much.'

'What makes you say that?'

'Her mum's an alcoholic and her dad is, like, addicted to gambling,' said Anja, suddenly sounding several years younger than she was, and with little empathy. A flash of light from the phone between the seats rescued Anja from a scolding. Charlotte angled the phone so that she could see the display.

A newsflash from a tabloid.

Leader of the Syndicates, Tony Israelsson, Released from Prison. Risk of Violence Escalating in Stockholm's Underworld.

The nausea in her abdomen came as a direct reaction. *Tony is out. Thank God I moved up to Umeå,* she thought, stealing a glance at her daughter who was thankfully now completely occupied with staring out the window.

3

Anton's mother was screaming at the police on her phone.

'He's on the bridge! Oh my God, our son is on the bridge!'

A dark figure sat on the bridge railing, looking up at the sky. Anton's bicycle was reflected in the light from their headlights as they approached. His back was bent like a C, and his hands were placed on the railing.

She stared at her husband in the car.

'Stop the car, Tomas! Stop!'

Her gaze went back to Anton on the railing. She pressed a hand against her mouth.

Tomas braked the car.

'Under no circumstances must you stop the car,' the policewoman said on the other end of the line. 'Drive past! We've sent officers. Your sudden presence may get Anton to jump. We have our negotiator with us, he knows what to do. Drive past – we're coming now.'

Tomas pressed the accelerator again. Cautiously.

'What are you doing? Stop the car, Tomas, we have to stop him!'

Her voice broke. She brought her hand to her head, running it slowly through her hair. An attempt to quiet herself, remain calm.

She breathed in. Held her breath. Only exhaled when her lungs demanded it. Wanted to crawl out of her body.

'Why didn't we listen? Just this time, when he was feeling bad. Stop the car!'

'You can't stop – drive past. We'll be there in three minutes.'

'In three minutes he may be dead,' she answered as the car glided past their son, who was sitting completely exposed. The slightest movement could topple him straight down. She wiped away the tears to be able to see him better. Anton let go of the railing and it appeared as if he was thinking – or praying.

'We can't just leave him . . .' She sobbed and looked at her husband. 'We can't just drive past!'

'The police know about these things. They're on their way. I'll turn around up here and then we'll drive back.'

He sounded calm, collected, but his hands were gripping the steering wheel tightly and revealed otherwise. His breathing was laboured and his movements jerky as he turned the car.

'We're coming in three cars but you must stay away,' the policewoman said. 'Let us take care of this.'

She did not take her eyes off Anton, but watched her son sitting on the railing. Tomas drove closer, slowly.

Snowflakes surrounded Anton in the air. It didn't look like he was cold.

She placed the palms of her hands against the window, bent both index fingers, tried to touch him through the glass. He was sitting right there. Why couldn't she rescue him?

She knew that it was almost forty metres down. He would never survive if he fell.

'I can't just stay here!' she shrieked.

She had to get out and pull him away from the railing.

'You see our car at the top of the hill? Please don't get out of your car!' The policewoman was shouting on the other end.

She ignored her completely. Tomas had turned off the ignition. He took a firm hold on her arm, trying to keep her from getting out, but his will was not as strong as hers. She tore open the car door and threw herself out. The wind made her hair swirl around her face. She squinted to keep the snowflakes out of her eyes.

'Anton! Anton!'

She screamed as her legs moved toward him. The wind was louder than her voice. She screamed again.

'Anton!'

The whiteness on the ground resisted her; he felt much too far away.

A car approached but she kept her gaze fixed on her son. Her voice made him turn his head to her. Just as quickly he turned it back and bent his face to the sky.

Then he disappeared over the railing.

4

Abbe used the crook of his arm to wipe the sweat from his forehead. The T-shirt stuck to his back despite the cold outside the window. He crouched before the young man in the chair, his knee cracking on the way down. He raised his hand toward the young man's face and let it strike the cheekbone. Considerably nicer than the previous blows. Abbe's black leather gloves had red spots on the smooth surface.

'Please, I don't know anything else, I promise,' the young man pleaded. His voice had reduced to a whisper as the assault got rougher. Abbe guessed that the young man was around twenty years old. His life would never be the same again. From his boyhood room in the affluent suburb of Lidingö to this shitty room on an estate in Mariefred. Abbe almost felt sorry for him. Blue-eyed and naive, he'd sold drugs and attracted the Syndicates' network and curiosity. The young rooster had delivered a rather considerable quantity of various narcotics, but he hadn't bought the drugs from the Syndicates. For that reason, on a late Sunday afternoon, he was now being worked over by Abbe, forced to answer questions.

With every blow Abbe delivered he hoped that the young man would talk, but it took a long time before he buckled and squealed like a piglet. He got his goods from Umeå, through a guy whose name was William. Several names were mentioned, especially one that made Abbe strike an extra blow. They knew where they should start their search.

'The kid has probably told us what he knows now,' said Abbe, turning to his boss, Tony. He had a particular henchman who usually took care of this type of task. Abbe hated when he had to step in; he was a bartender at Tony's club, not an assailant. But you didn't say no to Tony.

Tony took off his glasses and massaged the bridge of his nose. He looked like a kindly uncle, sitting in a chair that resembled a royal throne. Thin chest, his stomach concave, shoulders and hips like an eight-year-old. He was considerably more vicious than he appeared to be.

'Yes, it seems that way,' Tony replied, leaning against the velvet green back of the chair. He took out his phone. 'So we'll have to plan a trip to Umeå. I never would have figured that out. I would have guessed he bought from someone in southern Sweden.'

Abbe stretched his legs. *Damn it,* he thought, but kept the sentiment to himself. This was the worst conceivable scenario, Tony wanting to go to Umeå. He put his hands against his lower back and stretched. Stared at the stucco around the crystal chandelier in the ceiling, then again at the bloodied young man in the chair. He had emptied his bowels when he was dragged into the room with a hood over his head. Taken directly from the street and into the white van. No one who was delivered to the estate was allowed to see how you got there. Abbe hadn't tied him up. That hadn't been necessary.

With thumb and index finger Abbe took off one glove and met the young kid's gaze. He had given up hope of getting out of there alive. Terror was replaced with sorrow. Bloodshot eyes, hard lumps with cracks in the skin, blood working its way in between his teeth, a broken little finger that made his hand move jerkily.

Tony indicated with a slight head movement that he wanted to leave the room and Abbe followed. Left the crying young man in the chair unbound; he was too scared to dare do anything anyway. The floor creaked under Abbe's shoes as the wood bent under his weight. Tony stood in front of the open fireplace, which was black and cold. The room looked like a hall – gold chairs along the walls, several chandeliers, more rugs, uncomfortable couches, yellow wallpaper that seemed to be preserved from another time. Everything breathed wealth, old money.

'What do we do with him now?' said Tony, pointing to the little room. 'Shall we rub him out?'

'Let's let him go with a threat,' said Abbe. 'He's not going to talk.'

'He got beat up, he's going to talk,' said Tony, crossing his arms.

Abbe sat on a divan and massaged his knuckles.

'That kid in there is a rich man's Swede,' he said. 'An upper-class druggie who sells to his buddies on Östermalm. He's going to fabricate a lie that he was assaulted on the street if we tell him to do that. After that he's out of the game. Believe me. He'll want to crawl back into his mother's womb now. Let him go if he promises to keep his mouth shut, otherwise we'll come back and take out his mother, say that.'

'Damn, you're easy, like a fucking line of cocaine. But it doesn't matter. I trust you,' said Tony, imitating Abbe's accent. Tony thought he sounded like an immigrant kid and teased him often, even though he'd grown up in Bredäng outside Stockholm and lived in Sweden his whole life.

Tony pulled on the door, which creaked as it opened. At the same time a ringtone sounded from a jacket on the floor. The young man's. Abbe took out the phone. It said 'Mum' on the display. He turned it off.

'How the hell did you take over this shack?' Abbe asked, reaching for his sweater, which was draped over the back of a chair.

'This!' Tony said, laughing loudly. 'An aristocrat who bought my whores at the club. Gambled a lot, owed me money but couldn't pay off the debts, which was sad for me . . .'

'Sad? Why is that?'

'Ah, always good to be able to demand repayment of a debt from someone with contacts. You never know when such a service might be needed.'

Abbe looked out of the windows as they passed them. They were small in relation to the house and the glass made the landscape outside blurry.

'This place had been in his family's possession since some time in the nineteenth century. Felt fucking great to take it over,' said Tony, and the laughter echoed. 'A lot of land that gets put to good use.'

Abbe didn't want to know more about that.

'How would you have managed it if he had paid his debts?'

Tony stopped and turned to Abbe, who was a head taller.

'There were rumours that he liked young girls and slept with them here, among other things. There was talk that he smuggled them in through one of the wings when his wife was at home. Could have the girls there for days without her having a clue.'

Abbe clenched his jaw. Paedophiles made him boil over inside.

'One day the mistake came that I was waiting for. He asked me to get him a younger girl. Of course I arranged it, documented it and then bought this estate for a few million.'

'What's the value?' Abbe asked.

'Twenty-two million, with twelve acres of land.' Tony showed his yellow teeth. 'When we're finished up in the Umeå wasteland we'll have a party here to celebrate. I just thought of that. I'm a

18

genius. But first I'm going to finish what wasn't done before I spent six years in prison.'

Abbe fixed his gaze on Tony's gun, which was always in his waistband, like a caricature of a criminal.

'Pack your bag. We'll leave this evening,' said Tony.

Abbe let the air out of his lungs. He knew that the trip to Umeå would be the beginning of the end.

5

Viggo stared at the screen of his phone.

Leader of the Syndicates, Tony Israelsson, Released from Prison. Risk of Violence Escalating in Stockholm's Underworld.

Every muscle in his body stiffened. Tony was a free man. Viggo's eyes wandered between the screen and the edge of the table. He tried to analyse the situation. Viggo and his family were living in Umeå, Tony in Stockholm. Nothing indicated that Tony knew where Viggo was. Unless Abbe had told him.

He stole a glance at Estelle, who was sitting across from him at the dinner table. His wife was surprisingly sober this Sunday evening, but that would change if she read the headline about Tony. He was the reason she'd started drinking. After years of looking over her shoulder, she had developed anxiety and started self-medicating with alcohol.

Viggo put away the phone.

Their daughter Frida sat down at her usual place at the table. That chair was empty more and more often. She looked at the saucepan, which was full of spaghetti, ignored it and chose the salad bowl. As usual. He had stopped nagging her. She had just turned seventeen and Viggo couldn't bear to argue. He had given up because nothing he said or did changed anything. They just ended up arguing. Estelle said that it was about autonomy and that it had to work itself out, that it was normal, but Viggo wasn't so sure. Frida fought about literally everything she encountered. Wanted to have a reason to leave the house and disappear in anger. Sometimes it seemed as if she did it on purpose.

He looked at her. She set the thin lettuce leaves on the plate.

'Can't you eat a little pasta?' he asked, simply because it felt like the right thing to say. Viggo already knew the answer.

'No, it lies there like a lump of dough and my stomach swells up like a balloon.'

'You can't live on salad.'

Frida demonstratively tossed the salad tongs in the bowl but did not reply to the comment. Estelle looked up from the table to her daughter and smiled. Stroked her arm.

'Sorry,' said Frida, picking up a spinach leaf and putting it in her mouth. Viggo looked at her hand. One knuckle had a little sore with a thin scab. As if she'd run into something.

'What did you do to your hand?' he asked.

'Nothing.'

'But you have a sore there,' he said, pointing.

Frida leaned back against the chair, ran her hands through her hair.

'Dad, it's nothing. Okay? Stop worrying about everything.'

She seems to be doing fine at least, he thought.

Frida had also been strongly affected by life in hiding. All because of his crazy decisions. As a youngster she was always being moved around to new homes and cities. Viggo's guilty conscience meant that Frida got away with everything. As an only child she had no competition for attention, yet it felt as if she always needed more.

He looked at his daughter. She moved the fork around the salad on the plate while she poked at her phone.

'Frida, can't you put away the phone at the dinner table?'

She looked up. Set it alongside the plate. 'Satisfied?'

He laughed. *Always defiant,* he thought.

'Are you happy in Umeå?' he asked.

She shrugged her shoulders. 'What choice do I have?'

Viggo had no answer.

The day when Tony had been sentenced for a series of crimes, they decided to stop moving around and settle down in Umeå. They had lived calmly for so many years that he himself had almost forgotten his past. He still played poker but only on the internet, mostly on closed sites that were invitation only. A precautionary measure. But sometimes he missed the sound of the cards being shuffled and the ego trip of being at the heart of it all. Or the chance to be able to read his opponents' facial expressions. Viggo had made a lot of money on his talent and had no need for more, but it was hard to completely go without the excitement and feeling of winning. That was how the mess had started, when Viggo was a winner and got to know Tony at his gambling club in Stockholm. Tony surrounded himself with people of power and money. Viggo had been seduced and let himself be drawn into an operation where he would launder money through gambling. When Viggo said no, a price was put on his head. The police had rescued him by chance after they wiretapped Tony for another matter and heard him ordering Viggo's murder.

There and then their lives were changed, and he and his family were forced to leave everything and hide from the Syndicates. The police didn't think that the threat demanded new identities with changed personal identity numbers; they were given protected registration through the tax agency instead, meaning access to their personal data was restricted. The requirement was that they move to another town and live under those conditions. The witness protection unit within the police did what they could, but he didn't get the benefits that fictitious personal information would have provided. So the family did not dare to settle down for the first few years. Then, when Tony went to prison, life became a little more secure.

For Frida the hardest thing was not to be on certain social media. Viggo thought that the everyday things were the toughest, such as buying a new mobile phone or shopping on the internet. Because it wasn't possible to run a credit report on him, little issues became big ones.

What happens now that Tony is out? he thought, looking at Frida, who had picked up her phone again. Viggo had been advised to move to Norway, but Estelle wanted Frida to grow up in Sweden. It had been Abbe's idea to take the family to Umeå, and in retrospect that was a good choice. Viggo trusted Abbe, who'd thought that would put them outside the Syndicates' domain. It was far enough north to be safe and at the same time a good city for Frida to grow up in, with the university nearby. She had made friends here and she could live like a normal teenager, apart from certain restrictions, such as just not using social media.

With Tony in prison Viggo had been lulled into a sense of security that was treacherously dangerous but incredibly liberating.

All he could hope for was that Tony wouldn't try to find him now when he got out. That he had other problems that were more important than Viggo.

'Viggo? Hello?' Estelle's voice cut through his musing.

'Yes, sorry, I was thinking a little.'

'What do you say? Should Frida get to go to a party next weekend?'

Viggo looked at Frida, who had stood up with her plate and glass in hand. Ready to leave. He had missed the whole dialogue between Estelle and Frida and didn't know how to answer.

'Can we talk about it later?'

Frida sighed. 'As always, I can never plan anything because of that fucking Tony. I hate him!'

He watched as she left the kitchen, her heels pounding the floor.

6

Per Berg aimed his index finger at the button on the police station lift. He was only going to Level 1. The domain of Major Crimes. When the doors closed again, he pulled up his sweater and guided the thin needle into his stomach. Six units of insulin. He'd eaten a light breakfast, so no more than that was needed to keep his blood sugar in order. He saw the unit's data analyst, Kicki, as soon as the doors opened with a hissing sound.

'Sheesh, it's cold,' she said, pulling up the zipper on her black down jacket as she stepped into the lift and he stepped out. As usual she looked like a bohemian. Kicki always wore her Doc Martens boots with a pair of colourful tights and a knitted sweater that truly looked hand-knitted.

'Good Monday morning to you too,' Per replied. 'Where are you headed? Don't we have a meeting soon?'

'Left my phone at home. I'll be back for the meeting.' Kicki kept on talking as the lift doors came together. 'Check the log. We have a suspected homicide of a female, just came in. Not a very good start to the morning. You and Charlotte will have to take it . . .'

Per stood there. Bent his neck back and looked up at the ceiling.

Damn, can't people stop killing each other? he thought.

He strode off to his department. Charlotte was already in place at her desk. She was his assistant detective inspector and the best partner he'd ever had. Despite the fact that she was from Stockholm.

'Hear about the woman?' he asked, making her take her eyes off the screen and turn around. Her dark hair was loose, looked curled. She usually had it in a tight back bun and she always wore red lipstick that accentuated an extremely white row of teeth. Like a toothpaste advert. She wore her hair down more and more often, which made him happy.

'Yes, I have. The murder is supposed to have happened sometime just before the weekend. That's what the patrol that responded to the call thinks, at least. The Forensics team is on their way.'

Her Stockholm accent was of course stronger than the few words she used in the Norrland dialect. But it wasn't the choice of words itself that revealed her aristocratic upbringing but instead that she spoke correctly and with good articulation. She never swore, which made Per feel a little ashamed every time he did.

Sometimes Per caught himself changing his behaviour because of his colleague. Like when he visited her at home, and kept his shoes on.

'Wasn't it today you were going to get signed off by your diabetes doctor?' she asked, getting up from the chair.

Even in her movements you could see where she came from. Straight-backed and head held high. Per had tried to walk just as straight as her but only managed to keep his shoulders back a short time.

'That was last Friday. I'm going to see Kennet during the day. Don't think it should be a problem.' He patted himself on the stomach. 'I've taken care of myself. Lost twelve kilos in one year. Racquetball, you know.'

Per was pleased with himself. Kennet, who was his boss and the district chief of police in Umeå, had given him an ultimatum following the previous summer when Per had almost died. *Manage your diabetes or transfer to a desk job.*

'So how's it going with the psychologist?' Charlotte asked.

'Okay, I think,' said Per, taking off his coat. 'If I hadn't gone to talk to her, my police career would probably be over, and my marriage too.'

'Anja and I have found a house we want to buy. Would you and Mia consider taking a look at it?'

Per shrugged his shoulders. 'Yes, of course. Where is it?'

'On "The Island".'

'Of course,' he said, smiling at her.

She rolled her eyes in response and sat down beside Anna, their quick-witted young colleague who was part of the investigation team. She was the police station's number one health guru, or, at least, the whole building's guilty conscience because she reminded everyone how lax they were compared to her. She always drank tea instead of coffee, ran to and from work, hiked in the mountains on holiday. Anna's cheeks were always light red after all her outdoor activities. Her greatest skill in the unit was patience and precision. Per sometimes called her Breathless Anna when he saw her because she was always raring to go.

Per sat down so that he could see Kennet Eriksson, who was standing in front of them. It was uncommon that a district chief of police was engaged in investigations, but Kennet was known for getting involved in the work. Other deputy chiefs were bothered by that, but Per wasn't one of them. He liked Kennet simply because he was so engaged. Kennet had just opened his mouth to say something when the door slowly opened. Kicki. She got an irritated look from Kennet as she sat down.

'I know that you've received a report of a suspected homicide this morning and soon you'll get to focus on that,' said Kennet. 'I just want to report another matter first. Last night a sixteen-year-old boy killed himself by jumping from the West Beltway bridge. He did it right in front of his parents. Incredibly tragic.'

There were five police officers in the room. No one said anything. Per thought about his own sons, Simon and Hannes. Suicide cases were something that all police had to experience, but no one got used to children and youths who had seen no other way out.

'I've asked Mats Söderström to be present at our meeting. As you all know, Police Region North's new department works solely with missing and deceased persons from our four police districts. They are placed under the Investigation Section for the four counties of Norrbotten, Västerbotten, Västernorrland and Jämtland. Mats is the new section chief and responsible for the group.'

'Nice,' said Charlotte. 'Do you know how the kid could jump if his parents were there?'

'Who knows?' Mats replied. 'We'll have to find that out.'

Kicki carefully raised her hand. Kennet pointed to her.

'What will the new department do, in purely concrete terms?'

'Well, when a person is reported missing in our region, initially it will be handled by external operating personnel, and Mats' group will then be brought in as needed. Then they're going to look at how the matter has been handled and whether everything is correct, or if any other action needs to be taken. Sometimes we – Major Crimes – will have to take over. If it concerns suicide, as in this case, then measures will be taken for that. But you all know that we also have a number of refugees and homeless persons that we can't identify and who are sometimes found dead – it will be Mats' group's task to establish their identities. And so on.'

Everyone in the room already knew Mats because he had worked closely with Major Crimes for a long time within their surveillance unit.

Kennet cleared his throat.

'Well, the thing is, we've seen a great increase in drugs like tramadol and Dolcontin. The Danish customs authority reported a record large confiscation of more than a hundred thousand tramadol tablets. The address for the delivery was Stockholm but the increase we see with us is startling and Customs suspects there are transports up here. The boy who committed suicide had the drug both in his body and . . .' He paused mid-sentence. 'Mats will go and talk to the parents, see if we can trace where he got the pills from.'

'That's a Schedule II drug,' said Charlotte. All the police knew very well what that was. 'Do you really think there's a doctor in the county who prescribed it?'

'We don't know yet. It's closely related to both morphine and heroin, and used primarily as a pain reliever in healthcare. For that reason it's worrisome that there are such large quantities of it out there . . . Where does it come from?' Kennet asked.

'Given there are such large quantities, I don't believe it would come from forged prescriptions, but smuggling instead,' she said. 'It's extremely addictive and according to hospital emergency departments and youth clinics, more and more young people are coming in with it in their blood.'

'What does that have to do with us?' asked Kicki.

'I want you all to keep an eye out and have it in mind when you're questioning people. We need to stop the import of the drug into the county and we'll do that in cooperation with all units, including across county borders. Someone seems to be selling the drug like it is gummies. Tobbe Antonsson and his team at the investigation unit have been informed because narcotics is of course their jurisdiction. Now it's yours as well.'

'Why was an autopsy done on the boy if a crime isn't suspected?' Kicki asked. A relevant question, in Per's opinion.

'Because around the boy, scattered on the ice, were packets of these very drugs,' said Kennet.

7

Linn looked at her friend, who was lying on her back beside her on the bed. Tears from Frida's eyes were running down toward her ears. She'd been crying ever since she found out that Anton had taken his life.

'Why did he do it? How can you voluntarily jump right off a bridge?' said Frida, turning to Linn.

'Everyone who knew Anton knew he had problems. He said it himself – without drugs he couldn't exist.'

Frida nodded. 'But he was doing better – he said that when I talked to him. He was feeling better and got help.'

Linn sat up, unwound toilet paper from the roll and tore it off. Carefully she wiped away the dampness from Frida's face, but Frida waved her hand aside and twisted away from her.

'There's a pain in my chest. You don't understand,' she said.

Linn sat quietly, tried to think of something wise to say, but couldn't. Frida had been closer to Anton than Linn had, but she couldn't help being bothered by the drama. They didn't know each other all that well.

'I'm going to miss him so damn much,' Frida whispered.

The mattress moved when Linn sat up on the bed and looked at the quote she'd framed and hung on the wall. *Don't let yesterday take up too much of today.*

Linn liked her room. It was neat and furnished in light pink, white and grey. A white orchid stood in the left corner, matching the colours. Over on her desk, schoolbooks were piled on each other by size.

Frida's room looked like a war zone. She and Linn were different in that way.

'When are you going to die, if you had to guess?' Frida asked.

Linn raised her eyebrows at the uncomfortable question. 'Let's see . . . maybe when I'm seventy.'

'Seventy? God, I won't stand living that long.'

'What do you mean?' asked Linn.

'Who can bear to live that long? I think maybe age twenty.'

Drama queen, thought Linn, inspecting Frida's face, trying to see if there was any trace of irony.

'Not a chance,' she said, making a pouty face at Frida in an attempt to lighten the atmosphere. 'Now it's Downer Frida who's talking.'

Frida picked up her iPhone with the pink case and browsed through her pictures. Seemed to be searching. Stopped at one that showed Anton. Frida always insisted on saying that Anton was in love with her, but Linn wasn't so sure. Anton mostly seemed interested in pills and protecting himself from bacteria. It was like he was consumed by himself and his health problems. What presumably brought him together with Frida was the love of drugs and the talk about how you best treated anxiety.

Linn knew that Frida burned herself with hair straighteners. The scars were usually hidden by clothes but she never tried to hide it from Linn. On the other hand, she refused to talk about it when Linn asked. That was a place in Frida's life where not even Linn could be. The burn marks were clearly visible where she lay on the bed with her sweatpants riding down over her hip. Some of the marks were quite fresh and red with a thin scab. Others

32

were light violet or had become white scars. The sore on her hand came from when she had a hard time vomiting and had stuffed her fingers, hard, far down her throat. Frida had told Linn about this and laughed.

When there was a knock on Linn's door they were both startled by the sound. Before Linn had time to call 'come in' her mother opened the door. *Why knock if you're just going to come in anyway?* she thought, but didn't say anything.

Her mother leaned against the doorframe. Linn wished that she had her slender body. Instead it was clearly her dad's genes that had been passed on to her. Sturdy bone structure and a crooked front tooth. A positive gene was her big, dark eyes. Her mother didn't have those.

Linn's dad lived in Stockholm. She'd met him once when she was around age seven. Linn had a picture from that time on her computer. When she was younger she often asked whether she could go and visit him. She never got to. She hadn't even ever heard his name.

'Hi, how are you two doing in here?' her mother asked. Linn noted the gentle tone because it was usually harsh. As if she was asking because that's what you did as a mum, not because she really cared.

Frida didn't reply. She was looking at her phone.

'So-so,' said Linn. 'We're trying to understand why Anton jumped.'

Her mother just stood there. Looked at Frida. 'I'm sorry, but that boy wasn't healthy. There was nothing you could have done,' she said, letting one hand rest against the door handle. 'Linn, it's okay if you stay home from school today, but tomorrow I want you to go. Agreed?'

Linn nodded, just wanted her to leave.

'Let me know if you want something to eat. We can bake cinnamon rolls,' she said, leaving them with the door open.

You can take your fucking cinnamon rolls and go to hell, thought Linn.

Frida and Linn took each other's hands and intertwined their fingers in silence. Frida smiled faintly at the same time as her eyes filled with fresh tears. She held up her phone with her free hand.

'Has Mama Camilla taken any Instagram pictures today?' she asked, opening the app on her phone.

Linn was lying on her back beside her. Let go of her hand. Sighed loudly and raised both her arms toward the ceiling. Let her index finger make figures in the air.

'This morning, take a look,' Linn replied and watched as Frida clicked into the account *camillahappymum.*

'Why did she call her account that?' Frida asked, without really expecting an answer.

She scrolled to the picture that Linn's mum had posted. It showed Linn at the breakfast table, wearing make-up as always. The long ash-coloured hair sat lightly over her shoulders and framed her face. She smiled broadly and had a new Moncler sweater on. It was hella good-looking, in Linn's opinion. They had a lot of brand-name clothes that her mum bought to be able to display them on Instagram.

Breakfast had been set in front of Linn. There were eggs, a bowl of sour milk topped with mixed berries and a glass of bright yellow juice. A professional sandwich that looked good enough to have been picked up from a cafe, which it had been. It was all completed with a vase of colourful flowers in the background. Under the picture was the caption:

Cosy breakfast with my darling #happymamma

'That picture took an hour to take,' said Linn, grabbing Frida's phone. 'Can't bear to see that shit. I have to put up with enough at school.'

Linn had a crazy mother, but at least she wasn't like Frida's mum, who drank all the time.

Linn crossed her legs like a pretzel. There was less fat around her thighs. She was surprised at how easily her calves and thighs touched each other. A reward in the midst of all the shit. She knew that Frida did it too – almost all the girls stuck their fingers down their throats. But they seldom talked about it. Their conversations were mostly about parties, guys, clothes and what their lives would be like when they were done with high school and life could begin.

'There's something I have to tell you,' said Frida. She did not meet Linn's gaze as she continued. 'Anton knew what happened in the Nydala house.'

'What do you mean, "what happened"?'

'Well . . . uh . . . I told him that I'm seeing William and that. A little about that he, like, runs the parties in the Nydala house.'

Linn jumped up. 'What! You had no right to tell him that!'

'I know, but Anton pressured me to tell him about William, so . . .'

'If our parents find out about that, all hell will break loose! Do you understand?'

You didn't talk about the Nydala house or about the drugs; if you did, you were excluded. They were in their first year of high school and didn't want to end up on the outside.

It had started with William inviting Frida. Linn didn't understand why; Frida shouldn't have interested him. He was twenty-two years old, he was handsome and had a car and went to the university. Seemed to be constantly high. The girls at the Dragon School called him Pudd-Willy. Or The Pudd, as in pudding. William could sleep with anyone he wanted to, and he did.

Everyone knew that William was the guy who could get you what you wanted and he ruled the party house at Nydala. If you weren't invited there you were a nobody. A grey mouse. When you started high school, to get invited to the Nydala house was the major goal. It was a hazing that made many depressed. The parties there divided the students into approved and not approved. Some would do almost anything to get an invitation.

'Anton told me something a few weeks ago,' Frida continued, running her hand through her long hair.

'What was that?' Linn sat down on the bed again.

'That he was involved in something that had to do with drugs.'

'But that was no secret, was it?'

'No, but he gave me a whole pile of packets to hide. He didn't dare have them at home, he said.'

Linn looked at her best friend. Tried to decide whether there was anything serious in what she was saying. 'Do you have them at home?' she asked.

Frida nodded. 'I hid them. It was a little exciting, almost – hiding drugs like in a movie.' She giggled.

'When was this?' asked Linn.

'He asked if I could take care of them a few weeks ago,' said Frida, and although she always sounded over-dramatic, Linn thought this was exciting. 'But they were gone when I last checked, so he must have come and got them. I mean, he knew where they were.'

'Did you take any of the stash for yourself?' Linn asked.

'Yes, of course. I mean, like, what was he going to do with all that? I filmed everything.'

'Can I see?'

Frida shook her head, laughing.

'But come on, we know everything about each other,' Linn said, leaning to Frida. 'Come on! Show me.'

Frida picked up her phone and held it toward Linn. She had hidden the drugs in her dresser drawer and the video showed more packets than Linn could count.

'Where did he get all that from?' asked Linn.

'Don't know. Who cares?'

8

Charlotte put her beanie on as she left the police station, pulling it down as far as she could over her ears. The weather had cleared and the snow was like a soft blanket over everything. She wrinkled her nose and squinted to block out the sun. The news about Tony Israelsson occupied her thoughts. Did he know who she was?

Charlotte turned to Per, who was walking right behind her, fastening the small metal buttons on his blue coat.

'Don't you have a hat?' she asked, dismissing the thoughts of Israelsson.

Charlotte stepped back so she could address Per. The snow hadn't been cleared from the police station car park and she had left deep tracks behind her.

'No need, I have my helmet,' he answered, running his hands through his thick, dark hair.

'That coat looks really nice. I'm glad you don't dress like all the other men in this city,' she said, walking alongside him. Everyone dressed in identical jackets of the same brand: Peak Performance. Another thing she'd noticed since she moved up here was the women's enthusiasm for coveralls in the winter. In Charlotte's world that was a garment for the ski slopes, not the supermarket or for after work. But here protection against the cold was more important than fashion. Charlotte had promised herself never to wear them outside the ski slopes.

Her lips tightened and her breath was visible every time she exhaled. She brought her index finger against her lips, carefully wiped them. She looked at her hand; the lipstick was gone.

'I wonder how long it will take before I get used to the winters up here?' she said, admitting to herself that coveralls would be practical anyway.

'Stop whining. We're just going across the street, Miss Frost,' Per answered, pulling on a pair of black leather gloves. He slapped his hands together so that it echoed in the police yard.

'What was the address of the crime scene?'

They passed through the revolving gate with a code lock – part of the external shell of protection that virtually every police station in Sweden had added. Nowadays their workplace was a protected place.

'Number five Dressyrgatan. Walking distance from here. A peaceful area for a homicide – the middle of town. Mostly elderly people and families with children live here. Crime is pretty rare.'

'Forensics is on the scene so perhaps we can get a good picture of what happened fairly soon,' said Charlotte.

When they reached the shovelled pavement, they stamped their feet to remove the snow. They turned on to Dressyrgatan. A snow-plough was approaching from behind so they kept far in on the pavement, and masses of snow were pushed up against the kerb as it drove past. Charlotte loved that they didn't salt the roads up here. That kept the roads white and free from dirty slush.

Arriving at number 5, Charlotte saw the Forensics car before she saw the building number. She leaned back and observed the three-storey building. The brick facade was in a shade of yellow that was deepened by the intense sunlight. Some apartments had enclosed balconies. There was a fire escape up to the second floor.

'Which floor?' asked Per.

'All the way up.'

'The perpetrator may have come in by way of the balcony,' said Per, pointing up at the victim's apartment.

The entryway was propped open. They took the stairs instead of the lift. The grey stone steps had been dirtied by snow and gravel that crunched under their shoes.

A group of people had gathered on the first floor, behind the blue and white plastic tape that blocked the stairs to the second floor, the crime scene. They followed the plainclothes police with their eyes as they passed.

Per stopped and turned around. Took hold of the black plastic railing with one hand. Charlotte waited a few steps up.

'Are you neighbours in the building?' Per asked.

They all nodded.

'Has anyone taken any witness statements from you yet?'

They shook their heads. A young woman was the only one who seemed able to speak.

'What has happened to Unni?' she asked. Her eyelids were swollen, the whites of her eyes more red than white.

'We can't go into that now, but a police officer is going to ask you all a few questions. We would appreciate it if you'd help out and try to remember as much as possible.'

No one responded. The young woman wiped her eyes. A man in the group hugged her.

Charlotte realized that the woman was important; she seemed to know the victim. She made a mental note to speak with her privately.

A police officer who was standing by the victim's front door held out a pair of plastic shoe protectors. He gave Charlotte a protective mask and plastic gloves. They would not be allowed to move freely in the apartment because the forensics team was fully occupied with the crime scene investigation.

'They're far from done,' he said, giving Per a similar set.

Charlotte pulled on the gloves and brought one hand to the lock of the front door, stroked the cylinder with her fingers.

'No signs of a break-in,' said the policeman. 'The balcony door is locked, so either she left the door unlocked or simply let the perpetrator in.'

'Someone she knew – fairly common with assaults,' Charlotte replied, thinking about the red-eyed woman in the stairwell.

A gust of wind met her as she stepped into the hall. She crossed her arms over her chest, despite the down jacket. Straight ahead was the kitchen, where a window was wide open. Charlotte fixed her gaze on the angled glass sections.

'We're airing out a little,' said a woman dressed entirely in white.

'No sign that the perpetrator came in that way?' Charlotte asked.

She could only distinguish the brown eyes with no make-up. The forensic officer's mouth was covered by a protective mask.

'No windows have been forced open,' she replied.

Per came up beside her. He had his protective mask around his chin.

'You have to put that on properly,' the woman with the brown eyes said, pointing at Per's chin. 'We're not done yet.'

The woman took off her own mask briefly and exposed a slight underbite with a prominent chin. White teeth. Charlotte was struck by how much she resembled Crown Princess Victoria with her high cheekbones and lively eyes. She introduced herself as Carola and said that she was the supervising forensic technician on the scene, then she pulled up her mask again.

'We seem to have a particularly strange homicide,' she said, leading them further into the apartment, which was furnished in a functional modern style.

'The victim, female, age fifty-two, Unni Olofsson. She opened the door, or else it was unlocked. It seems as if she was attacked here in the hall,' said Carola, pointing.

Charlotte saw nothing unusual. Everything seemed to be where it belonged. But the label on the floor, evidence item number seven, revealed a blood stain no larger than a coin. They continued down the hall, toward the kitchen, and passed the bedroom without Carola saying anything. Charlotte looked in. The bed was unmade and a jeans jacket was on one end. It had a sun sewn on to one sleeve.

'So we're going on the theory that she let the perpetrator in and was first attacked in the hall,' said Per.

'Yes, that seems probable,' said Carola. 'We suspect that the perpetrator stabbed her in the arm with a knife here in the hall. Then she tried to flee from the man, into the bathroom.'

'The man?' asked Charlotte.

'Yes, you'll see why we're quite certain that it was a man.'

They found themselves in a generously sized hall with light grey walls where framed photographs were hanging. Unni with her student cap. Unni with some other women and a wine glass in her hand. Unni dressed in a helmet on a ski slope . . . Charlotte didn't have time to look at them all. They stopped between the bathroom and the kitchen. Label number eight was on the floor. Blood on the doorframe into the bathroom – fingers had smeared the red along the white wood.

'To think that a murder scene can be a cliché,' said Per, pointing at the blood.

Charlotte didn't know how she should respond to Per's comment. Carola also ignored it.

Straight ahead was a toilet. Black tiles on the floor, white walls. Large mirrors. The bathroom had a double sink but there was only one toothbrush in a glass beside one of them.

Carola conferred with her colleagues, then she told Per and Charlotte how they could move.

'We're done with the search for traces of evidence on the floor and for that reason you can come with me into the bathroom. Do you understand?'

'We know,' said Charlotte, and Carola disappeared inside.

The odour was tangible as they came closer. Charlotte saw in the mirror how Per buttoned up his coat, his face white. Carola called to them.

'Come in now. We don't have all day.'

They crossed the threshold. There was a tiled shower stall to the left and beside it was a bathtub in the middle of the floor. A block candle with four wicks revealed that Unni liked burning candles when she bathed.

Unni was lying in the bathtub. It looked as if someone had thrown her down in the tub.

Charlotte turned her eyes away. It felt as if she defiled the victim simply by looking at her.

'Oh dear,' Per whispered, bringing his hand to his nose. Carola kept on talking.

'So we believe that she tried to flee into the bathroom but obviously didn't succeed. There were traces of blood on the inside of the door handle, so the injury must have happened before she came in here. The traces of blood on the doorframe also seem to be hers, so her hands weren't tied behind her back at that time. That presumably happened here in the bathroom. We found traces of blood on the floor that the perpetrator tried to clean up.'

'Did she die in the bathtub?' asked Per.

'Wait,' said Carola.

Unni's red sweater and black bra sat above her breasts, which were exposed. She had jeans on. The bathtub was drained and one leg was hanging over the side. The arms were bound with duct tape behind her back, making the body lean to the left. Her head and gaze were aimed in their direction. A label with the number nine was placed on Unni's stomach.

'We've found traces of semen on the body, and she has a head wound that we suspect comes from the edge of the tub.' Carola pointed to a light red speck on the porcelain. 'She has classic pressure injuries and bruises around her throat.'

Carola put both hands on her waist and sighed before she continued.

'But there's something strange about it all,' she said, pointing toward Unni's throat. 'The cause of death is presumably strangulation. Someone strangled her with their hands, you see that by the marks on the throat. We'll have to see if the internal injuries confirm that. But strangling someone to death requires tremendous force. She must have been lying on the floor for that, then moved to the bathtub. We think that the crime scene has been constructed.'

'Why do you think that?'

'Unni was already dead when her arms were tied, or taped, behind her back. It's done sloppily. It would have been ineffective if she was alive. The body was presumably placed in the tub after she was dead. Perhaps the murderer didn't realize that she was dead and tied her up to keep her from putting up resistance.'

Charlotte tried to understand. 'But why not just leave her on the floor? Why place her in the bathtub?'

Carola nodded. 'It's strange the perpetrator wiped away the blood on the floor and presumably lifted Unni up from there. I have no answer as to why.'

'The semen found on her, what do we know?' asked Per.

44

'We don't know if she has been penetrated – the autopsy will have to reveal that, but she has trousers on, which suggests that she wasn't raped. We'll have to keep our fingers crossed for a DNA match.'

'When do you estimate that she died?' asked Per.

'In my opinion, sometime between Wednesday and Friday of last week. I would guess Friday based on the odour and how the body looks to the naked eye. But the autopsy should tell us more. A neighbour heard a strange sound from the apartment and when that person couldn't get hold of the woman over the weekend, she called us. And one more thing,' said Carola, pointing at the body. 'Someone has urinated in the bathtub. The DNA test should show whether it's the same person that the semen comes from.'

'Feels like degradation,' said Per.

'Why a golden shower?' Charlotte said to herself.

'What do you mean, "golden shower"?' asked Per.

'Look it up on Google,' she answered, leaving the bathroom.

9

The road conditions became more and more wintry the further north they drove and Abbe wondered whether the rental car had snow tyres. Tony was sitting in the folded-back passenger seat with his mouth open, eyes closed. There was a rumble every time he breathed in. Abbe could not connect that sound with the thin body.

His eyes stung after a night behind the wheel. His back was stiff and he'd finished the coffee in the holder next to him. They would be staying in a house that had formerly been owned by Hells Angels. He hoped there were beds. Ironically there was a hotel next door, but checking in there would be like announcing your arrival in a newspaper ad.

Abbe had been in Umeå a few times before, but Tony didn't know that. The GPS was on to conceal the fact that he knew his way around fairly well. He nudged Tony with his elbow. Tony woke up in the middle of an inhalation. Looked up.

'Damn that's a lot of snow,' he said, straightening in the seat. 'How cold is it?'

Abbe looked for the thermometer on the dashboard. 'Seventeen degrees below freezing.'

'We'll have to buy heavy jackets – we're not dressed for this weather,' he said, making sure that his glasses were straight. Abbe wanted to ask why he hadn't changed frames since the 1970s, but was afraid to offend.

'And a pair of sunglasses,' said Abbe, pulling down the sun visor.

He turned left at the roundabout and IKEA ended up on their right-hand side. The shopping centre next to it was open but the car park was almost empty.

'Should we stop here and buy jackets?' Abbe said, pointing.

'Yes, but not now. I need coffee and a sandwich. Breakfast.'

Abbe looked at him. 'I think they probably have coffee in there,' he said, easing up a little on the accelerator.

'No, I want to go to Mekka Bakery Cafe. Find it.'

Abbe sped up again.

'Why that particular place?' he asked, taking out his phone, pretending to search the internet.

'I was there once a long time ago. There was a babe I was in love with, when I still had hope that women were good people. My only positive memory of the female sex is from that cafe. Mekka.'

Damn the way he talks, thought Abbe, took the turn by Max Burgers and realized that he was going the wrong way, not following the guide but instead driving by his own compass.

'You're going the wrong way – follow the GPS,' said Tony, starting to root through his jacket pocket, taking out a bag of raspberry gummies.

They were redirected by the robotic voice and Abbe knew that they would pass the police station.

Tony stuffed a fistful of red candy in his mouth. 'You want some?' he asked, holding out the bag.

'No, thanks.'

Tony poured out another batch of sweets into his hand and was just about to toss them in his mouth when he stopped himself.

47

'Hmm, the police station . . . Shall we go in and see if we get a reaction?' Tony said, laughing.

'In order to . . . ?' Abbe replied.

'Just for fun, see how well-informed they are up here.'

Abbe drove past the fire station and glanced at Tony, who was consuming another fistful of raspberry gummies. 'I'm checking up on which cops we need to know more about. But honestly, Tony, let's do what we came here to do, so that we can go back home as fast as hell.'

'Good. Do that. Work out the most important ones in case we need to apply pressure.'

10

Viggo's office chair creaked as he stretched. He closed the poker site, satisfied with the day's winnings. What was supposed to be two or three hours of playing had lasted into the afternoon. The heavy curtain kept the daylight out and the only visit he'd had all morning was from Frida, who had slept poorly. Thoughts of Anton had twirled in her head and Frida had been around Viggo a lot, mainly when he was playing. Maybe she wanted to learn but didn't dare ask. Or else she simply wanted to be close to her dad right now.

'Estelle!' He called out to see if his wife was up or if she was sleeping off her hangover when he heard the front door open and close. *Maybe she picked up Frida from school*, he thought, calling again but getting no answer.

Estelle had taken the news about Tony Israelsson better than expected and together they had decided not to get worried. They had to dare to live their own lives. He drew his hands through his blond hair, which was starting to get thinner on top, stood up and felt the signs of age when his lower back ached. Then he heard that someone was in the kitchen.

'Dad, did you buy eggs?' Frida shouted.

So she wasn't at school.

Viggo moved to the doorway, his arms crossed. His body wanted to lie down, struggled for it; his eyelids struggled too.

Frida stood with the refrigerator door open. She must have been out for a run because her hair was wet and her cheeks red.

'Where are my eggs?' she said sassily.

'Why aren't you at school?'

She met his gaze. 'I've been with Linn today. She's been consoling me and I feel sick.'

Viggo raised his eyebrows at the obvious fabrication and looked at her.

'Just lay off. I couldn't sleep last night. No point in going if you're too tired to take in anything anyway. Besides, I'm mostly thinking about Anton. I'm crying all the time, Dad.'

She closed the refrigerator door. Viggo was torn. She talked about how sad she was about her friend's suicide, but at the same time she behaved like her usual self. One plus one did not become two.

'We've talked about this, Frida. I'm worried about you. How you're feeling,' he said, sitting down on the kitchen chair.

She smiled at him, leaned forward and kissed him on the forehead. 'Don't be worried. You can't complain about my grades.'

Her thin body looked even skinnier than just a few weeks ago. He sighed. He truly could not complain about her grades, but he was worried about her. She was involved in something that was dangerous.

'I saw it on the internet, Dad. I know he's out. Do you think he knows where we live?'

Viggo looked at her. Sometimes he forgot that she was in the process of growing up. She had sensed his worry and taken for granted that it was about Tony Israelsson.

'I don't know, honey, but I don't think so. Nothing indicates that.'

Frida took a glass from the cupboard. Filled it with water.

'Do you think I'll ever be able to live a normal life, like Linn?' she asked, and the words made Viggo stop breathing for a few seconds.

'To be honest, I don't know.' He looked at his daughter, who was standing with the glass in her hand.

'Sometimes I wish you'd laundered that Tony guy's money, so we could live like everyone else. But I'm proud of you too, Dad. That you didn't let yourself be pressured into becoming a criminal. That's, like, a big deal.'

Viggo's love overflowed in his chest.

Frida took hold of one ankle and stretched out her thighs. Balanced on the other leg.

The kitchen chair scraped the floor as Viggo stood up. He went over to Frida and put his hand on her shoulder, patting it gently. She had to put the other foot down so as not to fall on the floor.

'Oh, come on!' she said, laughing. He kissed her on the forehead.

There was a ping on Viggo's phone. He read the text message on his way out of the kitchen. The number was not stored under Contacts, but he knew who it came from.

We're in Umeå. Lay low otherwise it will be dangerous.

11

Per's coat was draped over his right arm. Unni's apartment was a crime scene and there was no place to set it down. The forensics team was starting to wrap up their investigation. Charlotte had her jacket on; she was standing with her back to him, focused on something else. Per saw that she'd brought her service revolver with her after lunch. He was so used to seeing it on her hip that he noticed when it wasn't there. Charlotte carried a gun much more often than he did, almost obsessively. It seemed like she was always ready for a fight. He noted it almost immediately when they started working together. It was as if she was afraid of something, but at the same time she was also the bravest colleague he'd ever worked with.

Per also noticed that she had a new watch on her wrist. The Rolex variant had been exchanged for some black-gold thing with a black leather strap. He wondered what it cost. Probably not that expensive because she was wearing it at a murder scene instead of locking it in her desk drawer. But nothing she wore was cheap, except maybe the black beanie she'd bought in a cold panic the other day.

In her hand she had a sealed plastic bag with a blister pack of pills and loose tablets. She'd found them in Unni's bedroom and wanted them to be analysed while the body was at autopsy. They had learned that Unni was a pharmacist who worked in the Utopia shopping centre and also taught at the pharmacy programme at Umeå University. Unni was single and had no children. She was probably married to her job.

Per looked at his watch, scanned his arm with his smartphone and learned that his blood sugar was stable at 7.2. He loved this new technology with the built-in glucose meter.

He saw how Charlotte handed the bag with a few pills to Carola, who nodded as she received it. Per went up to the women.

'How quickly can it be analysed, do you think? There are warning bells here.'

'What kind of warning bells?' Carola asked.

'She was a pharmacist and these pills are classified as narcotics.' He pointed at the blister pack of Dolcontin tablets. 'What is she doing with a morphine preparation at home? The other pills are unmarked. We'll have to see if the autopsy shows if she has the substance in her body, but something is strange here.'

'I'll see what I can do,' said Carola. She was just about to leave when she raised her hand. 'Oh, by the way, we found a jacket in the bedroom that probably isn't hers.' She took a few steps toward a plastic crate. Fished out a jeans jacket that was sealed in a bag. 'It feels more like a young person's jacket with this childish sun on the sleeve. And it's a smaller size than the other clothes in the apartment. Unni didn't have any children, did she?'

'That's strange,' Charlotte replied, turning to Per. 'Could the murderer have left it behind?'

Per shrugged his shoulders. 'There may be another explanation that doesn't have anything to do with her death.'

'We'll check the DNA on it in any event, see if it's the same as what's on the body,' Carola said.

Charlotte buttoned her jacket. Took out the black beanie and pulled it over her head.

'Should we take a witness statement from the young woman in the stairwell? They're starting to canvas the area, but I want to speak with her because she was the one who reacted the most to Unni's death, and she was the one who called the police.'

'Which apartment does the girl live in again?' Per asked, going toward the door.

Charlotte took the lead and Per followed her with his gaze down the stairs. She pulled off the beanie, making strands of hair stand straight up.

'You look like the doll in the elf's workshop on Donald Duck, Elf-mother von Klint,' he said, having to suppress a laugh when it struck him mid-sentence that they were just leaving a crime scene.

Charlotte put her hair in place with her palms.

'I don't know anyone who makes up nicknames as often as you do,' she said, stopping at the first floor, where the group of neighbours had been standing earlier. There were two doors, both of which were open. 'Hello, it's the police,' she said loudly in the stairwell.

The sad woman appeared in the doorway to the left. An elderly woman looked out from the right.

'A police officer is coming soon to talk with you,' said Per, waving to the elderly woman before following Charlotte in through the other door.

The young woman extended her hand and introduced herself as Petra.

Per immediately gave her a nickname which he kept to himself. Fringe. It stopped two centimetres below her hairline. A typical Umeå hairdo.

'Come, let's sit down in the living room,' Fringe said, showing the way.

After five steps they arrived at the combined bedroom-living room.

The bed stood to the right – at most two steps from a two-seater couch in grey velvet. There was also a kitchen with a dining area for four persons. Per noted two wine glasses on the table, one of which was half empty.

Petra sat down on a stool and let Per and Charlotte take the couch. On the table in front of her were open books. Textbooks.

'What are you studying?' Charlotte asked.

Per stretched so he could read in one of the books.

'Becoming an archaeologist is the plan,' she said, smiling with her mouth but not with her eyes. Her dialect revealed that she had roots in Gothenburg.

'Exciting,' Per said, without revealing that he didn't know anything about the profession except that they get on their knees and brush off old things in the ground. 'So, how do you . . . How did you know Unni?'

Petra tugged lightly on her index finger. 'From here, in the building. At first we just ran into each other, said hello in the stairwell. Then we started talking and realized we both spent our days at the university.'

'How old are you?' asked Per.

'Twenty-two.'

'How often did you see each other?'

Petra shrugged her shoulders. 'Occasionally, mostly on weekends. We drank wine together. Sat and talked. I thought her rather lonely, but smart. She was sharp and the conversations with her were often deep.'

Petra wiped away a tear that had worked its way down her cheek.

'Did you do anything other than drink wine?' Per asked, getting a perplexed look from Petra.

'No, what do you mean?'

'Did you have a relationship?'

She shook her head. 'I think she liked men, like me. We were just friends and both of us were very busy. Unni was often away. She came over to my place last week and seemed stressed about something. I got the sense that she had a lot going on at work.'

'When was she here last?'

'Uh, it was last Tuesday.'

'In what way did she seem stressed?' Per asked.

'She was looking at her phone the whole time, as if she was waiting for something important and she seemed irritated. That was unusual. Unni was usually calm itself.'

'Did you ask if she was stressed about something?'

'Yes, but she just said that she had a lot going on at work.'

Charlotte wrote down everything Petra said in her notebook.

'Do you know if she was seeing any particular person?' Charlotte asked.

'I think she met someone recently.'

'What makes you think that?'

'Because I saw a man ringing the doorbell at her place in the middle of the night one Saturday, about three o'clock. I came home at the same time.'

'When was this?'

'Oh, must have been three weeks ago.'

'Do you know who it was?'

'No, unfortunately. No idea.'

'Can you describe him?'

'No, I didn't look that closely.' Petra's gaze wandered. 'I was pretty tired after a bar run with some other students.'

'Describe what you did when you came home the other evening.'

Petra sighed, looked up at the ceiling. 'Well, so, I came home and was about to open my door when I heard movement one flight up. Someone was ringing someone's doorbell, so I took a few steps back and saw him. Didn't think that much about it. He didn't say anything, just stood and waited. But I got a feeling that he didn't want to be seen. Cap, jacket collar turned up, head lowered, yes . . . the kind of thing you see on TV.' Petra laughed at her own comment.

'Have you seen the man since then?'

She shook her head. 'No, it's always quiet here. No one running around. Just people who live in the building and the postman.'

Petra stretched. 'Do we need to be afraid now? Is there a crazy murderer loose in Umeå? What happened to her?' Her voice broke. She dried her eyes with the sleeve of her sweater.

Per looked at Charlotte. She was still writing so he answered as he stood up.

'We see no reason for worry based on what we know today. This sort of thing is usually an isolated event. Please call us if you think of anything else or find out the name of the guy who called on Unni.' Per held out his business card.

'What did happen to her?' Petra asked again.

'Unfortunately we can't talk about that because of the investigation.'

The classic standard response.

Charlotte put the notepad in her pocket and stood beside Per, extended her hand.

'Thank you for your time.'

Petra nodded and looked at Per's business card.

Per stopped by the threshold into the kitchen.

'Just one last question. Do you know if she was involved in anything else, such as drugs?'

Petra responded with a long silence.

'We're not here to arrest you for anything, you can answer.'

She met Per's gaze. 'I don't think she was involved in anything like that. I never saw her take drugs, anyway. But one time she asked me how common it was at the university, if I'd seen or heard anything.' Petra blew her nose in a handkerchief.

'Why do you think she asked that?' said Per.

'No idea. I thought it was a strange question, but then I thought that she does work with pharmaceuticals and such.'

'How did you respond?' Charlotte asked.

'There's a guy who's generally known at the university . . . there are rumours about him, that he sells . . .'

'What's his name?' Per asked.

'Unni asked that too. William Gunnarsson. He's good-looking but shady. He's very friendly with everyone on campus, popular with the girls. There are rumours that he never delivers the drugs personally.'

Charlotte took the notepad out again and wrote down the name.

'There's one more thing I've been thinking about a little,' Petra continued. 'Unni had no children, but there was a fairly young kid with her once. I saw them in the stairwell.'

'Did you ask her who he was?'

'Yes, it was just someone she was helping, she said. Then she changed the subject.'

'So you don't know what their name is?'

Petra shook her head.

Per looked at Charlotte. Could the jacket with the sun on it belong to this kid? Was he the murderer?

12

What are you doing? Linn wrote on Snapchat.

But Frida's icon didn't pop up on the screen. No answer today either. Linn tossed the phone on the bed and lay on her back alongside it, in the same place that Frida had been crying.

Three days had passed since Anton jumped from the bridge and Frida had neither been at school or at Linn's place since the day after. Linn didn't know if it was because she was sad or if it was just her usual drama. She reached for the phone again, wrote a new message on Snap.

> *Have an invitation to the Nydala house this weekend. Of course we're going?*

She actually didn't want to go there with Frida because she always got too high or drunk. Once she started partying it was like she couldn't lay off it; there was no stopping her and it often ended with Linn having to drag her home.

She stared at the screen. Maybe it was just as well that Frida didn't answer. Linn wondered whether she would dare ask

Anja, if Anja was even here over the weekend. Maybe she was in Stockholm.

Anja was the most bad-ass girl Linn knew. Self-confident, good-looking, rich. Lived in Stockholm and was different somehow. Linn often saw Anja in clothes like she had herself, but they always fitted better on Anja. Like all of her was right out of *Vogue*. Whatever she had on she looked like a super-trendy influencer.

Linn had got to know Anja at a self-defence course that they both signed up for after a girl was raped in Umeå. Her mother had registered her and at first Linn refused because it sounded so lame. But as usual she was forced. Mum needed pictures for Instagram and took a bunch to get that perfect image of her daughter in a sweaty workout facility. Afterwards Mum told her to lose at least five kilos because now she was going to have to edit out the fat. But the course wasn't that bad. In the process Linn had learned self-defence, lost two kilos and then improved the results by vomiting, at the same time as she got to know Anja.

If Anja lived permanently in Umeå she would have been the most popular girl at school. All the guys wanted to sleep with her but no one succeeded. Anja wasn't interested. That no guy could approach her almost made her into a sacred cow.

Linn wanted to be like her, but it was too late. She'd lost her virginity three years ago, when she was fourteen. After that it had just rolled on with parties and guys. She actually would have liked to rewind and start over. Be like Anja and restrain herself. Not get too high, not have sex with two guys at the same time just because she was in love with one of them. Have a little self-respect.

Linn sat up in bed and looked at herself in the mirror. Drew her hand over her thinned-out fringe that reached to right below her nose now. She curled her hair like Anja – at the tips. Frida did too, and her dyed-blonde hair got more and more ash-coloured.

Linn raised her top, brought her hand to her stomach, and with thumb and index finger pinched the fat, released the hold and smacked it with her palm. The sound filled the room. She hated her stomach. She lay on her side and inspected her body. Pulled in her stomach, pinched herself on the rear. She had lost weight but not enough. She wasn't skinny and that was the goal.

Linn lowered her top again and decided to skip dinner and go out and run instead. With a practised movement she tied up her hair in a bun on top of her head, let her hands glide down her cheeks and looked at herself. She looked okay but not good enough to be one of the popular girls at school. Her lips were too thin and she already knew that she would fill them out when she got permission. Her cheekbones were high but her eyes were too small and her forehead low. She was content with her breasts and often heard how nice-looking they were, so she emphasized them. Let the guys stare.

Linn picked up her phone. Did she dare invite Anja to the party? She would be popular if she brought her there. William would go bananas. That Anja's mother was a police officer was probably what made Linn hesitate. She didn't think that Anja took anything, or drank, but she didn't know.

'Linn!'

Her mother's screechy voice interrupted her musing. It was almost five o'clock and that usually meant photographing for Instagram.

Before Linn could step out of the room she was standing there with a freshly ironed white Fendi shirt dangling on a hanger.

'I'm going out for a run – can we do this afterwards?'

Her mum stepped in and sat down on the bed. 'No, little lady, we have to do it now. Let your hair down, fix your face and put on the shirt. I've prepared the dough – you just need to do what you're best at.'

Linn knew there was no point in resisting. She had done it a thousand times and lost every time. Her mother had learned that pictures of Linn got the most likes. *Camillahappymum* had almost fifteen thousand followers and they loved seeing the perfect daughter in perfect clothes in the perfect home with the perfect mother. When Linn was twelve she had to fight to escape having that damn bow in her hair in every picture. A call from the social worker was required to put a stop to it because she was bullied at school. Even today Linn could not see a hair bow without feeling pressure across her chest.

Linn hated the dough pictures most of all. She even hated cinnamon rolls because she associated them with her mother's pictures, though she still ate them in secret in her room.

When she stepped into the kitchen everything was prepared. The dough was rolled out on the counter, not an edge out of place. There was an aroma of melted butter and flour. The white candles in the candelabras were lit and gave a cosy glow in the kitchen. The cupboard doors were clean, the sink glistened. Mum scoured it with steel wool every day. Everything on the kitchen counter had a function to reinforce the pictures. Spices that no one got to touch, a watering can. One time Linn left an unwashed dish out and her mother gave her a slap. When you're seven years old you learn from that. Her mother had cried and said she was sorry a thousand times. It was one of the very few times that Linn had a regretful mother. Mostly she was harsh. When other mothers hugged their daughters on the last day of school, Linn got a pat on the shoulder.

'Come, stand over here,' she said curtly and placed Linn in front of the dough on the counter.

Their home looked like an interior design magazine, which was also something her mother worked with. She sold furnishings on the internet and had done well. Her business had flourished. She had one employee, Hugo. He was a kind of handyman for her, made sure the things that were ordered were shipped, picked up and delivered, and he did whatever she asked him to do.

Her mother gave her the rolling pin and guided a floury finger along Linn's cheek, slowly stroking a line there.

'There, won't that be too perfect!'

Linn inhaled, holding her breath before she let out the air. She took hold of both ends of the rolling pin and rolled it over the dough. Her mother placed herself on the other side of the kitchen island, raising her phone.

'Linn, little lady, look here, into the camera. You look amazing.'

She did as she was told. The phone clicked.

'Wait, stretch out the shirt on your left side. The brand can't be seen.'

Linn brought her hand to her ribcage and pulled on the fabric.

'Good. Laugh now, this is cool,' Mum said, laughing herself. 'You are super-good.'

Linn smiled with her mouth. It was a bit like leaving your own body – just do it and hope it passes quickly.

Mum came over and puffed up her hair. She used a clothes peg to gather the back of the shirt and aimed the phone toward her again.

'Linn, for God's sake, how many rolls have you eaten? Your stomach is sticking out – pull it in.' She stroked her hand across Linn's cheek. Harsh words were usually offset by physical contact.

Linn held her breath and pulled her stomach in as far as she was able. Mum had tightened the fabric hard at her back.

'Stretch, you look like a sack of hay.'

Linn pulled her shoulders backward and rolled, smiled, sucked in her stomach so much that she almost couldn't breathe. Made sure that the label was visible. Blinked away the moisture that welled up in the corner of her eye. Wanted to die.

'So, you're starting to cry now? Come on, little lady, it will soon be over. This will be great. Think that you're helping yourself. See it as you who's the influencer for our company.'

Linn shook her head. Her eyes moved up and down in an attempt to blink away the tears.

She did her job until her mother was satisfied. Swallowed all she felt and let it settle in her stomach. She knew that Camilla had grown up in foster homes in Stockholm, that she had a thick case file at the social services office and had left the big city to start a new life in Umeå. Showing a perfect surface was important because she came from shit. That was Linn's own analysis of her mother.

'Are we done? May I go now?' she asked when her mother stood and looked at her phone.

She waved with her hand that Linn could leave the kitchen and without looking up said, 'Thanks, sweetie, you were awesome. Take off the shirt, please, and hang it in my wardrobe.'

Linn moaned audibly. 'Can't I wear it to school tomorrow? It looks nice.'

She already knew the answer because she had asked before.

'That shirt is mine, little lady. We're running a company that is doing well, but we can't advertise it by always wearing expensive things in town. Sometimes you have to have clothes from H&M or Zara too.'

Linn decided to ignore what she said and hide the shirt in her bag. She could wear it at the party. She closed the door carefully so as not to irritate her mother. Took hold of her phone. Shuddered because the picture would soon be up for everyone's viewing. Carefully folded the shirt and set it in her school bag. There was a humming sound from the phone.

Frida had answered on Snap.

Feeling good! Got an invitation to Nydala too! This week-end there'll be a party!

13

Charlotte handed her credit card to the cashier in the police station lunchroom.

'What kind of special card is that?' Kicki asked, who was behind her in line.

Charlotte had other things on her mind and hadn't thought about it. The platinum card was not something she usually used in the cafeteria, especially not around Kicki, who interfered with everything she did.

'This? It's an ordinary card that looks flashier than it is,' she lied, feeling hot blood pumping across her cheeks. Kicki was always trying to expose her as a diva, as someone who thought she was superior.

'Listen, Kicki, do you know an estate agent in town who you trust?'

Charlotte got her card back and put it in her pocket, took her tray of food and waited for Kicki. Meeting meanness with friendliness made it harder for Kicki to bully. Charlotte refused to get down in the sandpit and throw back.

Kicki lit up at Charlotte's question. 'Of course, but have you asked Per?' she said, looking at the table where he sat, talking with Mats. 'His best buddy is an agent. I think they're neighbours in Degernäs.'

'Do people have neighbours in Degernäs? It must be twenty kilometres between the houses,' Charlotte said, laughing. Kicki didn't get the joke.

'Are you going to move?' Kicki said, taking her tray.

'Yes, I've found a place but would like a little advice from someone who knows the market in Umeå.'

'How are you going to find something in little Umeå that's good enough, when you're used to fancy Stockholm?'

The old Kicki was back.

'Where's the house?' she asked.

Damn it! thought Charlotte.

'Uh . . . on The Island,' she answered, setting her tray down next to Mats.

'Of course you're going to live with your own dock in the city's most expensive district. Not where us common folk live.'

Charlotte ignored the comment and turned instead to Mats, who was sitting with her colleagues.

'How are things with the new group? Does it feel like a good team?'

Mats finished chewing before he answered. 'Yes, it's going surprisingly well, I must say. I've hired two new officers today. We're moving into the space next to you at Major Crimes.'

Charlotte cut up the meatball on her plate, adding a little mashed potato and lingonberry to her fork. 'Cool,' she replied, putting the food in her mouth.

'Yes . . . whether it's cool or not God only knows. We've had two suicides and six missing persons since we started up a few weeks ago.'

'My God,' said Charlotte, putting more food on the fork.

'Yes, what is it?' Per replied, smiling at her. He raised his eyebrows but directed his attention back to Mats.

'How's it going with the kid who committed suicide over the weekend?' she said. 'Did you find anything interesting about the drugs that were around the body?'

'No, not yet. But thanks for the tip about that young guy that you identified with the murder investigation of Unni Olofsson. What was his name?'

'You mean William Gunnarsson? The one they think sells drugs at the university?' Charlotte asked, putting the forkful of food in her mouth.

'Yes, exactly. Surveillance has started following him a little. Then we got the parents' permission to go through Anton's computer and phone. We know that he's been on some shady sites on the internet, maybe on the dark web. We'll see what IT Forensics comes up with.'

Per pushed his tray forward to make room for his elbows on the table. 'Maybe he bought the drugs? He was a sixteen-year-old with an OCD diagnosis. It's not uncommon that they self-medicate with cannabis or pain relievers,' said Per.

'Yes, that may be the case. Both tramadol and Dolcontin are common on the internet, or benzo tablets. We confiscate a lot of that, unfortunately,' Charlotte replied.

'Yes, he probably self-medicated a bit and seems to have received padded envelopes at home in the mail that his parents didn't react to. They thought they were ordinary things he was getting by mail order.'

'On the dark web you can buy everything from narcotics to tanks and women. But guns too, children and every conceivable kind of shit between heaven and earth.'

Mats nodded.

'On the other hand maybe the kid only used the message board to process his thoughts,' Per continued. 'Everything is encrypted, so who knows.'

'Yes, it's shitty. And the poor parents . . . it was terrible to have to tell them that he didn't survive,' said Mats.

Charlotte nodded; she'd had to convey similar news many times over the years. Many who were going to get such news already understood when they opened the door and saw the police. Others couldn't take it in even after the police told them – they asked for more evidence and could even become threatening and call the police liars. Sometimes they were in so much shock that the next of kin didn't believe it was their child even when they saw the body.

'According to the parents, Anton had been at the psychiatric emergency department a couple of times,' said Mats. 'They sought help everywhere for his OCD, but got the cold shoulder and ended up on a waiting list, or simply fell between the cracks. On the other hand, he had been at the paediatric and adolescent psychiatry clinic in Umedalen, but there he only got a prescription. No psychological help for his anxiety. It's incredibly tragic that our society can't help people with mental illness.'

There was silence around the table.

'We'll have to see what we find,' Mats continued. 'But we're understaffed and we're only investigating because we want to know why the kid had large quantities of narcotics around him. By the way, how's it going with the murder of Unni Olofsson? I hear she also had drugs in her apartment?'

'Yes, as Kennet reported at the briefing. There's a lot of drugs everywhere.'

'Isn't it strange that the media hasn't reported on the murder?' Mats said.

Charlotte nodded. 'They have reported, but just a brief announcement. They don't know the circumstances.'

'Did any of the neighbours see or hear anything?'

His chair scraped the floor as he pushed it backward with his legs. Charlotte followed him with her gaze as he stood up. The silver chain around his neck had a tag that stuck to his collar. His grey shirt was well-ironed. No tie. It suited him to be a boss.

'No, nothing that can lead us further. The tips we've got are a dead end. Her computer and phone have been sent to IT Forensics. We'll have to hope that they produce some interesting leads. The motive seems to be sexual, but we're not sure.'

'Do you miss the surveillance group?' Kicki asked Mats before he managed to leave the table.

Kicki's eyes were fixed on her tall co-worker. She smiled in a way that she didn't usually smile at anyone at work. At the same time she drew one hand across her short hair.

Mats met her gaze but turned away just as quickly.

'Yes and no. You miss being out in the field and such.'

Mats left and Per turned to Charlotte.

'Listen, come over to Mia and me tomorrow. We're having friends for dinner. One is an estate agent and he'll gladly help you with questions about the house.'

'That's so nice! I'll be more than happy to come. Can Anja come too? She's up for the weekend again.'

'Do you even need to ask? Simon and Hannes are at home too.'

Charlotte's phone vibrated on the table. She looked at the screen – it was a colleague she worked with in Stockholm who was calling. What did he want?

'Excuse me, Per, I have to take this,' she said, getting up from the table, leaving Per alone with Kicki.

'Hi, it's been a while,' said Charlotte as she left the cafeteria. She stood by the entrance to the police station reception.

'Hey there, lady, how's it going up there? We miss you down here in the capital.'

The entrance opened, cold air swept in and blew her hair in front of one eye. She pressed the phone to her ear.

'Okay. A little more ordinary police work now. What's on your mind? Are you on your way up here?'

Her colleague coughed. 'No, but we've got information that I thought might be good for you to know about.'

She made her way into reception.

'Uh . . . I'm telling you this in confidence because you have personal experience of this person and maybe would like to know if you run into him in town. Do you understand?'

Charlotte looked up at the ceiling, shuddering at what he was going to tell her. 'Tony Israelsson,' she whispered, thinking about his favourite sweet. Raspberry gummies.

She turned and walked away from reception. Looked around for an open space.

'Yes, he's still the leader of the Syndicates and is occupied with the usual crap. Well . . . you know yourself . . .'

'Yes, thanks, I know what he's capable of.'

'We've received information that he and a few of his closest associates are on their way to Umeå. We still don't know what business they have up there, but it may be good for you to know. But this didn't come from me, okay?'

'Okay,' she said curtly.

Charlotte took out her pass card, held it against the card reader and entered her code. She pulled open the door before the beeping stopped, entered the empty room, sat down at the desk used when someone needed to file a report. The chair was a bit too low.

'This isn't good. It worries me that he's on his way.'

Time caught up with her; it was so long since she'd had anything to do with Tony that she'd almost forgotten him. Charlotte remembered his children, who were in nappies then. She remembered his outbursts of fury at his wife, who always had bruises.

'I just thought it might be good for you to know,' he said.

Charlotte leaned over the desk again.

70

'Hello, are you still there?' her colleague asked from the other end.

'Yes, I'm just thinking. Can you find out what business he has here?'

'This information landed in our lap by chance in connection with another matter. But if I find out more I'll call you. Okay? Maybe he's going to a wedding. Who the hell knows?' he said, laughing at his own comment.

Charlotte got up from the chair. 'Right,' she said with a sigh. 'Listen, thanks for calling. I know it's not customary. Thanks.'

'Well . . . it's your history with the guy that makes me bend the rules here, so please do keep it to yourself.'

'Of course,' she replied and tapped him away with the red circle on the phone screen.

That Tony Israelsson was on his way to Umeå was not a good sign. The Syndicates were a criminal gang who killed people as casually as she might step on a spider. She wondered whether she should tell Per about her background with Tony. She would prefer to bury it to avoid talk, because talk easily led to leaks, which in turn led to Tony. Charlotte closed her eyes. Before she opened them again she had made a decision.

She would wait and see how it all developed.

Charlotte pressed the exit button to her left and when the click came, she opened the door, her heart pounding hard in her chest.

14

Linn's eyes were drawn to the bag of crisps her mother had set out on the coffee table. The aroma of barbecue seasoning made her reach out her hand to take one but Frida's facial expression made her pull it back. Her mum always nagged at Linn to lose weight and now she'd set out a bowl of crisps. That was insane.

'Maybe she's testing you like this before a cosy Saturday,' Frida said, laughing. Linn had asked where she'd been earlier in the week but got no answer to that.

Linn pushed the bowl away. Frida was probably right.

It was the first time in several months that they were sitting in a room other than hers. Frida was already made up for the party at Nydala.

'You do know that it's bitter cold out, huh?' Linn said, pulling lightly on Frida's short skirt.

'Yes, and? My legs are the best-looking part of my body, so why not show them off?'

'But it's cold,' said Linn, feeling like Frida's mum.

'William hates it when I have trousers on. He loves my short skirts,' she said, laughing and tossing her hair back.

William this and William that, thought Linn. She was tired of him, but Frida was in love, and it was impossible to talk sense with her.

'I think you're worth someone much better than William,' said Linn.

'Knock it off. William is the world's dreamiest guy, but you haven't seen that side of him and you're never going to either. I'm the one he gets cosy with, got it?'

Linn's gaze was once again drawn to Frida's legs. The perfectly shaped tapers had a large gap between the thighs. How could Frida stay so thin? How much did she actually vomit? Linn felt a lump in her stomach at the same time as her shoulders collapsed. She put a cushion over her stomach to conceal the roll around her waist.

'Have you met Camilla's friend Hugo?' Linn asked.

Frida looked at her. 'Why do you say Camilla instead of Mum? It sounds shady somehow. I always say Mum.'

Linn shrugged her shoulders. 'I don't know, it just comes out like that. I've been doing it for years.'

Frida seemed content with the reply and came back to Hugo. 'What do you mean, then? Has Camilla started hiring people?'

'Yes, she hired Hugo a couple of months ago. He's started hanging around here at home loads.'

'Why a guy and not a girl? She's still selling home furnishings?'

'Don't know. I think she feels more secure with a guy who she can run things with,' said Linn, laughing.

'Maybe they're sleeping together,' said Frida, winking.

The thought had struck Linn too but she didn't say that. Frida stuck her hand in her little handbag, took it out and extended her palm. The size of the tablets varied, some were round and white while others were oblong with a pink plastic coating. She poured them out on the couch between them. Girl things, as William called them. Frida got them from him for party nights like this.

Linn had taken a tablet before a test one time, to have energy to study. Otherwise she only used at special parties. Linn preferred to party with alcohol because the drugs gave her crazy anxiety. In the pile there was a new pill that Linn hadn't seen before – a turquoise one.

'What kind of thing is that?' she asked.

'Dolcontin, like morphine or something. William said that you sleep super-good on it.'

Linn heard her mother's footsteps approaching and set the cushion over the pills. With a quick movement Frida stuffed one in her mouth and smiled at Linn just as her mother stepped into the room. They could hear the TV showing the news on TV4; it was about the increase in drug use among young people, ironically enough.

'Frida, how nice that you're here this evening,' she said, sitting down on the arm rest. Hugo also stepped in and fired off a smile at them.

'This is Hugo, he . . . does a little work for me,' she continued as he held out his right hand to greet Frida.

'Frida is my daughter's best friend,' she added.

Hugo looked good. Long black eyelashes, thick dark hair. Linn thought that he was a copy of Jon Snow from *Game of Thrones*. Frida apparently thought so too because she ran her hand through her hair and slowly placed one slender leg over the other. She also brought her shoulders back, emphasising her breasts.

Drama queen.

'So what will you ladies be up to this evening?' Hugo asked, looking like he wanted to sit down, but he stood there with his hands in his pockets.

'Just hanging out with friends,' said Linn.

Frida sat quietly, inspected Hugo as if he were a mannequin.

'Just say the word if I can drive you anywhere. I'm going home soon anyway,' said Hugo, but did not take his eyes off her mother. The green eyes didn't even try to hide what he was thinking.

Linn knew that Hugo helped her with orders and keeping track of inventory and such, but he also worked as a mail carrier and newspaper distributor sometimes. Her mother was much older than Hugo but still looked okay. Linn guessed that he was about twenty-seven, but maybe he liked older women.

Mum and Jon Snow. Linn couldn't blame her. Hugo was good-looking but a little behind the curve; he thought slowly and didn't talk too much. It was hard to put your finger on it; he seemed normal but somehow not. Talk about weather and such was fine, but if you asked a real question, you noticed that something was not quite right.

Mum drew her fingers through Linn's long hair. 'You've started to thin out your fringe,' she said, firmly pinching some strands of hair between her thumb and index finger. Linn moved her hand away.

'It's the Anja syndrome,' Frida said, laughing. The pill had started to take effect. Linn tensed up, placed one hand over the cushion that hid the pills in an attempt to look relaxed.

'What do you mean?' asked Camilla.

'A girl from Stockholm that Linn worships because she's upper class.'

Linn wanted to punch her for that comment. Her mother raised an eyebrow but didn't ask more about it.

'So how are your mum and dad doing?'

Frida's gaze moved over toward the TV. She shrugged her shoulders before she replied. 'I guess they're okay.'

'They still haven't given you free wi-fi?' Linn's mother asked and smiled.

'Jeez, she doesn't even have Instagram,' Linn added.

Camilla took out her phone and snapped a picture of her daughter before she and Hugo went to the door.

'I'll drive you. Just say when you want to leave,' he said.

'Thanks, we'll let you know,' said Linn.

Frida looked after Hugo and mimed 'wow' with her mouth.

'Knock it off, you can't sleep with him,' said Linn.

'Why? Who doesn't want to sleep with Jon Snow?' Frida laughed loudly and reached for the crisps. 'I have to eat anyway,' she said, letting her hand slowly pass Linn's face before she demonstratively stuffed the crisps into her mouth. 'I'm so damn excited.'

She took away the cushion that hid the drugs, and put them in her handbag again. 'This is going to be such an awesome night,' she continued, patting Linn on the shoulder.

'I know, it's, like, it's so great to be alive,' Linn replied, but didn't agree with that herself. She held out her palm to Frida, who gave her a pill. Linn placed it on her tongue. Leaned back on the soft couch and waited for the rush.

Camilla had lit a candle on the table and the flame flickered from her movement. The big picture window facing the street made the room feel bigger than it was.

'I know that William has been back and forth a lot with me,' said Frida. 'But lately I've felt closer to him. He's more there, do you understand? He asks me to do things that he never would if he wasn't interested.'

'What kind of things?' Linn asked, looking at her friend.

Frida lowered her gaze. 'Just things, harmless, not sex or anything like that. All the girls want him, but I'm the one he asks about things.'

Linn let her gaze wander out through the window. Frida exaggerated William's reputation as popular. Many people laughed behind his back. Called him a failed druggie. But she didn't say that now. Didn't want to ruin the mood.

Instead she enjoyed the calm she felt in her body. That warm sensation, like being wrapped in a blanket of self-confidence. She stood up and went over to the window. The snow outside appeared to be dancing under the streetlights. The flakes moved in various directions.

She looked at the car that was parked down on the street, lit up by the same streetlights. A white car, similar to the one William had.

'Check it out, Frida. It looks like William is picking us up.'

'Huh?' said Frida, standing beside her. 'He didn't say that to me. How does he know where you live?'

An orange dot moved back and forth in the otherwise dark front seat. The smoke slipped out through the open side window. Frida took out her phone and sent a text to him, but the person behind the steering wheel didn't seem to look at a phone. Instead the car drove away.

Frida's phone vibrated.

What do you mean pick you up? I'm at Nydala.

15

Abbe tossed the cigarette out the side window of the car and started the engine. He'd seen what he needed to. The girls were on their way out. He pulled away and headed to the place by Scandic Hotel where Tony was waiting. At the time when Hells Angels made use of the little brick house it had been surrounded by a high fence, but now that was torn down and the house was unprotected. Abbe wondered whether they knew that the Syndicates had confiscated the building. Temporarily, in any case. The two groups had battled over cities and territories for a long time but in the past few years the Angels had pulled back and found other hunting grounds further north.

Abbe followed the traffic laws so as not to attract attention to himself, lightened his foot on the accelerator, took it easier than usual because the idiots in Umeå didn't salt the roads.

Tony had sent a text that it was time, so the only thing to do was obey. Abbe bent his neck to the side, cricking the vertebrae. The six-hour-long drive from Stockholm had not been kind to his body. His clothes weren't made for the cold air and the chill made its way deep into his bones. Working for Tony was a hazardous job. He was constantly under observation by both the cops and other criminal organizations. Wearing body armour was a no-brainer, even if Tony usually neglected to and counted on the fact that his closest associates would take the bullets for him.

Abbe thought back to how it had all started. How he ended up in this damned position. He was a young bartender in Stockholm when Tony got him into the fly nightclubs full of celebrities. And just for a little return service in the form of keeping track of his gambling club. Making sure that everything went smoothly when he couldn't be there himself. Pounding on those who made mistakes. Keeping the women in check. In the beginning it was a role he played in order to blend in. Then it became normal, and after a while he started liking it. He got to fuck as much as he wanted, but the more he took of the women for himself, the less he wanted them. He wanted to leave Tony and the whole mess. But right now that wasn't possible, so he let go of the thought and turned up the music. Bruce Springsteen echoed in the car as Abbe drove over the Teg Bridge. Saturday night had just begun and a few individuals were walking across the bridge in the direction of the city, toward the nightlife. They looked cowed; the wind made them bend their backs in order to protect themselves from the worst of it.

He wondered whether there were any noteworthy gambling clubs in Umeå. A place where people got their needs satisfied. Everything here seemed tightly arranged. Politically correct. Abbe knew that Umeå was the fortress of the Social Democrats and left-wingers. Culture was heavily subsidized and the Sweden Democrats were exiled. Abbe himself didn't vote because he thought that politicians were just as criminal as himself, albeit with a salary from the government.

He flicked on the indicator and turned off Blå vägen toward Teg, drove past a petrol station and stopped the car in front of the discreet little house. Tony came out with his trigger-happy buddy who had taken the train up. The gun was quite visible in front of his stomach, stuck into the waistband like a real cliché.

Abbe leaned over the passenger seat and opened the door. Tony got in, holding one of his phones in his hand. He was always simply dressed. Looked like any working man in jeans and shirt, topped with a Gant sweater and a generic jacket. His shoulders were thin and he leaned forward slightly. He was funny like that, Tony. Extremely hungry for money and brand-name objects, while he looked like an anonymous office rat. There were no characteristics to describe him with. No crooked nose, no high cheekbones or forehead. No tattoos, no piercings, no scars. Just an ordinary old guy who looked like a million others and Abbe wondered how the police would describe his appearance.

'I've found a person for you,' said Abbe. 'One I know you want to get at.'

'Who? There are many to choose from, my good friend. Do you mean here in Umeå or in Stockholm?'

'Umeå,' Abbe replied, taking out his phone, showing Tony the picture he had taken earlier in the evening.

Tony whistled, stuffed a fistful of raspberry gummies in his mouth and laughed out loud. 'Do you have an address too?'

'Of course,' Abbe replied, checking off yet another betrayal on his list.

'You're a genius. This will be an exciting night,' said Tony.

If you only knew, Abbe thought.

16

Per moved close to Mia and embraced her. Set his chin on her shoulder. She was dicing onions.

'How's it going with the murder of that woman in the bathtub?' she asked.

Per raised his eyebrows. He wasn't used to her caring about his work.

'We haven't found a motive or anyone who wanted to harm her. None of the work we've done has brought us closer to a solution. Crazy frustrating.'

Mia nodded. 'What are the boys doing?'

'Showering. Hard to imagine that we'd become hockey parents – the sort who hang out in ice-cold rinks,' he said, leaning against the kitchen counter beside her. Mia had make-up on, her hair pulled into a ponytail.

'I'm mostly worried about the cost,' she said, scraping the chopped pieces into a bowl. 'My God,' she continued. 'That Bauer stick that Simon wants costs three thousand kronor.'

'Yes, I know, but the way they love skating around on the ice . . . He'll have to play with the stick he has until it breaks.' Per smiled, with his gaze on the white floor. 'Björklöven seems to be an okay club anyway, and think how nice it would be if the boys could devote themselves to a sport instead of other things. You know that Simon is going to want to hang out with friends soon. He's ten now. Man, how time goes fast.'

Mia laughed. 'Yes, pretty soon girls will be running up to their room.'

'I know how quickly it can go downhill, even for the youngsters who have the best circumstances in life. If I can keep him or Hannes from starting to run around with the wrong crowd by putting a hockey stick in their hands, I'll finance that one way or another.'

Mia set down the knife. 'Shall I remind you of the sighs and moans you made when we bought the original equipment for them?' She took her index finger and pressed it on the tip of Per's nose. 'We took it from the holiday account – remember that next summer. Eleven thousand kronor less to have an experience with.'

Per was about to reply when the doorbell rang. Mia went to answer it. He followed her with his gaze and came after her to greet Charlotte who had stepped into the hall.

'Hi! Did you come alone?' Mia asked, closing the door behind her.

Charlotte extended a bottle of wine and hugged them. 'Yes . . . it turned out that way. Anja is going to a party.'

His wife and colleague had found a friend in each other. In the beginning Mia was not that interested in getting to know Charlotte, but because Per had seen how Kicki harassed Charlotte at the police station, he decided that she and Mia should have the chance to meet. Then Charlotte had worn down Mia with charm and warmth. Now she loved his colleague and Mia had also become Charlotte's closest friend in Umeå.

The door opened again and a few snowflakes whirled down on the doormat.

Per crossed his arms over his chest, tensing his muscles as protection from the cold. Nils and Annelie's clothes were covered by snow that fell to the floor as they stepped in.

'Oh, hurry on in, it's so damn cold out,' Per said, closing the door. They went into the kitchen where it was warm and laced with the aroma of his risotto.

'You didn't bring the kids with you, either?' Mia asked, looking at Nils and Annelie. The wine glasses clinked as she took them down from the shelf.

'No, they wanted to stay at home and watch movies.'

Nils and Annelie greeted Charlotte politely and Per took a sip of red Italian wine. Barolo. A heavy wine that not everyone enjoyed. Per knew that Charlotte loved it but it wasn't certain that the others would cheer in delight. Nils had just started to drink wine; he was more a beer drinker.

'Take the opportunity and enjoy that the kids want to be at home and watch movies,' said Charlotte. Her wine-red dress had sleeves that broadened from the elbow and were about to end up in her glass. *It matches the wine,* thought Per. The smooth bun on her neck sat perfectly as always. Per's gaze moved to her mouth, the red lipstick sought attention and she had eyeliner on too. A pair of glistening earrings that could probably support a whole family for a year. Charlotte had placed one foot on the other. Maybe she was uncomfortable without her indoor shoes.

Nils laughed at her comment about the children. 'Yes, we've gone through the teenage phase with one, now we have the other one left,' he said, raising the glass to his mouth, and stopped mid-motion. 'Where's your daughter?' he asked.

'She got permission to socialize with some friends at a party, with a guy at some house in Nydala.'

Annelie cleared her throat and turned her gaze to Charlotte. 'Do you mean that abandoned house on Stenson's lot? I hope that's not where she is.'

Per could see on Charlotte's face that that was exactly where Anja was.

'I don't know if it's an abandoned house, but she did mention something about Stenson,' Charlotte said, setting her glass down on the table. 'What do you know?' She took her phone out of her handbag.

'We shouldn't worry you unnecessarily,' Annelie said. 'But two years ago we picked our daughter up there. She actually called us and was . . . well, to speak plainly . . . drunk off her ass. We never went into the house because she was standing outside waiting when we came, but she told us a few things when we came home.'

Charlotte held the phone in her hand. Per saw that she was starting to get irritated.

'What did she tell you?'

'Evidently both alcohol and drugs were flowing there. There's a VIP room where some of the kids have entry. Then the house has a top floor with three rooms that only have mattresses on the floor. The less popular girls end up there in the hands of the boys.'

Per listened and watched as Charlotte raised her phone to her ear.

'Yes, it's just terrible,' Annelie continued. 'Our daughter was offered lots of alcohol and then led up to a room. A boy tried to take her clothes off but fortunately she managed to get out of there and call us. Think about the girls who don't have that presence of mind.' Annelie shook her head. 'It's just crazy. I didn't think they still had parties there!'

'But, Charlotte, Anja's a smart girl. You don't need to be worried,' Per said, knowing at the same time that those words would not calm Charlotte.

'Maybe we should have reported the guy for assault,' Annelie continued, 'but we didn't think that far and instead were just glad that she got out intact. But this MeToo debate has made me wonder if we were wrong. Easy to be wise in hindsight.' She looked at Nils, who stroked her back with his hand.

Per didn't want to put any blame on his friends, but the fact they didn't report or at least flag that something was wrong in that house? That he couldn't understand.

'How the hell can we be unaware of this? We're police officers, for Christ's sake. Some patrol must have gone there on a call over the years,' Per said, setting down his glass. It spilled over from the hasty movement.

'There's a pact at the school. You don't talk about it, much less call the police if anything happens,' said Nils.

'I see . . . so you can be raped and no one calls,' said Mia.

Charlotte paced back and forth in the kitchen while she tried to call Anja.

'I'm only reaching her voicemail. I have to go pick her up. Can one of you come with and show me where it is?'

'Of course,' said Nils, going to the door. 'I can drive. I've only had a few sips.'

Charlotte's jaw was clenched. She walked toward the hall, her heels pounding on the floor.

'And in which room am I going to find Anja? In the VIP room or on a mattress? So crazy! This is so crazy!'

17

'What are you up to?' said Linn, pressing her palm against Frida's forehead so that her head moved backward. Frida giggled and every movement she made was in slow motion. Linn had just witnessed how William almost had sex with her on the speaker in front of lots of people, where several of them were filming everything too. Linn had tried to pull her away from there, but Frida refused. It was sick and degrading and Frida didn't even notice it. Everyone was laughing at her. They'd been at Nydala for an hour or so and things had already spiralled out of control. Anja was here too and Linn wanted to hang out with her, but didn't know where she was.

Linn saw that William was looking at Frida, how he drew his hand through her thick blonde hair. He had ice-blue eyes and looked like a surfer.

Frida smiled at him. The music was deafening, an old Katy Perry song pounding out of the speakers. Frida's skirt wasn't pulled down completely after the adventure on the speaker and had got stuck around her rear. Linn grasped it with both hands and pulled the fabric down with a sturdy tug. Frida held her palms up toward her.

'Whoops,' she said, taking hold of another girl's plastic cup, yanking it out of her hand and draining the red liquid. The girl shook her head but put up no fight over the drink.

William moved close beside Frida, put a pill on his tongue which he then guided into Frida's mouth before he took two steps backward. He caressed Frida's hand, cocked his head. It looked like he was going to take her right there where they were standing. His gaze was foggy, his lips moist. William whispered something to Frida, then he turned around and left.

Linn watched him as he went to the stairs. He kissed a few girls on the way up but didn't take any with him.

'Pull yourself together, damn it,' Linn screamed into Frida's ear. 'You're not going up to the top floor with him. Do you hear me?'

Frida let her scream. The music had drowned out most of what she said.

'I'm not going up there, you know that. I'm not a lay for him,' she said in Linn's ear. 'He wants me to go home with him. His friend is going to drive me.'

Frida shook her head so that her hair straightened out on her back. She took a lip-gloss from her handbag and brought it to her lips. The movement was slow and she had a hard time keeping her upper body still.

Linn looked at her. 'Which friend?' she asked.

'Don't know, he just said that his friend would pick me up.'

'Isn't it better that Hugo drives you? I can call him,' Linn said, looking around.

'No, I'll wait for William's friend.'

'You can't ride with someone you don't know,' said Linn, trying to make eye contact with her. But Frida pursed her lips, smiled and started moving her legs in time with the music. The group that had filmed her crude necking on the speaker had scattered. Frida leaned toward Linn.

'Does it matter? It's William's friend – like, what can happen?' she said, raising her arms in the air trying to follow along with the music, but her movements always ended up in the wrong tempo.

'I'm thinking about sleeping with him tonight. He's so damn fine and if I get to go to his house it's serious. That's just how it is. I want him.'

Linn shook her head. 'Then you'll be one in the crowd of girls who have slept with him. Is that what you want?'

Frida smiled. 'You don't get it, I'm his woman now. Not just any girl.'

18

Charlotte stared out through the windscreen at the oncoming snowstorm. Nils drove with low beams even though it was pitch black out. Charlotte had called Anja so many times without a result that she'd given up. Her daughter still hadn't called back. Charlotte clenched her jaw so hard that a little point of pain made itself known just above one eye.

'You know we're not going to ticket you if you exceed the speed limit,' she said to Nils, getting a faint laugh from Per in the back seat.

Nils kept his eyes on the road. 'It's slippery as hell. I don't dare drive faster.'

'I understand,' she said, but wanted to scream at him to take the brick off the brake pedal.

Per undid his seat belt and leaned forward between the seats.

'Anja isn't as wide-eyed and innocent as other girls her age. She's tough, she'll speak up.'

'If she's been offered alcohol or drugs, though, who is she then?' said Charlotte, inhaling and holding the air in her lungs as long as she could.

Nils was driving on Blå vägen; she could see The Island straight ahead. There was her future home. Maybe. Anja loved it. The airport on the right was vacant and silent. With an accustomed movement she moved her hand to her hip. *Shit,* she thought. *No gun.*

'Calm down. Do you honestly think you'll need that now?' Per asked.

'I'm ready for anything,' she replied, realizing herself how crazy that sounded.

She looked at Nils. He had no hair, kind eyes, glasses. The thick jacket hid a slight bulge on his stomach and tattoos that Per told her were from his time at sea. He didn't look like a sailor, but Per called him the Captain.

'We're going to Lake Nydala?' said Nils, pressing down on the accelerator a little.

'An abandoned summer cottage maybe?' Per asked. 'There are quite a few of those in the area.'

'Yes. Stenson's house is maybe a kilometre or so from the lake. Otherwise it's mostly forest and cottages all around. This time of year they can probably party undisturbed, I would think.'

When they turned off to a smaller road, Nils had to put the brights on. Just about the same time, a pounding bass could be heard distantly, along with laughter and singing. Nils stopped the car in front of a rather large house that had once been red. The tyres had barely stopped rolling when Charlotte had her first foot out on the ground.

'Easy!' Per opened the door and took a couple of quick steps toward Charlotte, and tried to get hold of her without succeeding. Charlotte didn't shut the door but instead marched straight toward the house. Per caught up with her, took hold of her coat sleeve and forced her to stop.

'Charlotte, breathe. You have to be calm when you go into the house. For Anja's sake.'

Two girls were standing in front of the entrance. Smoke was puffing out of their mouths. They were wearing thin black tank tops and tight jeans. Both of them had hairstyles similar to Anja's, but platinum-blonde curls.

Is everyone cloned in this town? thought Charlotte, tearing herself loose from Per's grip and going up to them. Her boots got a poor hold on the snow.

'Have you seen this girl tonight?' she asked, holding up the phone screen to the young women who were each taking a puff on the cigarette. They looked at the picture. Both nodded at the same time.

'Anja. She's probably in there somewhere.'

'How old are you?' Charlotte asked angrily.

'Are you Anja's police mum?' asked the one with fake eyelashes, kohl around her eyes and way too much blusher.

'Yes. How old are you?'

'Eighteen,' the taller girl replied. Short but still tallest.

'Bullshit,' said Charlotte, calling her colleagues at the station as she took two steps at a time up to the entrance.

She heard Per close behind her.

The front door was open, yet it still felt warm when she stepped into the house. The eyes of the young people went straight toward the two adults who had come to the party uninvited. They stopped talking and stared. Some were too drunk to notice them.

'It's barely nine o'clock and they're already completely out of it,' she said to Per without looking at him.

She took a few steps inside and found herself in a large room that was completely empty of furniture. The dance floor. The music pounded in her ears. A computer was placed on the windowsill, giving off a faint glow – that was where the music was controlled. Charlotte could hardly make out what type of music it was. A pressure wave passed through her body from the speakers. Some youths were dancing in a circle, moving in time with the music. Two girls stood and talked, or rather shrieked at each other. A guy was standing next to a girl whose head was hanging down; she was having a hard time standing up. The guy leaned forward, lifted up her head and guided his tongue into her mouth. The plastic cup in her hand turned to the side and liquid ran down on the floor.

Charlotte went up and tapped the guy on the back. She was just about to hit him when Per took hold of her arm and stopped it mid-motion. She glared at him.

'He's exploiting her!' Charlotte screamed at Per, who nodded and mimed *I know* at the same time as he made signs to her to calm down. The guy left them and went into another room. Charlotte took a deep breath and turned around in the room so that she could see every corner, every person. No Anja.

While Per stayed behind to talk with the drunk girl, Charlotte moved toward the room the guy had gone into. The lighting was dim and the music not as deafening. Charlotte was relieved when she saw youths whose heads seemed to be clearer. Three red wide couches. Boys and girls who sat and talked. But Charlotte could not see her daughter. One of the guys noticed her and stopped talking mid-sentence. The others followed.

'Well now, seriously good-looking boots!'

Charlotte turned to the girl who had noticed her Gucci.

'Thanks,' she replied and looked at her. It was too dark to make out her pupils but Charlotte could swear that she was high. The focusing. The presence. Classic cocaine. Besides, it must be impossible to be in this house without being anesthetized by something. She held out the phone to the girl. 'Have you seen Anja?'

'Are you joking? Everyone knows who Anja is. We know who you are too. Come on, I'll show you. She's in another room. I was just there but went out to . . .'

The girl stopped herself, then she met Charlotte's gaze and fired off a big smile. 'To smoke,' she finished, winking.

A brave young lady, thought Charlotte, and realized that she looked like she was out of a fashion magazine.

'Then you know that I'm a police officer?'

The girl angled her index and middle finger at her own eyes, then toward Charlotte's.

Cocaine, thought Charlotte, and was reminded of her own quite different youth. She had tried cannabis once but didn't like it. After that she had never tested anything. She prayed to the gods that Anja hadn't sampled. That she'd stood up for herself. Charlotte followed the girl. On a table she noted the remnants of white powder. It had probably been removed in haste because of their sudden presence. *So much cocaine and shit,* she thought.

Her stomach was in a knot. Her pulse rose as the stairway to the top floor came closer, and when the girl took the first step Charlotte could no longer contain herself.

'Is she on the top floor?'

The girl turned around, smiled and continued.

Charlotte pushed past the girl and took the stairs two at a time. A guy on his way down bumped into her shoulder so hard that she almost fell backwards.

'Excuse me, take it easy!' she said loudly and turned around and looked at him. But he disappeared quickly downstairs without answering.

She looked around on the top floor. Four doors. All closed.

'So, where is she?' Charlotte's voice sounded more panicky than she intended.

The girl stepped up to the door at the far end of the corridor. Charlotte took a deep breath and followed. *Whatever you've ended up in, I love you,* she thought, looking at the young hand that carefully pressed down the door handle.

'Mum! What are you doing here?'

Anja was sitting in an armchair a short way into the room. Fully clothed, thank God. Next to it was a corner couch that housed a girl and four boys. All clothed.

'Anja, my God,' she said, thinking about rushing up and hugging her. Anja's look made her change her mind.

'What are you doing here, Mum? God, you're a pain.' Anja stood up. The young people remained sitting on the couch and looked at Charlotte. They seemed calm. Some had their feet on the table where there was an ice bucket with beer and some plastic bottles that no doubt contained self-mixed alcoholic beverages.

No drugs.

'Are these your friends?' she asked, trying to smile at the group of young people.

Anja put her hands on her waist. 'Yes, this is Linn – you know, the girl I mentioned,' said Anja, and Linn held out her hand to greet her. *Well brought up,* thought Charlotte and looked at Linn. Clearly under the influence of something, but exerting herself to seem unaffected. Kind brown eyes, like a deer.

'Then this is Jesper, Nille, Kalle and Oscar. They play hockey in Björklöven,' Anja continued, moving the focus from Linn.

'It's chill here tonight,' said the sassy girl who had led Charlotte to the room.

'Like every night,' Jesper added, and they all nodded in unison.

Charlotte ignored them.

'What kind of place is this, Anja? And why in the world don't you answer when I call?'

'Mum, this is the VIP room. Whatever happens in the rest of the house has nothing to do with me. Besides, you can't bring your phone with you in here, everyone puts them there.'

She pointed at a crate by the door with several phones inside.

'May I speak with you? Come with me here,' said Charlotte, moving toward the door.

Anja rolled her eyes. 'Sorry about my mum,' she said to the people on the couch. She followed Charlotte and picked up her coat on the way. Anja had borrowed it from her. Max Mara, cashmere.

'You know that you're embarrassing me, right?' said Anja, closing the door behind them.

'Listen, I don't care if I'm embarrassing you. You shouldn't be in this kind of place. This house is soon going to have a visit and hopefully be shut down forever.'

'Knock it off, Mum. This is nothing out of the ordinary – it's exactly the same in Stockholm, even if the address there is finer and the rooms better decorated. Otherwise it's the same.'

Charlotte snorted.

'When are you going to get it in your head that this is what it's like to be young now?' Anja continued, putting on her coat. 'It's not like in your medieval times.'

She knows that I'm not going to let her stay here anyway, thought Charlotte and inspected her daughter who was tying the belt around her waist demonstratively hard.

'Anja . . . have you taken drugs?'

'No. What the hell? Do you think I would dare after all your scary talks about how easily you can become an addict? I'm never going to try them. Believe me.'

Charlotte breathed out. She intended to trust her daughter because she wanted to trust her. She intended to live in denial a while longer. But that topic of conversation wasn't over – just for the moment.

'Do you know a guy named William?' she asked, thinking about the murder investigation.

'Yes, how do you know who that is?'

'What do you know about him?' Charlotte asked at the same time as blinking blue lights could be seen through the window.

Anja searched for a picture on her phone and showed it to her mother.

'He runs this place. A charming guy that I would never touch.'

Charlotte looked at the photo. *A dangerous young man for young, impressionable teenage girls,* she thought.

'We're going to arrest him, because what he runs here is illegal.'

'What do you mean illegal?' Anja said defiantly.

'He sells or distributes drugs and alcohol to minors. That's illegal in so many ways. You know that. I want you to get in the car outside while I talk with him. Do you know where he is?'

'No idea. He's probably somewhere with some girl.'

19

Viggo supported himself with his hands to sit up in bed. He leaned his back against the headboard and looked at his wife Estelle. They were alike, her and Frida, though Estelle was the only woman he knew of who wore a nightgown with matching silk bathrobe. *Like in* Dallas, he thought. The light violet fabrics glistened as she moved in the bedroom. She'd wanted to have sex. He hadn't said no to that and now they were wide awake, even though it was the middle of the night.

Viggo observed his blonde wife. Her long legs were natural but she had paid for the ample breasts. *Worth every penny,* he thought. The first time he saw her was at a bar in Stockholm. She stood out from the other women because she was always sober. It was almost ironic, considering how things were now. He hoped that Frida wouldn't inherit the love of alcohol.

Estelle was quiet, but extremely charismatic. She drew men to her simply through her existence and that made her exciting. She could just stand there and they came like bees to honey. She chose, and that evening he got the winning lottery ticket. Viggo had been completely sold.

They started talking, went to her place and since then they had stuck together. That was eighteen years ago. Viggo had wanted to separate many times during those years. But he stayed. Partly because he still loved Estelle, and partly because of all the shit he'd dragged her into – the escape from Stockholm, which had always been her home. Estelle's whole identity was in Östermalm, where she'd gone to school, made her friends, had her first drink, built up her yoga studio . . . Now she was living in Umeå of all places. She hadn't moved there voluntarily. The consolation was their finances – Viggo's money, which gave them the opportunity to travel abroad often. She didn't need to work and they weren't dependent on each other. They took care of themselves.

When Viggo's phone vibrated, he was wakened from his thought bubble.

'Aren't you going to see who it is?' said Estelle.

Viggo took hold of the phone. A text was visible on the screen.

Just wanted to check if Frida came home. – Linn

Viggo read the message to Estelle and she met his gaze.

'What the hell?' he said, tearing the bedspread off his body. He grabbed his bathrobe in passing and followed Estelle to Frida's room.

'What time is it?' Estelle asked, taking a firm hold on the doorframe.

'Almost two,' said Viggo, running right into her when she stopped abruptly at the threshold.

The bed was empty, untouched. As she'd left it.

Estelle brought her hand to her mouth. 'She's not at home.'

Viggo entered Frida's number. Estelle was standing so close that he felt her breath. The ringtone sounded again and again. At last he was connected to voicemail.

'Frida, it's Dad – call when you get this. We're worried about you. Where are you?'

He hung up and entered Linn's number.

No answer.

'Damn!'

He wrote her a message. *Frida isn't at home. Isn't she with you?*

Viggo pounded his hand on the wall so hard that a picture shook.

'Where was she going?' Estelle asked.

Viggo sat down on Frida's bed and tried to think. They had talked at lunch but he'd been so engrossed in his own thoughts that he hadn't really listened.

How the heck did I give in? he thought. There and then it had been an easy way out. A way to avoid the nagging but also to keep her in a good mood. Her psyche was fragile and Anton's suicide made Viggo afraid that she would get strange ideas.

'She was going to a party, I think, at a friend's.'

'What friend?' Estelle asked, starting to tap on Frida's computer. Entered various passwords. When she failed the third time she slammed the lid shut.

'A guy, maybe someone in her class. Don't really remember.'

Viggo rested his elbows against his thighs and put his head in his hands.

'How the hell could you let her go to a party without knowing exactly where she was going? You know we have to be careful about such things,' Estelle said in a loud voice.

'We can't watch over her twenty-four hours a day – she's almost grown up.'

Estelle did not let herself be calmed. 'But we have to because she's living under threat, because of you!'

'Think about if you could stay sober longer than a few hours and Frida had a mother to talk with! Have you thought about that?' Viggo wanted to maintain control but his voice broke.

Estelle's eyes turned black. 'Don't lay the guilt on me! Who is it who put us in this fucking situation to start with?'

Viggo got up from the bed. 'I see, so you're going to play that card again. It's my fault that you're an alcoholic, it's my fault that you get depressed, it's my fault that you don't have a career. Everything – just everything – that you hate about your life is my fault!'

He took a deep breath before he continued. Fixed his eyes on her black irises.

'If it hadn't been for my talent at poker you couldn't have lived your glamorous housewife life with everything served up. You don't need to lift a finger and you just drink all day. Maybe if we'd had another child you would have taken care of yourself.'

He knew that he'd crossed the line the moment he said that, and Estelle's palm struck him so hard that his head moved to the side. It hurt but he didn't show anything.

'Sorry, I . . .' Estelle interrupted herself, tears running down her cheeks. She wrapped her arms around Viggo's neck. He let her come close.

'I'm sorry too. I didn't mean that.'

'We have to call the police,' she said, burrowing her face into his chest.

'Not yet, Estelle. Maybe she's sleeping over with a friend.' He wanted to buy time. His thoughts went to Tony, but it didn't feel right. If Tony knew that Viggo was in Umeå he would have been dead by now. Tony didn't play games.

His phone rang.

'It's Frida,' he said, pressing the phone to his ear. The tension in his chest relaxed immediately. 'Hi, honey, where are you?'

There was no response. Instead he heard something that scraped and faint breathing. As if she had pocket-dialled.

'Frida? Where are you?'

The pressure in his chest was back.

Viggo pressed the phone harder against his ear. Held up his other hand to Estelle, who wanted to take the phone from him.

'Hello? Frida?'

He held his breath so as not to miss a single sound from his daughter. Then came the buzzing. The call was ended.

'Damn!' Viggo called her back.

Voicemail.

20

Per pulled the scarf closer to his mouth, let the warmth from his breath meet his chin during the short walk from the car park to his workplace. It was late and the events at the party house had also changed the rest of the evening. Per and Charlotte had driven Anja home and so now they were here, on their way into the station. Colleagues were at the scene out in Nydala to close down the party house and they had taken a dozen young people into custody who they had found with drugs.

'A sad evening this was,' said Charlotte.

There was a click in the entry door and Per took hold of the cold handle. He stamped his feet, making the snow that covered his shoes run off.

'Yes, you can safely say that.'

He held the door for Charlotte, who could barely see anything under the edge of her beanie.

'Very sad that we couldn't have a calm, pleasant evening with Nils and Annelie,' she said, pulling off the knitted hat. Her hair spread in every direction.

'Yes, but they understand. I talked with Mia – she and Annelie drank a lot of wine, so some of us got to enjoy the evening anyway.'

'Can I get Nils's number so I can ask a few general questions about the house on The Island?' Charlotte said, greeting a policeman on his way out.

'Sure, then I'm sure he'll go home and do his research. Believe me, first thing tomorrow you'll have a PowerPoint on advantages and disadvantages and the market value and God knows what else.'

He knew Nils, who was a meticulous estate agent, would never stoop to being dishonest. That was also one of the reasons that Per liked him so much.

Charlotte pressed the lift button and Per noticed that her index finger was completely white.

'Are your fingers frozen? Already? You were only outside a short time.'

Charlotte massaged her left hand and held it up for Per.

'This is a reminder from a beastly cold week skiing in Val d'Isère a few years ago. Got frostbite on my fingers and now they turn white as soon as my hands get cold.'

Per had the same problem with one of his big toes. But that was from a day on little Bräntberget in Umeå when he was skiing with Simon and Hannes. He refrained from telling her about that.

The lights were on in the offices of Major Crimes, even though no one was there. Per undid the buttons on his blue coat and swung it off. He took out his glucose monitor and scanned himself. Showed Charlotte out of habit with a sigh. His T-shirt was sticking to his back.

'Ooh, two point six,' she said, stepping out to the kitchen. Per sat down on the nearest desk – Charlotte's. His scalp felt damp.

'I felt completely fine until we got into the lift,' he said, watching how Charlotte inserted the straw into the juice carton and gave it to him. 'Thanks.'

He slurped up the whole box and tossed it in Charlotte's wastebasket. It landed on a picture, a man Per had never seen before. He didn't look like a hooligan, more like a grey office gnome, but the picture was from the police register.

'Who is that?' he said, leaning down to pick up the printout.

'No one, just a criminal from Stockholm. I wanted to see what he looks like these days,' Charlotte replied.

'Evidently someone that you've taken the trouble to print out a picture of and then discard it.'

Charlotte stood quietly. Her face was expressionless but her gaze was directed at the picture. It looked as if she was about to say something but then they were interrupted.

'Hello, there's a lot of activity here on a Saturday night, I see. I heard about the call-out you made to the Stenson house at Nydala.'

Ola Boman had come in without them hearing anything. Charlotte turned her head toward him and Per saw how her cheeks had gone red. The man went by the name Hot-Ola in the police station.

'Don't you ever sleep?' she asked, straightening her back without taking her eyes off him.

'We had an incident today that dragged on,' he replied.

Per felt invisible. *Can't you two just sleep with each other and get it over with?* he thought as Ola took the picture out of his hand.

'Are you happy working in Witness Protection?' Per asked, and his gaze landed on Ola's nose. Perfect and straight. It wasn't just Charlotte who'd been seduced by his appearance. The whole fricking police station was of the same opinion. Per called him the Dressman because he looked just like the man in their adverts.

'Sure, thanks. It's pretty much fine, I have to say,' said Ola.

Per's gaze moved to Ola's stomach, which was hidden under a white shirt. *Irritatingly flat,* he thought and his hand went toward his own belt. Per had needed to add three holes after his weight loss, but he was a long way from Ola's six-pack.

Ola placed his hand on Charlotte's shoulder. 'I have something for you,' he said, handing a file to her.

Charlotte took it; her fingers had regained their normal hue.

'A transcript from a wiretap in Stockholm,' Ola continued, looking at Charlotte with an intense gaze. 'He's in Umeå now, but he may be on his way to Stockholm again. You can read it for yourself.'

Have they already slept together? thought Per.

'What's that?' he asked, pointing at the file.

'I haven't been here,' said Ola, and Per watched him as he left the room. Charlotte was reading from a paper in the folder.

'Charlotte?' Per went up to her. He picked up the picture that Ola had left on the desk. 'Who is this?'

She responded with silence and continued reading in the file.

'Charlotte!' Per clenched his jaw. 'What is it that Ola knows about, but I don't?'

'We'll deal with that later, Per.'

Charlotte snapped the folder shut and threw it in her desk drawer. The one with a lock, where she stored her jewellery when they were out in the field. Her service pistol was also there, which she took out and put in its place in the holster.

'I know, a prohibited place to store it. It won't happen again,' she said. 'Now I want to talk about what happened this evening.'

Charlotte went to the briefing room and Per followed her in the dark corridor.

The fluorescent light buzzed when Charlotte turned it on. A coffee cup was left on one of the tables. Per shuddered; it was cold in here.

Charlotte placed herself in front of the whiteboard, where the investigation of the murder of Unni Olofsson took up most of the space. The pictures of her in the bathtub made Per purse his lips.

'I can't help thinking about Unni after what happened in the Nydala house this evening,' she said, taking a step backward, right into Per. She excused herself and stepped to the side.

'What if the drugs we confiscated can be linked to the ones we found at Unni's apartment? Petra, the neighbour, told Unni that William Gunnarsson sells drugs at the university, and he is evidently the one who supplies the young people in the Nydala house with drugs, if I'm to believe what Anja says.'

'We have checked up on William, right?' Per asked.

'Yes. He comes from a rather well-to-do family and has never been charged with a crime. The guy doesn't even have a speeding ticket.'

Per looked at the whiteboard again. He thought about what Charlotte said.

'That the murder of Unni, or even the tablets we found in her apartment, would have any form of connection to what we confiscated in the house this evening is rather far-fetched.'

'I agree,' Charlotte admitted. Her phone screen blinked silently and she raised it to her ear.

'Hi, Anja, aren't you asleep?' Charlotte picked at a white spot on her dress with her finger. 'Yes, I know. Per and I just drove to the station to debrief the evening. I'll be home soon. Go back to sleep.'

Per listened to his colleague. She had just found her daughter in what was a mild version of a sex and drugs den. If it had been him, Per would lock up his boys until they were eighteen years old. At the same time he would preach about how bad things can go if you try drugs, as Charlotte had done with Anja. Scare the shit out of them so that they would never dare test it. He wondered whether he should show them pictures from drug dens. Or was that taking it too far?

Charlotte ended the call and went up to the whiteboard, took a marker and wrote with green letters:

She turned to Per. 'Anja just told me that a girl who'd been at the party during the evening can't be reached. Frida Malk. Anja said that none of the girl's friends can get hold of her, and according to the parents she's not at home and her phone is turned off.'

'This has happened before without any crime being committed,' said Per.

Charlotte heaved a deep sigh. 'Frida has a best friend named Linn who was at the party. According to her, Frida was extremely under the influence. Frida and William were seen necking in the house and that's apparently all over the internet now.'

She held out her phone screen toward Per. The film clip that Anja had sent showed William and a young girl necking wildly on a stereo speaker.

'Then maybe they're still with each other?' said Per.

'It feels iffy that she's alone with that William in her condition – he seems to take advantage of young girls.'

'Okay, let's do this,' said Per. 'Check with the operations room if the parents have called in and reported her missing. We'll send a patrol to William's house, find out if he and Frida are there. I'm sure there's no danger.'

Charlotte took a deep breath and slowly exhaled. 'You're right. Let's do that.'

At the same moment Per's phone started ringing.

'My God, what a lot of activity there's been tonight,' he said, taking the call. 'Yes, this is Per Berg here, Umeå Police.'

'Yes, hi. This is Petra Lanz, Unni's neighbour on Dressyrgatan. I apologize for calling in the middle of the night like this, but I didn't know who I should call. I just came home from a party and there seems to be someone in Unni's apartment.'

'Did you see who it is?' Per asked, moving to the door.

'No, but someone has broken in.'

'Okay, stay inside your apartment. We'll come there in a car. Thanks for calling.'

Per alerted the regional command centre as he and Charlotte ran toward the lift.

21

Linn wanted to go inside because she was so freaking cold, but she stayed sat on the kerb. Djurgårdsgatan was her home; here the small houses stood in a row, and right in front of her was the birch lane. The snow weighed down the branches of the trees, making them look tired. All the white snow lit up the night, which made her less afraid of the dark. She was sitting right in front of her old swing, the one her mum set up in one of the birches at least ten years ago. The rough rope was green when she was little; now it was more like grey. The round wooden seat she had sat on hundreds of times was hidden by a thick layer of snow. Her legs were shaking – she didn't know whether it was because it was so flipping cold or if the drugs were on their way out of her body. She saw her house on the other side of the lane. All the windows were dark. She wondered whether her mother was asleep, or if she wasn't at home. Probably the latter.

Linn had declined getting a ride home from the party at Nydala from Anja's mother. She had lied and said that her mum could come and get her. Linn was both drunk and under the influence of other things so she didn't want to be too close to Anja's police mother. There'd been an uproar when she got there. An ambulance and police car with blinking blue lights ended the evening. And no one knew where Frida was. *Damn you,* she thought.

Linn tensed every muscle in an attempt to stay warm. She had walked the whole way to Haga, past the university and turned off at the Motorcentralen car dealership where the serial rapist 'Hagamannen' had once worked. Her mother went on about that rapist for several years, forbade her from playing outside by herself when she was little. Linn knew everything about the guy, even though she was only a child when he was arrested.

Linn tried to understand what had happened with Frida during the evening. Had one of William's buddies driven her from the house? Why couldn't William do that himself?

Linn had told Anja about Frida on Snapchat, so now she was anxious that Anja would tell everything about Frida to her police mother. So flipping crazy. Frida would never forgive her.

Her rear ached and Linn stood up from the kerb. *Time to go home,* she thought and looked at her phone for the hundredth time. Still nothing from Frida, and according to her parents she wasn't at home. They kept calling Linn but she didn't dare talk with them, afraid that they would have a go at her because she hadn't watched out for Frida.

She took a shortcut through the lane toward her home. Saw obvious tracks in the powdery snow – a car had left their driveway. Probably Hugo. She stomped off the snow as she stepped up on the front porch. Put the key in the lock and turned it. She was stiff from cold so her fingers moved slowly. There was a creaking sound as she opened the door and stepped in. Camilla's jacket was not hanging in its usual place.

Her nose noticed first that something was different. She groped with her hand for the light switch. Then came the sound. A thud. Then a spot of light that moved jerkily between the kitchen and living room. A dark figure that wasn't her mother. Linn stood still.

Could not move. The point of light disappeared at the same time as she heard the patio door opening. Then, silence. Linn took a breath.

'Camilla!'

There was no answer.

22

Charlotte placed her hand on the black steel at her hip, opened up the strap on the holster so that she could easily get out her SIG Sauer if needed. They didn't bring a police patrol with them – they were all fully occupied elsewhere tonight. Per went ahead of her up the stairs. Charlotte had to exert herself to see in the darkness. The glowing red button for the lights showed the way but they didn't want to switch it on. They stopped at Petra's door. Her eyes appeared in the narrow opening. Per brought his index finger to his lips and Petra nodded before she closed the door again.

Charlotte's boots risked waking the whole building so she put only her tiptoes on the step in the hope that it would make less noise. That would be fine as long as she didn't lose her balance and was forced to step on her heel.

As they approached the top floor she saw the broken-down door.

Per signalled with his arm that he would go in first. He took hold of his gun at the same time as Charlotte took hers out. The blue and white barricade tape was torn and hanging from the doorframe. They stopped, listened, looked at one another. Charlotte held her breath. She heard a faint sound. Luckily they'd confiscated Unni's computer, but the question was whether someone inside there was searching for something that the police didn't know they should be looking for.

Per peeked in through the open door. His coat fluttered as, with lowered gun, he went into the apartment.

Charlotte held hers with both hands, thumb against the butt, secured, and with the muzzle aimed at the ground.

'It's the police!'

Charlotte followed Per in. She looked around for the light switch.

Per called again. 'Police!'

At the same moment a person in a ski mask came straight toward them at full speed. Per was shoved to the side with such force that he lost his balance and ended up on his rear. Charlotte tried to aim the gun at the person but before she got that far she got a palm right in the face. When she regained her balance she felt metal against her forehead.

'Drop the gun or she dies.'

The barrel of the pistol was pressed so hard against Charlotte's forehead that her neck was jerked backward. She stared at the pistol, saw the lower side of the barrel and the man's hand. Between the jacket sleeve and glove a bracelet was visible. Pink, violet and green plastic figures. Mermaids that dangled. The pressure made Charlotte back into the hat rack where the hangers made a jangling sound. The adrenaline made her focus on one thing. The gun against her head.

'Don't do anything hasty. We'll let you go,' said Per.

The masked man took a couple of paces away and the barrel was eased from her head. He aimed his gun at them both before he backed out of the door, and closed it behind him.

Per took a few quick steps toward it. Heard echoes in the stairwell. He followed.

Charlotte ran to the kitchen, called for reinforcements and looked out of the window, down to the courtyard. A white van, Volkswagen. It must have been in the car park waiting when they arrived. The number plates had been removed. She took out her phone and snapped as many pictures as she could while she talked with the command centre and all active police cars in the vicinity – of which there were not enough.

'Armed man in white van, model Volkswagen, number plates removed, driving toward the Dragon School. Stop the car!'

The Gucci boots echoed as she ran on the parquet floor in the hall to the front door. Per was in the stairwell and Charlotte went after him, listening for the familiar sound of back-up. Down the stairs they went. She cursed her dress that didn't give her the chance to move freely. Thoughts were whirling in her head. She still felt the point where the barrel had been pressed against her forehead. The headache that had already appeared on the way to Nydala several hours ago had now parked right between her eyes.

She reached the entrance just as reinforcements arrived at the address. Charlotte's lungs met the cold air. She tried to calm her pulse with deep breaths as she heard the police cars further away take up the chase after the van. She brought one hand to her stomach, leaned over. With her body doubled over she focused her gaze on the snow, on her boots, on the sounds around her. She heard Per's and her own breathing. The nausea went away, and she straightened up and put the gun in its holster.

23

Sunday, 24 January

The grey, natural-stone windowsill was cold against his butt. Abbe's tailbone had started to ache from sitting on the hard surface. His body refused to relax, and while the others slept through the early morning hours Abbe thought about everything that was happening. His index finger moved over the knuckles of his hand. Obvious swelling that was sensitive to the touch.

Everything had got out of hand. Like a chain reaction. They had to withdraw from central Umeå and now they were in a cabin somewhere outside Vännäs. A back-up plan that was not meant to be used. How could the police already know they were here? With his gaze to the window, Abbe drew air into his lungs. *Spruce trees heavy with snow – perfect Christmas trees,* he thought. The snow gave light, otherwise it was endlessly dark and silent. But the darkness outside was nothing compared to what he felt inside. It all had to end. But how?

There was crackling in the open fireplace. Abbe turned his eyes toward the sound and saw how the sparks flew away to then die out a moment later. The house could not defend itself against the freezing temperature so the fire was necessary. He was sitting in the kitchen; was there anything edible in the refrigerator or just beer and liquor? On the table was a flowery waxed tablecloth that hadn't been wiped off. No one dared clear away the white powder. There wasn't enough to sniff up your nose, but more than you'd want to wipe off with a rag. Tony was sleeping in the next room, his trigger-happy buddy in the room opposite. An immigrant kid who had fled from deportation was lying on a mattress in the hall. He got to do the shit jobs, and was heavily exploited as free labour. Tony was a maniac about controlling all stages – pointed with his whole hand and did not tolerate disobedience. It was like a personal affront to him. The knuckles on Abbe's hand testified to the consequences. Then you got a beating. From him or someone else. But never from Tony himself.

'What are you sitting here thinking about?' Tony said, making Abbe start.

'Damn, you scared me. I thought you were asleep.' He jumped down from the window seat and sat on the wooden stool in front of the white powder.

'Things got out of hand last night,' said Abbe, letting his index finger meet his tongue to then gather up the dope on his finger. He rubbed it against his gums and let it take effect. 'How long will we keep the kid here?'

Tony sat down on the chair closest to the fire. He had a blanket wrapped around his body and looked pitiful. Barefoot.

I could shoot him here and now, thought Abbe.

'A while longer. This is nothing we haven't done before. I think it's kind of fun. The cops have no idea what I'm doing here, but they're going to chase me.'

Tony opened his mouth, yawning so broadly that Abbe looked right into his yellow teeth.

He was starting to feel the cocaine.

'Do you remember when you tried cocaine for the first time?' he asked Tony, who took off his glasses and set them on the table.

'Yes. What the hell? I was probably pretty old. When I started partying you mostly took amphetamines or weed. Cocaine didn't come along until the eighties.'

The first time Abbe tried drugs was as an eighteen-year-old after a shift at the bar. That was before he met Tony and had come up in Stockholm's underworld. But he didn't use it often; his father's drinking was always at the back of his mind. He was afraid to get hooked and mostly stayed away from it.

'I grew up with a whore for a mother and a father who hanged himself in the barn, so my life had nowhere to go,' said Tony, taking out a bag of white powder that he set on the oilcloth.

'How old were you?'

Tony divided the cocaine so that they got two lines of equal size.

'Ten years old. I was the one who found him and after that the men flowed freely at home. Ma didn't know any other way to bring in money. I got beaten up a lot by her customers, so I split when I was fourteen. The rest is history.'

'What happened with your mother?' Abbe asked.

'Died from an overdose a few years later. Just as well.'

Abbe thought about his own family and suddenly felt fortunate. 'My dad gambled away everything we owned and he was never at home. Mostly ignored us kids. Hit my mother every time she looked at him wrong.'

Abbe leaned over his line on the table. Held his index finger over one nostril and breathed in. It was almost comical that they were sitting here talking about life like two completely ordinary Swedes.

'So you've inherited your father's temperament,' said Tony, doing the same.

Abbe laughed before the next string of cocaine disappeared up his nose. 'He was a fucking zero who couldn't control himself.'

Abbe thought that his admiration for Viggo was a response to his father's gambling addiction. When Viggo stepped into Tony's club, he reminded him of Abbe's father, although the opposite. Viggo was a pro. Abbe observed him to start with, watched him at the tables. Self-confident, controlled. Never drank while he was gambling, kept the strippers at a distance. Abbe saw something special in the guy who won more than he lost. New players streamed in every day to Tony's club but no one captured his attention like Viggo had done. There was a gentleman in him that was reminiscent of heroes in old American movies. He conducted himself with self-respect.

Over time they built up a real friendship outside the world they found themselves in. They understood each other, knew each other's secrets. Their hanging out in the bar continued after closing time and Abbe knew that if his life was in the balance, Viggo would help him.

It was Abbe who tipped off Tony about Viggo; he told him about the gambler who was a whiz at poker and who could transform his criminal money into clean money. Tony took the bait and suddenly Viggo found himself among celebrities, hanging out at the trendiest clubs in town together with Tony. To start with Abbe was happy that he had brought them together. Viggo even met his wife during this time. When he could no longer duck out of the demand to launder Tony's money, the death sentence came. Even today Viggo had no idea that Abbe was the reason that he lived in hiding with his family nowadays.

'By the way, I've checked on the cops in town,' said Abbe, getting Tony's attention at once.

It was a routine the Syndicates had, to find out about the weaknesses of individual cops – they all had them. Usually it was the family; that could always be used if necessary. Although most Swedish cops lived a rather sedate family life.

'What have you found? Anything nasty and usable?' said Tony, leaning across the table.

'One police officer stands out,' said Abbe, taking out his phone.

'I see . . . in what way?'

Abbe held up the screen to Tony.

'This woman – Charlotte von Klint. She's from an aristocratic family and made of money. Has a daughter who lives in Stockholm. She worked in Stockholm previously but not against our organisation, she did other things. But with her we can probably—'

Tony tore the phone out of Abbe's hand. Enlarged the picture of the woman, then stood up so quickly that the chair fell backward.

'What the hell, Abbe!' Tony drew his hand across his face. 'My old nanny,' he said, laughing out loud. 'I think she called herself Maria Andersson at that time. How long has she been a cop?' He took off his glasses and rubbed them against his sweater.

Abbe hesitated. This had taken a turn that he wasn't prepared for. 'Twenty-three years.'

'Now I understand why my gun smuggling took an abrupt end long ago. Pretty little Maria, who I actually liked – the kids loved her. She was so . . . she was pleasant. Maria was like a light summer breeze.'

Tony put his glasses on and looked at the picture again.

'I never understood how in the hell they managed to gather so much evidence against me. When I was arrested, I was cooked. Impossible debts to the Albanians. They tried to take the club in exchange but then I'd had enough.'

'What happened?' Abbe asked.

'I killed their leader and his three closest men,' he said, laughing even more. 'There wasn't much left of their gang of thieves when I was done. Now I know how the cops gathered all the evidence. I even rubbed out a dude close to me that I was sure had squealed. Oops.'

Abbe stared at Tony and realized that this would not end well. He had opened Pandora's box.

24

Charlotte leaned against the front door as soon as she had closed and locked it. Her handbag hit the floor of the hall, her jacket followed, likewise her hat and mittens. She closed her eyes and thought about the evening that had started so pleasantly at Per and Mia's home, and which then had gone downhill. They didn't succeed in capturing the man from Unni's apartment, despite persistent searching. It was as if the vehicle had disappeared from the face of the earth. Presumably they would find the white van abandoned and burned out somewhere. Per and Charlotte had gone through Unni's apartment while the search was going on. Nothing seemed to be missing from the crime scene. The big question of course was why the killer had taken the risk of returning to the murder scene. From experience, both Per and Charlotte believed that was the case.

Charlotte felt her forehead where the man had pressed his gun. It was sore and she had a slight bump. She tried to ward off the tears by taking deep breaths. Charlotte had been threatened with a pistol before but never like this. For some reason the man with the bracelet didn't shoot. What stopped him? Criminals shot at police without batting an eye nowadays. Per? Hardly – he acted according to regulations when a colleague was threatened. Backed off. Safety first.

She'd made a sketch of the bracelet at the police station, as a description. Otherwise there wasn't much to go on because he'd had a ski mask on. The guy was of medium height and build, neither heavy nor slender. She silently thanked someone up there that she was still alive.

The pads of her feet ached from the high heels of the Gucci boots and she pulled them off. *Never again,* she thought as the pain in her feet made her limp. She started to put them in the wastebasket in the kitchen, but changed her mind and took them out again. Maybe Anja would like to have them.

The door to Anja's room was ajar, a faint glow of light coming from inside. Charlotte stood in the doorway.

'Hi, Mum, are you just home now? Haven't you been home all night?' Anja sat up in bed. Her light blue pyjamas were wrinkled.

'No, we followed up the events from earlier,' she said, leaving out the fact that she'd just been threatened with a pistol.

She went in and sat down beside Anja. Her daughter leaned her head against her shoulder, like she had when she was little. Charlotte drew her hand across her long hair.

'What a night,' she said, kissing Anja on the head.

She had lots of questions for her daughter but didn't want to appear too prying or suspicious.

Instead she let silence work. She fixed her gaze on Anja's armchair. It was full of brand-name clothes. The heavy, light grey velvet curtains had been a must for Anja when she furnished the room. But her daughter had good taste, Charlotte thought, even if it was expensive.

'Have you heard anything about your friend Frida?'

Anja shook her head. 'Nothing new.'

'We sent a patrol to that William's place. They'll be in touch with me when they've located her. I'm sure there's no danger.'

The scent from Anja's hair disappeared when she raised her head from her shoulder.

'Mum, just so you know, I don't take drugs. Do you remember when I was, like, eight years old and you showed me that picture?'

Charlotte smiled. 'Yes, I remember.'

'You said that she was twenty-seven and had lived just as good a life as me when she was little, but started taking drugs when she partied as a teenager. That she got stuck in drug abuse and was living in misery, completely broke and with no contact with her family.'

Charlotte had been doubtful about showing her daughter that picture. She had done so anyway.

'I think about that every time someone asks if I want some. Then it's not as hard to say no.'

Charlotte met Anja's green eyes, so like her own. She embraced her daughter.

'I know that you're crying, Mum. It's cool – out with it,' said Anja, laughing.

Charlotte wiped away the tears. 'What do your friends say when you don't want any? Do they get upset?'

Anja first shook her head, then she seemed to think about it. 'You know my friend from Djurgården, that I hung out with a lot before? She always tried to convince me to try, not be so flipping mainstream, and when I refused a couple of times she stopped calling me. Started hanging out with other people instead.'

'Does she take drugs?' Charlotte could not conceal her surprise.

'Yes, she does drugs every weekend now. Mostly cocaine but also pills. If you see her on Stureplan sometimes, she's usually high.'

'Do her parents know about it?'

Anja shrugged her shoulders. 'No idea.'

Charlotte wanted to ask more questions but let it be. She yawned. The sun was coming up and she needed a few hours of sleep. Luckily it was Sunday. Just when she'd decided to go to bed her phone started vibrating where it sat on Anja's bed.

'Who's calling now?' said Anja, crawling down under the covers again.

'It's an unlisted number, probably work,' said Charlotte. She limped out of the room and answered.

'Yes, this is Charlotte von Klint with the Umeå police.'

Silence.

'Hello?'

All that was heard was static.

'This is Charlotte.'

No response.

She pressed the phone harder against her ear.

'Hello?'

The person hung up.

25

Viggo stared at a sticky note with the police department logo that was stuck on the back of a computer screen. A woman in reception had moved him and Estelle to a separate room at the police station. It was Sunday afternoon and Frida was still missing. The police had not managed to locate either her or William. They had sent canine patrols to search around the house in Nydala in case Frida, in her state of intoxication, had wandered away and ended up in a snowdrift, but without a result.

Now he and Estelle were sitting with a female uniformed police officer. She did not appear to be any older than twenty-five. Blonde hair tied in a twist. Blue eyes. Narrow lips. Rather round at the waist. The room had white walls that were completely bare. The heating element was only lukewarm – Viggo had felt around it with his hand. The blinds in the window were pulled down halfway even though it was just after four o'clock and dark outside.

So far they had needed to answer simple questions, such as about Frida's circle of friends, what school year she was in, the name of the form teacher, phone number and other things that he thought was a waste of time.

'Does Frida have any distinguishing marks on her body, such as tattoos, scars or the like?'

That question made him take his eyes off the sticky note and look right at the young policewoman. Her fingers glided across the keyboard.

Viggo turned to Estelle, who nodded and started speaking.

'On the inside of her left thigh there is a rather large birthmark. At least five centimetres.'

'Is she in the dental registry? That is, have her teeth been X-rayed?'

Viggo felt how the question made him flare in anger. 'Yes, of course she's been to the dentist, she's seventeen years old.'

The woman asked more questions about how Frida was dressed. Questions that Viggo had to try to answer because Estelle had been too drunk when Frida left the house. But she was sober now and let out a piping sound every time a tough question landed on their side of the table.

The woman took her hands off the keyboard and met Viggo's gaze. 'Has Frida been missing before?'

'Uh, no, not as far as I recall, can you?' he asked, turning to Estelle again, who shook her head and remained silent.

'Does she associate in any so-called risk environments? That is, places where there are drugs, or other places where there is a risk she could be the victim of a crime?'

'What the hell do you mean?'

Viggo raised his voice and the policewoman quickly shook her head.

'It may concern drugs, for example. Does she use drugs – do you know that?'

Viggo looked down at his hands. Estelle reacted more forcefully.

'She sure as hell does *not* use drugs! She's a well-behaved young woman who does well in school and does things that normal seventeen-year-old girls do. Puts on make-up, talks about boys, and exercises. Frida exercises a lot. Runs several times a week. She probably doesn't even know what drugs look like.'

Estelle took a deep breath, largely to stop the fury that was coming out of her. How simple it would have been for them to blame the disappearance on the fact that Frida took drugs and that was why she was gone, but Viggo said nothing. Estelle had stated their point of view.

'It's rather common that parents don't know whether their children use drugs, maybe at parties and such. You mustn't see it as an accusation against you as parents. You can't just lock them up,' the woman said, laughing a little.

Viggo decided that she must be a little older than she appeared.

'But we need to know,' the female police officer concluded.

Both Viggo and Estelle shook their heads.

The woman inspected them. As if she was trying to see through them. 'Then I have a question that we must ask with this kind of report – that is, a standard question. Has Frida expressed any suicidal thoughts?'

Estelle hid her face in her hands. 'God, my God.'

Viggo understood that the question itself was hard for her, but as far as he knew Frida had never even had such a thought, much less talked about it. So he said that to the policewoman, who entered his answer into the computer.

'She got a little shaken up when her friend killed himself just over a week ago, but she seems to be handling it well, doesn't she, Estelle?'

She nodded and the policewoman looked at them.

'What was the friend's name?'

'Anton Ek,' Viggo replied.

She seemed to react to the boy's name, but left that and asked the question that Viggo had feared.

'Do you know if there have been threats of any kind against Frida? Has she been subjected to threats, harassment, bullying or anything like that through social media?'

Viggo felt like a jack had been placed over his chest. Estelle turned toward Viggo and hissed at him.

'Will you tell her or me? Huh?'

Viggo shook his head. The room felt warmer.

'Yes, we're all living under a threat,' he started. 'And because of that we have partly shielded personal information. Tony Israelsson is a criminal bastard who put a price on my head, so we're registered in another town and have a confidential classification with the authorities.'

The woman stopped her writing. Looked at Viggo as if she was trying to decide if he was telling the truth or not.

'Okay,' she said, getting up from the chair. 'Wait here.'

She left the room and Viggo leaned back against the hard metal chair. He looked up at the ceiling and drew his hand across the beard stubble.

'Thanks,' said Estelle, her voice sounding gentle again.

Damn how he'd chased around after her since they alerted the police. They'd called every single person, driven and searched all over the damn city. Screamed her name out loud in places he knew she often visited. He'd searched through her social media for clues. Called Missing People, who wanted to wait for the police. Been at the hospital, at the Dragon School and now he was sitting here. Viggo's fear was that Tony had found them and taken Frida in revenge or for blackmail purposes.

Every second was like a damned eternity.

He moved his legs back and forth under the desk, left a damp stain on the floor from his heavy winter shoes. Estelle sat in her thick down jacket. Her hat and gloves were on her lap.

After a while the door handle was pressed down and into the room stepped a tall man who introduced himself as Mats. Viggo did not catch his surname but he stood up and extended his right hand. A woman also came into the room.

'Hi, my name is Charlotte von Klint and I'm the assistant detective inspector,' she said, giving Viggo a firm handshake. He registered her surname immediately.

'A detective?' said Estelle, picking up her gloves and hat, which had fallen on the floor when she stood up to shake hands.

Mats sat on the edge of the desk, and indicated with his hand that they should sit down again. He crossed his arms over his flat stomach. Under the black, knitted sweater a checked shirt was visible.

'It's like this: my group is responsible for individuals who are reported missing. From experience, we know that girls Frida's age sometimes stay away for various reasons and come back fairly soon. But your special situation means that we need to take precautions, do you understand?'

Viggo felt his face getting warm. 'What do you mean, "precautions"? It's pretty damned obvious, isn't it? You need to start searching. I've searched all alone. What's the problem? Our daughter is gone! Don't sit here talking, do your job now you know our situation!'

Charlotte leaned over the desk and fixed her gaze on him. Her green eyes were calm but intense. 'We sent out a description of your daughter to all cars already last night. On the other hand it would have been good to know that there is a threat against her and your entire family. If you'd told the police that immediately we would have taken greater measures from the beginning. Now we've lost time.'

Viggo did not say anything.

'Do you know who this guy is?' she asked, extending a picture. Viggo was just about to take it when Estelle tore it out of the hands of the policewoman.

'We know that your daughter and this man had some form of relationship and that they met up yesterday,' she clarified and Estelle brought the picture closer to her face.

'Yes, we've heard that from her friends but we've never seen him before,' said Estelle, letting go of the picture, which sailed down to the floor. Then she brought her hands to her mouth and tried to stop the crying.

Mats stood up from the edge of the desk and picked up the photograph, giving it to Viggo.

Something was familiar about him, thought Viggo. He was sitting in an armchair dressed in a V-neck T-shirt. He was tanned, so the picture must have been taken in the summer. Full lips, upturned nose, narrow face, chiselled jaw, curly blond hair. *Damn,* he thought. The guy appeared to be completely Frida's type.

'Who is he?' Viggo asked, without taking his eyes off the picture.

'His name is William and he's a student at Umeå University,' Charlotte explained. 'And he has a fondness for drugs. He runs the party house by Nydala Lake, which is also the last place Frida was seen.'

Viggo set aside the picture and drew his hands through his hair. This was so confusing that he was starting to go crazy.

'We've heard that Frida was going to meet William at his place,' Charlotte continued. 'But neither Frida nor William have been seen since the party in the house.'

'Could this guy have taken Frida?' Viggo asked, feeling a little hope. Better than having Tony take her.

The female police officer answered. 'We don't know if anyone has taken Frida. I understand your worry, but it may also be that she's at home with someone. The most common thing is that there is an everyday explanation and that missing youths show up again.'

Viggo opened his mouth to answer but was interrupted by knocking on the door. Charlotte stood up and pressed on a button that beeped, then she opened the door. She talked with someone outside and left the door ajar before she turned to Viggo and Estelle.

Viggo leaned forward and his elbows pounded the table. His stomach hurt, and his chest. He felt Charlotte's hand against his shoulder and straightened up again. He dried the tears from his cheeks and blinked repeatedly to remove the fog from his eyes. Obviously he should have told them about Tony immediately. *Idiot.*

'You're going to meet our guy at Witness Protection, Ola Boman. Does Tony Israelsson know you have a daughter? You see, we have reason to believe that he's in Umeå,' Charlotte said.

Viggo stopped breathing. What if Tony had been at Nydala to push drugs and met Frida there? Viggo's heart dived right into the abyss. Charlotte might just as well have said that she was dead.

26

Monday, 25 January

Per was sitting at the desk, a place he mostly used when it was time to write reports. He preferred to be out on the floor with his colleagues, especially now, after the weekend, when they started dropping into the police station. The ones who passed his office had the usual Monday tiredness in their eyes. He sent a text message. *No racquetball for me tonight, sorry about late cancellation.*

There would be a lot of backlash but he needed to work overtime. The weekend had been incredibly dramatic. A murder, a missing seventeen-year-old girl and an absent young man had made the whole police station come to life. And the kid's suicide just a week earlier besides. Per was most worried about the fact that Frida had disappeared at the same time as William. Maybe someone wanted to get at him and she'd been in the wrong place at the wrong time. Or else it was the other way around. There were many question marks and they needed to be figured out. Mia had taken it unusually well that he needed to work overtime, which also made him worried. Was that a sign that she was starting to lose interest in her husband?

His phone chimed.

Replies trickled in on the group racquetball thread.

We understand, you need an upper body to play.

If you can't get hold of transportation service I can pick you up.

Understandable after last time's humiliation . . .

Per was good at racquetball after his years in tennis as a youth, and he was just about to respond to the taunts when he was interrupted by the district chief of police Kennet Eriksson.

As chief, Kennet was usually on the other side of the pay gap, which was also the nickname for the glass footbridge that separated the top-level managers from those who did the work out in the field. But recent developments had brought him to the Major Crimes side of the bridge more often.

'We need to gather our sections and review new events,' Kennet said, taking off his scarf.

'Our briefing?' said Per, pushing his chair back from the desk.

'What measures have you taken concerning the young woman?' Kennet asked.

Per collected his thoughts. So much had happened that he was afraid he'd missed something.

'Well, where Frida Malk is concerned, Mats has turned it over to us and we've started an investigation on suspected kidnapping with the extra resources we requested.'

'Okay, fine – and have you seen this?' said Kennet, holding up *Västerbottens-Kuriren*, the local newspaper.

Per moved closer and read the headline.

'It was the pits that he got away. Who's been talking with the media?' Per asked, following Kennet to the briefing room.

'A source inside the police, it says, or else we'd assume from one of our witnesses.'

'Yes, but the choice of words – "bathtub murderer". We haven't mentioned that in any way other than internally.'

'To be honest I'm surprised it hadn't reached the press sooner,' said Kennet. 'Why was the masked man at the cordoned-off crime scene?'

Per had no answer, and they stepped into the familiar briefing room. A few police officers were already there.

'Where is everyone else?' said Per, looking at Kennet.

'We have an incident that requires discretion. Charlotte and Mats are going to tell us more shortly.'

Per raised his eyebrows, but he knew that with this type of incident, developments could change from hour to hour.

Charlotte stepped into the room with her head raised high. Dark trouser suit, shirt and jacket were matched with a pair of heavy black boots. Her green eyes were anything but energetic. She looked exhausted.

'I've been looking for you like a ferret,' she said, pointing at him.

'I know, sorry. I went home and rested for a couple of hours. My diabetes, otherwise the blood sugar goes haywire.'

Per sat down on a chair at the front, ready to listen. Once again it struck him that Charlotte was ready to take care of a separate group of investigators. She had taken over when he gave her the confidence to do that.

But it was Mats who started talking – about Frida. She got a separate whiteboard next to Unni's. Then Charlotte took over and set William's picture up on the whiteboard. Drew a red line between him and Frida and wrote *Missing/kidnapped?*

'So, we have two missing youths, William and Frida. None of the usual measures have produced results. We're in the process of producing the young people's phone contacts lists. We also know that they met up the same evening they disappeared. But it has turned out that William is perhaps interesting for our other investigation.'

Charlotte went over to Unni's board. 'The murder of Unni Olofsson may be drug-related because we found pills, including unmarked ones, in her apartment. But nothing indicates that she took them herself. So we're looking at a possible connection between her and this William. We know that he sold drugs at the university and ran the Nydala house, which we closed down over the weekend. The house was full of the type of drugs that we found at Unni's place. On her side, she taught at the university alongside her position at the pharmacy. We have to work broadly and without preconceived notions, and for that reason we want to find out whether Unni may have bought drugs from William.'

Charlotte worked methodically and then set up a photograph of a white guy in his fifties, above which she wrote *Viggo Malk.*

'Frida's dad,' she stated, and then continued to put up another photo. Per noted that it showed the man whose portrait she had thrown in the wastebasket. Under that picture she wrote *Tony Israelsson* and started to explain the connection between him and Viggo. How long had Charlotte known about this, without telling Per? That made him irritated.

'Frida has a threat against her. This man, the leader of the Syndicates, Tony Israelsson, has put a price on Viggo's head.'

No one in the cramped room said anything.

Per looked at his colleague. 'A nationwide search needs to be put out for Frida,' he said.

'But not William?' asked Kennet.

'Eventually,' said Charlotte. 'At the present time we don't know if William is a victim, a perpetrator or only temporarily missing, but we're carrying on a dialogue with the National Operations Department. And we've asked for files from all relevant surveillance cameras that are in the city and broadened the witness interviews.'

Per was about to stand up to ask a question when Ola Boman from Witness Protection came into the room. Per sat down again. He noticed that Ola had on a pair of brown corduroy trousers and could hardly contain himself until he got to laugh about it together with Charlotte. *Who the hell wears corduroy these days,* he thought, *and brown besides?* But he had to admit that they sat well on the guy anyway.

Ola pointed at the picture of Tony. 'My group at Witness Protection has just now put highest priority on investigating whether, and if so, why, Tony Israelsson is in Umeå.'

Per looked at Charlotte. She stared down at the floor.

Ola said a few words about the cartel called the Syndicates. Everyone in the police knew about it but few in Umeå had ever had anything to do with it.

'Viggo has a price on his head, signed by Tony. His family has been in Umeå for seven years. Frida is Viggo's daughter and she disappeared about the same time as Tony rolled into Västerbotten. It's just too improbable that there wouldn't be a connection. But until we know more we've put the parents in custody in a secret location.'

'Yes, I guess it's obvious that he came here for Viggo – what business would he have up here otherwise?' said Anna, taking a sip of tea. She looked like she had run to work but hadn't had time to shower because there was still sweat in her damp hair. After Charlotte, she was the best investigator they had in the group.

Charlotte pointed at Frida's picture. 'We don't know for sure that Tony has anything to do with her disappearance, but we have to proceed on that basis in order to release enough resources . . . But Frida's disappearance must be kept out of the media – we don't want her face in the newspapers. That would be instantly dangerous for her, if it isn't already.'

'What do you mean? Isn't it good to get tip-offs from the general public?' Anna asked.

'Not yet. If Tony has Frida, she could become a burden if everyone knows that she's missing, and at the same time she can't be released alive, since she's a witness. Do you understand?'

'Why, then, isn't it better to send out a description of her and bring in Missing People?' Anna asked, draping a sweater over her shoulders.

'But think if Tony *isn't* here because of Viggo. Maybe he doesn't know that the family is even here. It may be a coincidence. If he sees Frida's name and picture in the newspaper he'll make a connection to Viggo. If she's still alive we have to keep her out of the media so as not to risk her life.'

Anna seemed to accept that explanation and Charlotte switched to talking about the murder investigation of Unni.

'Per and I encountered a masked man in Unni's apartment on Saturday. What was he doing there? What was he searching for? Was it the same person who murdered Unni? We have to prioritize finding all this out.'

Kicki raised a hand with fingers full of metal rings.

'I've checked in the log about the white van, which is being searched for after your blunder. It turns out that a similar vehicle is owned by a car mechanic in Stockholm – a mechanic that we know is a front man for Tony Israelsson. We also have pictures of him in that very van. True, it was logged a year or two ago, but it's still interesting. The white Volkswagen van has registration number

ADS 667. Because what you saw on Saturday was lacking number plates, I've compared the photos you took of it with pictures from surveillance cameras in Stockholm. And there is a feature that Israelsson and co foolishly enough haven't thought of.'

Kicki took two pictures from a folder she had in front of her.

'Previously there have been decals on the back hatch of the van that there are still traces of.'

Per took the pictures, stood up and put them on the whiteboard as Kicki continued.

'Look at the red strip on the lower edge of the left door. It's the same on both pictures, in the exact same place. It almost looks standard, but it wasn't there originally.'

'Good job, Kicki,' said Charlotte, writing on the board.

Kicki responded to the compliment by shrugging her shoulders.

'It strengthens our theory that it was someone from Tony's gang that we ran into at Unni's,' said Charlotte.

'Could it just as likely have been Tony himself we met in Unni's apartment?' said Per.

She shook her head. 'The man we met in the apartment wasn't Tony – that I know from my encounters with him in Stockholm. His voice didn't sound like his and Tony is thin – and an experienced man would never do the shit jobs himself.'

The service pistol was still on her hip and Charlotte's large movements made it visible under the jacket. Her cheeks turned red, as if she'd been out skiing. *This Tony person affects her,* Per thought.

'But regarding DNA traces, we still have no match on any of his probable associates,' she continued. 'The question is, what were the Syndicates doing in Umeå in Unni's cordoned-off apartment? She was murdered just before Tony came here to Umeå.'

Per's phone chimed and he took it out of his pocket, listened to Charlotte while he read the text he received from Carola in

Forensics. When he was done reading he cleared his throat and put the phone back in his pocket.

'We have two perpetrators,' he said, looking at the group.

'Excuse me?' said Charlotte.

'According to Carola, they've found two different DNA traces on Unni. The first is from bodily fluids, the other from a strand of hair on the tape that was used to bind her hands. Thus two perpetrators. But neither of them is in our database.'

Per was about to continue when he was interrupted by a knock on the door. No unauthorized persons were allowed in the briefing room, so Charlotte opened it and went out.

Per turned around and looked at the whiteboard. It was starting to get full of suspected perpetrators and victims. Charlotte came back. She put both hands on her hips.

'We have a dead man at the university.'

'What? Who?'

'Don't know, but the body is in a snowdrift and visible to everyone. They've sent a patrol to cordon it off. The only thing left is for us to go there,' she said, looking at Per.

27

It was Monday and Frida had been gone for two days. Linn jumped off the bus and started walking the two hundred steps over to the main entrance of the school. The sun was high in the sky and forced her to look down at the ground in order not to be blinded. She followed her feet. The red Vans were dirty but she loved them. She felt as if she was balancing on a tightrope – keeping her thoughts in check, not losing focus and falling down into the hole where she admitted that something awful had happened to Frida. She used every muscle in her body to keep herself on the rope as she walked toward the school, convincing herself that Frida had slept the high off somewhere and then just stayed there.

When Linn got to the school building, she pulled open the door. The sun was reflected in the glass and she turned around. It felt like someone was watching her. A vague feeling she had that she couldn't understand. She let her gaze search among the students in the schoolyard, squinted from the light when the sun met the white snow, looked for someone who deviated from the norm. No one was looking at her. Everything was as usual. Linn shook her head. She was starting to get paranoid.

The entrance to the Dragon School was a cube entirely made of glass and well known in Umeå. She and Frida met up here every morning. Out of habit or hope she placed herself just inside the glass cube and waited. Linn looked at the entrance to the garage. Thought about how much fun they'd had down there. The heated garage that they'd partied in several times, a perfect place to warm up in when it was bitterly cold outside and no one's parents were away from home. Actually Linn's home was the best place – there was just her mum, and she, like, worked constantly. Frida used to say that Camilla needed a man to relax a little, someone that made her less angry and uptight.

Linn agreed. But Hugo was the only guy that seemed to be in her life these days. Linn felt sorry for him. Being born with that appearance but not being able to use it. Like having a whole sweet shop but no teeth.

Linn stamped off the snow from her shoes against the thick rubber mat and took off her hat. Turned her head to look out at the garage one last time. No Frida. This was where she often sensed the familiar lump in her stomach, here in the cube, and today was no exception. Linn leaned her forehead against the glass, once again searching for Frida with her gaze. She looked at her phone. Nothing.

She left the glass cube, but the uncertainty about what was waiting in the corridors made her move toward the wall. She kept away from the people who self-confidently walked in the middle, often in a group. The school had a familiar smell, like rubber mixed with damp clothes.

The corridor was in front of her like a shark's jaw. The stone floor needed to be scrubbed and the fluorescent lights in the ceiling made no difference when the big windows let in daylight. The high school was one of Sweden's largest, with two thousand students, so she could easily disappear into the crowd. The lockers were lined up along the corridor. Black, white and green. She turned left, past the cafeteria and onwards to the bleachers, which was an obvious meeting place. No Frida. Over toward the ping-pong table where there were always people, mostly guys. On Mondays the mood was often subdued in the corridors, then the sound level rose in pace as the weekend approached, like a drum roll.

'Hey, Linn, whadup? Were you at the party on Saturday? Or maybe you were home with your mum?'

Linn turned around. The comment came from a guy that Linn recognized but didn't really know – one of the popular guys. He walked in the middle of the corridor along with his crowd.

She opened her mouth and pulled in her stomach. But the guy disappeared before she could respond. Linn ran her fingers through her hair, which was straight and unsprayed. She regretted not making herself look nice. The jeans were good, on trend, but the jacket was an old one she grabbed because she was cold. Why did *that* guy have to come up today when she was uglier than usual? Linn saw her reflection in the window, pulled the big jacket away from her stomach and saw her outline. She wanted to see what the guy had seen, if she'd embarrassed herself by being unprepared.

She sneaked a glance at the cafeteria. Her stomach was rumbling because she hadn't eaten breakfast, but the risk of getting a comment or a scornful smile made her turn and continue toward Frida's locker. When Linn turned to the right, the corridor became narrower and the walls changed to brick. Shit brown. The light from the ceiling landed on the colourful lockers. Hers was lime green and Frida's had a dent on the door from a previous student. She dumped her things in the locker and sat down on the stairs alongside it. Linn's class wouldn't start for twenty-five minutes so she had plenty of time. She stared absent-mindedly at her phone. Sometimes she had to turn her shoulder to let students past who were going up or down the stairs. She avoided eye contact and stared at their shoes. Vans, Nike, Lacoste, mostly sneakers. Linn picked at her cuticles, tore one so that a red drop was forced out on her thumb.

142

She wiped it off on her sweater and thought about something Frida had said one time. About pretending to disappear. Get attention and then be found. Become someone everyone wanted to know more about.

There was a flash on her phone screen.

A Snapchat message from Anja.

Linn had almost forgotten about her in all the chaos. She looked at the picture of Anja, read the text: *Back in sthlm, have u heard anything from Frida?*

Linn aimed the phone at her face, fixed her hair and snapped a picture where she was sitting. Then she wrote: *No, waiting by her locker.*

Anja answered immediately: *OK, let me know.* She ended with a red heart and Linn smiled for the first time since Saturday.

The clock showed 8.20 a.m. and still no Frida. Linn got up from the stairs and heard two guys talking while they rooted in their lockers.

'Did you hear about Horny Sabinje?' one of them said, laughing.

Linn tried to hear what they were saying.

'Yeah, what the hell? What a whore she is. Apparently she sandwiched with two dudes over the weekend, in the house.'

More laughter.

Linn listened to the talk. *Damn you,* she thought, hearing how metal met metal when the lockers were closed. She knew that guys could be brutal; it was like they didn't understand anything. Called girls whores as if that was a sweet nickname. She wanted to jump out and show herself, tell them what pigs they were. But if she attacked them, they would attack her, so she just stood there. Kept listening.

'She got so much cock that she couldn't stand afterwards and ended up in the hospital. Now she refuses to come to school. Disgusting female.'

More laughter. Their voices moved away.

Linn looked after them. Wanted to throw something, hit them. They wore their caps with the brim in front, flannel shirts, jeans. *So fucking mainstream,* she thought. Closed her eyes. She had pain in her abdomen, a sensation that made her want to vomit. She leaned against the brick wall and inhaled in an attempt to quiet her stomach. She thought about the drugs that she stuffed in herself sometimes. One pill too many and she could end up in a situation that gave her a bad reputation. Any girl could end up there. The guys decided autocratically which girls were good and who was bad. You couldn't be boring and skip the alcohol, drugs or sex. You couldn't drink too much either, take so many drugs that you lost control, and if you slept with the wrong guy you were finished. And you should be slender, good-looking and just cocky enough – anything else and you were fat, a whore, a bitch. Once a rumour was started it couldn't be stopped, whether it was true or not. Like their talk about the girl now. The talk was in motion. She was already a whore at the school.

28

Per and Charlotte were at the university campus with a new dead body.

William Gunnarsson.

It was as if he'd fallen from the sky like a dead bird.

Swollen eyes and a wound on his cheek testified to rather rough handling, but what had killed him was a shot to the forehead. A pure execution. He was lying in a pile of snow, but his face and head were clearly visible, as were one arm and both legs.

'How can someone be shot like this without it being noticed?' Charlotte asked, leaning her head forward to observe the young man. Bluish-red discoloration from livor mortis had appeared on his face. His eyes were closed and he was missing a shoe.

'It's most likely that he wasn't killed here,' said Carola.

Carola's co-workers on the forensics team had set up a white tent to protect any evidence from being disturbed, but also to shield William from curious gazes. They took a few steps out of the tent, away from William. The body was lying right next to Lindell Hall and the library, in close proximity to the pond which was now drained. Massive window sections in the hall aimed the sun's rays straight at them. The five pillars in front were snow-covered and sparkled. Everything was glistening, apart from the nearby corpse.

'There isn't a single drop of blood in the surrounding snow,' Carola continued. 'And from what I can assess he'd been dead a while before he ended up in the cold.'

'It's one hell of a risk to dump the body here, right out in the open for anyone to see. Why would someone take that risk?' said Per, turning around, scanning a relatively open landscape. Lots of windows, so someone might have been watching.

'We've confiscated a tractor that was parked down by the roundabout toward the hospital. We suspect it was used to carry him here,' said Carola.

'But why? What symbolism does the university have? It almost feels like this is a statement,' said Charlotte, and Per fixed his gaze on the steam that came out of her mouth as she spoke. As usual you could barely see her eyes because of the beanie.

'The guy sold drugs here – a deal that maybe went wrong?' said Per.

'This is a brutal murder and he's been missing since Saturday evening.'

Carola pulled down her mouth protection but continued speaking. 'The person who called in about the body was here at five fifteen just this morning. At that time, he was lying here, but we'll have to see how long he's been dead – maximum ten hours, I would think. So he died some time before midnight.'

'So where has he been until he was dumped here?' asked Charlotte. 'He was last seen Saturday evening at the Nydala house. That's a long way from here.'

'He could have been anywhere at all. Carrying a dead body here attracts more attention than hiding it in the snow on a tractor scoop,' said Carola.

'And where is Frida, if William is here?' said Per, turning to a policeman who was talking with witnesses. Blue and white plastic tape fluttered in the wind. 'Have you found his phone?'

'Yes. With a solid list of customers.'

'Footprints in the snow?'

'It will be hard – lots of people walked around here and looked before we arrived.'

Charlotte placed herself beside Per. She was standing so close that he smelled her perfume.

'Unni worked at the university, William was a student here – what is it we're missing?' she said, wiping away the moisture that ran from her nose.

'Yes, and where is Frida?' said Per, turning toward the body in the snow. 'Maybe he had the answer to where she is.'

Carola turned around, browsing in the evidence that had been collected in bags. 'This note was in his hand.'

Per took the small slip of paper. Held it up in front of his face and saw a string of numbers, more than was possible to remember.

'What's this?' he asked Carola.

'Don't know. We're sending it to IT Forensics, so we'll see. But it doesn't seem to be an ordinary computer password.'

Per's phone vibrated. He left the tent to answer and was met by young people who were standing outside, whispering.

'Per Berg, Umeå police.'

'Yes, hi, my name is Tomas Ek. My son Anton died a week ago, he . . . he committed suicide.'

The man whose name was Tomas cleared his throat. His voice sounded as if he'd been drinking whisky every day for the past two weeks.

'I'm sorry about your loss,' said Per. 'Can I help you with anything?'

'My wife and I are trying to understand why he did what he did. We've searched through everything to find a suicide note or something that can give us an answer. But we're not finding anything.'

Per heard a sigh.

'But, well . . . the policeman I talked with said that I should call you, because I did find something that neither my wife or I understand at all. But maybe you will.'

Per pressed the phone against his ear so as not to miss anything.

'What is it?' he asked, taking a couple of steps away from the curious students.

'Do you know who Unni Olofsson is?' Tomas asked, and Per's ears perked up.

'Why do you ask?'

'Anton wrote her name on a slip of paper along with a time. We found the note in his desk drawer. According to the online directory she lives on Dressyrgatan and we tried to call her but only got her voicemail. We wanted to know who she is and how he knew her, so I went there but you'd cordoned off her apartment. So I talked with the police and they said that I should call you.'

29

Viggo sat up in the hotel bed. He loathed their protected residence. Estelle was lying in the other bed, sleeping with her back to him. He only saw her head, the rest of her body was encased in a thick white coverlet. An hour or so ago she'd come up from the hotel bar, staggering, supporting herself against the wall as she took off her shoes. Slurred something about Frida and said that she would kill everyone. *You can start with yourself,* he'd thought, and immediately felt guilty. He didn't mean that. Her drinking was his fault, from start to finish. A life in flight was of course not what she'd imagined. When they met she stood out as irreplaceable. Now the balance of power in the marriage looked different; she was the weak one and he was the stronger.

Ola Boman had asked them to pack the most important things from the house; their home was no longer secure. The hotel room that they'd been temporarily placed in was small: two single beds with a nightstand between them. Parquet floor, wardrobe, straight ahead a desk with an information folder that said Quality Hotel Skellefteå. There was no minibar here, which led to an outburst from Estelle.

Viggo couldn't sleep, and he couldn't be up. It was Monday afternoon and Frida would soon have been gone for two horrible days. He'd run out of tears, only the empty space in his body was left. He couldn't stop thinking about all the terrifying atrocities Frida might be subjected to. In the worst case, a guy like Tony might have sold her, forced his innocent daughter into prostitution. When the darkness took over his thoughts he considered suicide. Nothing else would take away the pain. It was like being flayed alive. The desire to avoid thinking and feeling became just as strong as the will to survive had been previously. He'd considered jumping from the window – it was high enough. What stopped him was that he couldn't leave Frida. Not until he knew. That would be just as cowardly as getting drunk every day. Instead he'd started to direct his fury at the police who had caged him in this shitty hotel and didn't let him go out and search. Viggo struck the bed with his fists.

How had they revealed themselves? They had followed the directives to guarantee security. Frida had even accepted not having any of the most common social media platforms. Viggo and Estelle had talked about her perhaps having a secret account that wasn't in her real name. But if such was the case, it didn't matter anyway. Just as long as she didn't post things about her family. He'd gone through all the scenarios and analysed every aspect of their lives, but he still didn't understand how Tony had managed to find them.

This must be what it's like to lose your mind, he thought, stealing a glance at his wife.

Viggo reached for the computer. His usual phone was confiscated, but he still had a phone with a prepaid card.

He clicked on to the Tor network, which worked more or less like any other web browser, apart from the fact that through it he could reach forums that other search engines didn't produce. Because of the security it worked slowly and Viggo stared at the screen. He knew that the search would jump between at least three different servers before he got what he wanted. But it was also the reason that it was so hard to trace IP addresses on the dark web. When the green page appeared on the screen he looked at Estelle.

Out like a dead fish. He'd written in the onion address several times previously so it started up on its own. PHD-CASINO.COM.

Viggo had made serious money here. Some bitcoins were still in the gambling account so that he would be able to play, like now. When Estelle's blanket moved he turned the computer screen away from her. She was lying on her back, her blonde hair spread out on the pillow and a little way down over the end of the bed. Her face was bare, with no make-up. The red lacquer that she so carefully put on before the hell started up had come loose from some of her nails. A scratch had just begun to heal on the top of her hand. He realized that he hated her. When they needed each other the most, the wall was higher than the one Trump had wanted to build by Mexico.

He logged into his account, ready to burn a few hundred bucks out of pure anxiety. He looked at his balance, which was no longer a total. It was zeroed out.

He bent his head closer to the screen, logged out again and then back in. Something must have been wrong.

No. It was no mistake. He had no money left in the account.

'Damn it!' He glanced at the other bed. The drunk was still asleep.

Where in the world were his bitcoins?

Viggo got up from the bed. The glow of the computer was the only source of light in the room. He'd dropped the case like a hot potato, so that it was hanging just over the bed. Bitcoins were missing at a value of at least five hundred thousand kronor in ordinary currency. He wasn't anxious about the missing amount – he used e-currency to gamble on the dark web, nothing else. His real millions were in other bank accounts around the world. Some were invested in properties via shell companies and Frida had a fund that she would get when she turned twenty-one. No, what he was anxious about was that someone had got into his account. Infringed on his private sphere. How the hell had someone managed to reach his wallet?

Viggo was careful about his passwords. The account was impossible to get at.

Damn, someone has got much too close, he thought, bending his knees, letting his rear meet the edge of the bed. Then he reached out his hand and grazed the keyboard. Looked at the disbursement history. Everything had been withdrawn at the same time and to a single wallet, which he would never be able to trace.

Viggo closed down the page. Clicked up a news site instead. While he thought about who could have done this, the screen lit up with the newspaper's website.

The headline hit him just as hard as the empty account.

Police Tight-lipped About Investigation of Murdered 50-year-old.

But it was the picture that made him clench his jaw so as not to start screaming.

It was taken in Unni's stairwell.

Now he understood why her phone had been turned off.

30

Charlotte closed the door on the unmarked police car, fastened the seat belt and leaned back as Per started the engine. She loosened the buttons at her throat. The tyres squealed against the concrete ground as the car left the parking garage. Daylight was about to disappear. William had been taken for autopsy and they had reported to the others in the investigation group.

'Where do we start?' Per asked, lowering the sun visor as the car came out into the light.

'We'll go back to the academy, I think. We need to talk with Unni's colleagues and students again,' she said, taking out her personal phone. Held it in her hand.

'Academy?' said Per. 'You mean the university?'

Charlotte laughed at herself. Academy was a word her father always used.

'In any case,' she continued, 'Unni had no traces of drugs in her when she was murdered. She did have drugs at home. Could she have been an addict? We see many people who end up there but still live a normal life for quite some time before it falls apart. Dolcontin isn't that easy to get hold of.'

'No, but she was a pharmacist. Maybe she'd brought some home with her from work?' said Per. 'We'll have to see. She may just as easily have bought the shit from a pusher on the street, or acquired it on the dark web.'

'Why did Anton Ek write down her name on a piece of paper?' asked Charlotte.

'We have to find that out,' Per replied.

'As we suspected, the autopsy confirmed that Unni died two days before Anton took his life. And before Tony came to town. Frustrating to have two such good pieces of evidence from a crime scene but not be able to connect them to a perpetrator – or two perpetrators in this case.'

There was a lot that didn't add up. She watched the shopfronts while they drove through her new hometown. When they passed the Run and Walk clinic she was reminded to go there and buy new soles for her exercise shoes. Her scoliosis meant that she couldn't exercise without them.

Per had his eyes directed at the train station opposite.

'Do you know that there was a murder here in 2013?'

Charlotte listened and leaned forward to see the brick-red station building with the green metal roof.

'It was a twenty-one-year-old guy who, completely unprovoked, shot a young woman in the back. They had no relation to each other whatsoever. Just completely crazy.'

Charlotte had heard about the case. The newspapers dubbed it the 'Platform Murder'.

'Now the media have started digging into the murder of Unni,' Per said with a sigh, driving along Järnvägsallén where for some reason there was a traffic jam.

'Yes,' said Charlotte, leaning forward to change her sitting position. 'You wonder what they're thinking when they write the headlines.'

'Now it's the "Bathtub Murderer",' said Per.

154

'A lot of nasty things happen here. Instead of *Good Evening* maybe you should broadcast *Crime Journal Umeå*,' she said, looking at her phone.

Per laughed. 'Yes, things happen, like in all big cities,' he said, stopping for a red light.

Charlotte opened her mouth to comment on what he'd just said, but stopped herself. She thought it was sweet that to him Umeå was a big city. In her world New York was a big city.

'So, just say it. I know you want to,' said Per, pressing on the accelerator when the traffic light turned green.

Charlotte laughed. 'Umeå is a big town in comparison with many other towns in Sweden and—'

Per interrupted her in mid-sentence. 'Towns! You can't very well call Umeå a town. It's a city, damn it!' He shook his head. 'You're so snobbish sometimes it drives me crazy. But sorry, I interrupted you, so what do you think is a *big* city?'

'This is just my personal opinion, I'm not saying that I'm right.' She paused. 'Stockholm is a big city, of course, the capital of Sweden, but it's not a *big* city, if you understand what I mean?'

'Continue,' Per said with a grin.

'Los Angeles, have you been there? That's a big city.'

As Per turned off toward the university area her phone rang. The estate agent.

'Yes, this is Charlotte von Klint.'

Per drove on to the big car park that belonged to the university. It was full. She heard him swear but was focused on what the estate agent had to say to her.

'Yes, but that's good, thanks! Then we'll meet this evening and sign the papers. Wonderful. Thanks again.' She smiled broadly at Per. 'Anja and I have become homeowners here in town.'

'What? Did you already make an offer on the house on The Island?'

Per stopped the car and let it idle while he waited for someone to leave their parking space.

'Yep, won the bidding war today – so fun. I have to call Anja and tell her!'

Charlotte had come to life at the joyful news. She longed to get away from the apartment in the city centre. Now they would have a real home.

Per raised his hand and she slapped his palm with her own. 'Congratulations! What did you get it for?'

'Twelve million.'

Charlotte leaned back in the seat. She knew it was provocative that a single mother with a police salary could buy a house for that amount.

Per whistled. 'Wow, I knew that you don't live like other police officers so I won't say anything. But wasn't it offered for ten million or something like that?'

'Yes, but I got so tired of the bidding. Three of us were interested, who were raising it ten thousand at a time. So after two days I raised it by five hundred thousand.'

She avoided looking at Per. The words came out with a guilty conscience.

'Looks like it took the edge off the bidding.'

Per squeezed her arm. 'I'm glad that you feel so much at home here that you want to buy a house. But you have to think about two things. The last thing you told me? Perhaps you shouldn't mention it at the police station. Kicki would never let it go. Plus, count on having Simon and Hannes swimming there in the summers. Just to forewarn you.'

'I'd be delighted,' she replied as she pointed at a parking spot that opened up. 'But does that mean you won't be going there to swim?'

'I always swim in the reeds, you know that.'

'Says the man who lost twelve kilos and has become really fit. Mia must be pleased.'

Per sighed as he got out of the car. Charlotte followed him. Put on her hat. It was just past three thirty in the afternoon and now the little daylight that remained had definitely disappeared.

'I don't know. Her tone has been rather curt recently. She hasn't argued or sulked about my overtime like she always does. Something's going on. Her behaviour worries me.'

'What do you mean? In what way?'

'When I came down to the kitchen this morning she'd made breakfast and started eating without me. That never happens. Her tone was silky when she talked, although nervous too, but it was what she said that worries me.'

'And?' Charlotte said eagerly.

'She said that we need to meet this evening without the boys and talk, and when I asked about what, she turned around and left.'

Charlotte searched for words that could lessen his worry.

'I may soon be a divorced man,' he said while they walked toward the university.

'What? No, I don't think so. She would have told me. Mia and I talk several times a week. She's never said anything about it.'

'Well, maybe it's not so strange, because technically I'm your boss. She probably didn't want you to know. Even if the two of you are friends.'

It was cold out, but also refreshing. They continued talking on the way to the university building.

'Mia doesn't want to divorce you. By the way, do you remember when she and I first met, at your house?' Charlotte laughed at the memory.

'Yes, she thought you were a little strange in your expensive designer clothes. But I was convinced that you would get to like each other and I was right. That evening drinking wine was what was needed. I'm extremely happy about that.'

'Me too,' said Charlotte, taking him lightly by the arm.

'We'll have to see what she says this evening,' said Per. 'But now we have to focus on Unni's workplace, which may be a narcotics den.'

Charlotte mused about what Per had told her. When she thought about it, she realized that Mia had kept her distance recently. Being best friends with your boss's wife was perhaps not ideal. But Mia was her only real friend in Umeå, apart from Per.

Many students were done for the day and on their way out of the campus. A few stood by their bicycles and brushed off the snow that had fallen lightly during the day. The most experienced had seat protectors with lambskin, like Charlotte's mother had when she was little. Many bicycles also had grooved tyres, which impressed Charlotte. *Incredibly practical*, she thought as Per got a phone call.

He slowed his steps and while he was talking, Charlotte looked over at the building where the library was. She loved the university library. Not long ago she was here with Anja in the hope that she would apply to study here when she finished high school. But Anja had complained about all the boring people. Sometimes the snobbishness really came out in her daughter. The friends she hung around with in Stockholm were anything but humble. Really spoiled snot-nosed kids. Anja had high standing in her circle of friends thanks to her mother and father's aristocratic titles and money. Charlotte's ex-husband was high up in the peerage and well-known in the business community. Things had gone well for him. Charlotte had fallen for him when she saw his picture in a trophy case at the elite Lundsberg School where they were both students. Carl's golf talent had given the school a respected title and when Charlotte saw the photograph she fell in love on the spot. Without even having met him. Ten years later came Anja. A name her daughter was often teased about. Anja didn't exactly sound aristocratic. 'The Russian' was a recurring nickname she had to put up with. Mostly in jest, but Charlotte knew that Anja hated it.

Carl had never forgiven her for that choice of name, even though he'd actually been involved and approved it. He voted for Victoria, or Caroline ending with an e. Important. But Charlotte would not fall in line and through a little manipulation it became Anja. She was rather pleased with herself. Charlotte could have convinced a criminal to sell flower pins, so a Carl in love was no problem. The name Anja itself she'd loved since she was a child because that was the name of her favourite nanny.

Per caught up with Charlotte and they entered the building together. They'd been told that Unni's students were at a lecture so they had to wait a while.

'If we'd just got a hit from the DNA from where Unni was murdered, something to go on from our database . . .' he said, sitting down on a bench inside the entrance to the library itself. He unzipped his coat. Scanned his arm to check his blood glucose. No action was needed. Charlotte sat down beside him. A wave of cold air struck them every time someone opened the entrance door. Shoes dragged in slush and gravel on to the floor and there was a crunching sound as the young people walked past.

'I'm worried about Frida,' said Per. 'There is no evidence of her around the house at Nydala, and with William dead it doesn't look good. We're limited by the fact that we can't use Missing People.'

Charlotte nodded. 'Yes, right now we can't get help from them because then the whole media circus will start up and Frida's identity will be known. We still have to avoid that.'

She stamped off her shoes a little and continued. 'With William murdered, it's Tony we should focus on in our investigation. William was seen with Frida in the house. She disappears. He is found dead. Could William have delivered Frida to Tony?

Although how in the world has Tony from Stockholm come into contact with William in Umeå? I can't fit it together.'

'I think that Tony sells drugs, which William did too,' said Per. 'Maybe Tony supplied William with the drugs. Can that be the connection? Then Tony found out that Viggo is in Umeå and so he used William. Many of the people around Frida that we talked with think it was strange that William showed so much interest in Frida. Was it perhaps to get close to her dad? An assignment he got from Tony?'

'But then Viggo should be dead by now,' Charlotte added.

'True. It's confusing,' said Per and continued. 'We've issued a national search for Tony. Wherever he is we'll find him. Although . . . when are you going to tell me about your relationship with this Tony?'

Charlotte turned her gaze to her hands. She picked at her signet ring, which was on her little finger. It had a blue stone with the family's emblem. Her jaw was clenched. Should she tell him now? She was uncertain, needed time to explain properly.

'We'll discuss that another time,' she replied, taking off her hat, not bothering to straighten her hair, and met his gaze. If Per found out he would immediately remove her from the investigation. She would actually be in danger now, when their work brought them ever closer to a confrontation.

Charlotte inspected the students; many looked tense. The big examination hall was in this building, which could explain some of the gloomy expressions.

'Unni was murdered by a sexually deviant person. It can't be Tony,' said Charlotte, trying to change track, fully aware that Per must wonder how she could know that. 'He can put the pressure on and be violent, even torture, but what Unni was subjected to is too . . . unlike his pattern. True, he may have hired someone to do it, maybe some local talents who aren't on our register yet.'

She took out her phone. Her ex, Carl, was calling, and she put it back in her pocket without answering.

'On the other hand, human trafficking is more his thing. He has girls at clubs, on the street, on the internet and they're constantly replaced by new, younger talents.'

She stood up.

'We have to check up on what's being said in town in the underworld. If she was murdered on Tony's orders there'll be talk about it. Criminals are like a gang of gossipy old ladies when it comes to impressing others.'

He couldn't help but laugh at the comparison.

'We'll talk with Unni's students, see if they remember anything new,' Charlotte continued and started moving away. Looked at the clock. Walked toward the hall where Unni's students were.

Per looked at his assistant detective inspector. *Why am I her boss? She should be mine,* he thought, following her.

The smell of chemicals was heavy in the narrow corridor. Sounds from various devices was all that broke the silence. Some students sat bent over their books outside a lecture hall. Fully focused, they didn't say a word to one another. Charlotte harboured enormous respect for what they were learning. *Smart kids,* she thought, showing her police ID. She introduced herself and said that the police needed to hold private interviews with each one of them due to what had happened to Unni.

'You all had her in the pharmacy programme, right?'

The students seemed satisfied to get a break from their studies and nodded. Several of them asked questions about Unni.

'Unfortunately I can't go into details because of our ongoing investigation,' Charlotte replied, looking over at Per. He was talking with someone who appeared to be a janitor.

'We're going to take your contact information in case we need to talk more with any of you. We can start with you,' she said, taking a female student aside. Per did the same and placed himself in a corner with another girl from the group.

The young woman met Charlotte's gaze, looked over at her study group, then back at Charlotte.

'Well, I don't know, but there was something strange about Unni towards the end, I think, anyway,' the woman said.

'Do tell,' said Charlotte, taking out a notepad.

'She asked our group about drugs – if we knew whether anyone was selling tramadol or Dolcontin. I perceived it almost as threatening. At the same time it's just the type of pharmaceuticals that we're learning about.'

'Threatening in what way? Did she threaten any of you?' Charlotte asked.

The woman crossed her arms. 'Well, no, but she seemed angry about something. I perceived her questions as aggressive.'

'What questions did she ask – do you remember?'

'Well, like . . . Do you buy drugs? If so, then where and from who? Those kinds of questions. As if she took it for granted that we used drugs.'

'What?'

Charlotte could not conceal her surprise. It felt like a complete invasion of privacy to ask students such questions if it wasn't part of the instruction itself.

'Yes, I thought it was a little strange, and now when she's been murdered it feels unpleasant, of course.'

'How did you respond to her?'

The woman turned to her group, appeared to think about how she should answer.

'Well, we said what everyone on campus knows. That it's William who supplies. Or *was*, he's dead now, too. Do you think it was William who killed Unni?'

Charlotte looked at Per. Thought about the DNA results that they hadn't found a match for. William wasn't on their register but the autopsy would show whether his DNA matched what was found where Unni was murdered.

'Well, I know that Unni talked with William here on campus. There were rumours about that anyway,' the young woman continued.

'What kind of rumours?' Charlotte asked, getting ready to write on her notepad.

'Yes, well, there was talk that Unni confronted William at the library. He apparently went completely berserk. A friend of mine saw everything and said that he, like, threatened to kill her if she talked a lot of shit. William shoved her so that she almost fell backwards. Screamed at her to stop snooping. But everyone here knows that he sells.'

Charlotte wrote feverishly. She needed to talk with the person who had seen the incident. But also to get in touch with Carola. There was a chance that the evidence they found on Unni, the body fluids or strands of hair, could be William's.

31

Linn was holding her phone in her hand. The glazed square she was standing in was a central place in Umeå and she was often there with Frida. They would pretend to search for reading material at the city library but mostly sat at the bakery drinking fizzy water and craving pastries they never ate. Linn looked at one of the tables where they almost always sat and her stomach knotted up.

It was Tuesday and her mother was in the Duå delicatessen. Camilla circulated among the shelves, a metal basket hanging over the crook of her arm. Still empty, Linn saw. It would be a long wait.

An arm hit her thigh and when Linn looked around she saw a little boy who was already moving away from her. Tableware clattered from the Gotthard restaurant directly adjacent; people were talking, laughing, chair legs scraped on the stone floor. No one seemed to care that Frida was missing, that soon she would have been missing for three days. Linn wanted to scream out loud that they ought to go home and worry, not sit here and be happy.

But she let that remain a thought. The feeling of being observed became increasingly intrusive. Sometimes she was sure she was imagining things, and at the next moment be dead sure that some-one was standing behind her. Linn had started holding on to the keys in her jacket pocket. With the sharpest key ready.

Linn noticed the guy who was working the register at Duå, one of the brothers who owned the place. She was annoyed by his big glasses, which were an attempt to look hip, but he was always cheerful and kind. He constantly poked at the frame on the bridge of his nose with his index finger.

Her mum's voice interrupted her thoughts. 'Linn, sit up straight – you look like a sack of hay!'

She waved at Linn to come into the store. 'Have you heard anything more from Frida?' she asked, putting a jar of green olives in the basket.

Linn looked at the screen of her phone for the umpteenth time. 'She didn't show up at school today either,' she replied.

Her mother straightened Linn's long fringe, looked sincerely worried, as if she actually cared. 'The police called. They want to talk with you again about Frida. Ask more questions that have come up during the investigation. What do you actually know?'

Linn shrugged her shoulders and tried to decide whether Camilla really wanted to know or was just playing worried mum.

'Nothing really, but now I don't know . . . She's strange,' said Linn.

Her mother started moving again, looking for something on the shelves. Linn followed her.

'She's alive,' Linn said firmly, grabbing a bunch of tomatoes that sat like grapes on a branch. Set it in Camilla's basket.

Her mother stopped mid-motion, looked at Linn with a seri-ous expression before she moved on.

'I'm sure she is,' her mother said.

'She has to be,' said Linn.

Her mother stopped again. 'Linn, you don't think that Frida has done something to herself? I mean, she hasn't been doing so well at times.'

'Camilla, leave it!' said Linn, feeling her heart start to race. The thought had struck her, but however she twisted and turned it she knew that Frida hadn't killed herself.

Her mother nodded, smiled and cocked her head, like she always did when she knew that she had pressured Linn too much.

'Okay. If you say so then it's so. She'll probably be in touch soon, you'll see.'

Linn wrestled with the thought that this was so typical of Frida.

'Do you want anything in particular, Linn?' her mother asked, ordering salami from the guy with the big glasses who was now at the meat counter. Or was it his twin brother? It was impossible to see the difference.

'No, thanks.'

Linn looked at her mother. She was so used to parrying her mood and need for control that she did it out of pure reflex. Camilla wanted it her way, because that was the only right way. Her truth was the only reality.

When Linn sensed the familiar vibration in her hand her heart had an extra beat. She stared at the screen.

'Yes, there you are!' she said out loud to herself, turning away from her mother. Her heart raced again. Frida's yellow icon showed up on the screen. Linn opened Snapchat faster than ever and looked at the picture Frida sent.

Forest. No picture of Frida. Only nature. But she was the one who had sent it.

Linn tried to see details but there were none, only trees and snow, that sort of thing. But Linn knew exactly where Frida was: by the I20 forest. In the background she glimpsed the athletic facility.

Linn sent back a question mark, and then the text: *What are you up to, you have to come home!*

She stared at the screen, waiting for Frida's icon to jump up in the chat. Changed her mind and called her instead.

Voicemail.

'Damn you!'

Back to the app.

No Frida.

You're so annoying! she wrote and snapped a picture of herself by the deli counter.

But this meant that Frida was alive.

32

Per guided the snow shovel ahead of him, picking up the pace as he approached the snowdrift. With a jerk he unloaded the snow and went back toward the house to start over. The snow blower had a fault so his exercise for today became snow shovelling. The cold made the snow as light as powder and it didn't affect his pulse noticeably, but his leather gloves still got damp from his body heat. His coat was in the way but he didn't want to go in and change. Kennet had forced them to go home for a few hours of rest; the whole police station was working in shifts to find Frida and further the investigation of the murders of Unni and William.

He hadn't said anything to Mia yet but instead tried to collect his thoughts. Per needed the snow-shovelling to be able to reset from work to focus on his own marriage. The short drive to Degernäs wasn't enough.

Per was sure that Mia wanted a divorce. There was something about her behaviour recently. Absent-minded. Distant. Nothing that was important before mattered any longer. His thoughts went to infidelity, that Mia had simply met another man. Or that she'd got tired of him missing the boys' hockey practices, coming late to parent-teacher conferences at school and not being able to be romantic with his wife in his free time. The only thing he'd done right was taking care of his diabetes.

What do I say if she wants to leave me? he thought, wiping his forehead.

Per had tried to work less after the incident last summer. But the police station was like a magnet; he was a police officer all the way to his fingertips. How did you switch off? He had no idea.

He looked up at the kitchen window, where he saw Mia sitting at the table. It was past eight so the boys were either asleep or at least in their beds. Per took a few extra rounds, making sure that the edges of snow were straight and even. They were up to mid-thigh height now and got a little higher every week.

He leaned the snow shovel against the wall of the house and stamped off the snow on the steps. Took hold of the door handle, hesitated for a second and took a deep breath. *This is going to be a tough evening,* he thought and stepped in.

Mia was sitting quietly at the kitchen table. She had a glass of red wine in front of her, which surprised him; she seldom drank on week nights. The bottle stood alongside it and suggested that more than one glass would be consumed.

She met his gaze with bloodshot eyes and Per's heart sank down to his stomach. She wanted to separate, now he knew for sure. He sat down on the chair opposite and brought his hand to hers. She didn't remove it. Per blinked several times to keep away the tears. He tried to keep panic at a distance.

'Forgive me that I haven't been here and that I've let work consume me.'

He sought Mia's gaze and she met it. She had her hair tied back in a twist which always made her look younger. She had pulled one leg up and rested her chin against her knee. A tear trickled down her cheek and he reached out and wiped it away.

'I don't know why I can't leave work, put it to one side,' Per continued. 'My psychologist says I have a fleeing behaviour. But I don't know what I'm afraid of.'

He looked at Mia's bloodshot eyes, the swollen skin below them and the chapped lips.

'Talk to me. Tell me what I can do to make this right,' he said.

Mia smiled cautiously and her grip on Per's hand got harder. She raised the wine glass with her free hand. 'There's something I have to tell you,' she said.

Per stopped breathing. His thoughts were screaming in his head. *She's met someone else. Damn it, she's met someone else!*

'Okay,' he said, sounding harder than he had intended.

'I have breast cancer,' she said, taking a sip of wine.

33

Viggo swirled the whisky around in the glass and looked at it. The ice clinked against the edges. Estelle had taken sleeping pills, slept the whole day and woken up in the afternoon. When she stepped into the shower he took the opportunity to slip down to the bar. He was on his second glass and the alcohol settled like cotton wool around his soul, slowly coating the pain in a soft covering. The image of Unni's doorway had been more than he could bear. He tried to understand who would want to kill her, but however he twisted and turned it, his thoughts came back to Frida.

'Hi there.'

Viggo interrupted his thoughts and looked at the woman at the bar who addressed him in heavily accented Swedish. He'd never seen her before. Her light hair reminded him of Frida when she was little. That whiteness you thought would never change colour. Before he replied he finished the whisky in one gulp.

'Hi, do I know you?'

The woman glanced at the ring on his left hand, and showed her own hand. No ring. She smiled ingratiatingly and he understood what she was. He'd met lots of them in Stockholm and everywhere he played poker. They swarmed where there was money and Tony loved them. Viggo turned to the bartender and asked for another glass. The guy nodded without hesitating.

'No, you don't know me,' said the woman. 'But we have a mutual friend.'

Viggo tried to look unmoved. 'I see, who is that?' he asked.

'He sent me to take you to him.'

Viggo observed the woman. She was perhaps a few years older than Frida. She was not naturally blonde – her hair looked like brittle grass. The short skirt got even shorter when she sat down on the bar stool and Viggo had an impulse to pull it down, cover her. She was wearing a pair of red tennis shoes. *I haven't seen those on a prostitute before anyway,* he thought, taking his eyes off her.

'Not without knowing who it is,' he replied after a long silence.

The bartender gave her an irritated look as he put the fresh glass in Viggo's hand.

'Someone who knows where your daughter is. What you can lose, huh?' she said, and Viggo's brain woke up from the fog.

'Who?' he asked again.

The woman stood up again and came closer. Her green eyes, with no make-up, stared into his. 'Follow me,' she said.

'Okay,' said Viggo, downing the whole glass. Then he stood up.

Would he meet Tony now? Was this the settling of accounts? Maybe he could trade his life for Frida's?

My God, let me see her, he thought while he walked right behind the young woman with the tennis shoes. She turned around to check that he was following her. Viggo ran his hands through his hair. His brain was about to explode from all that was whirling around inside. He was aware that perhaps he was going straight toward his own death. Would it be painful or would Tony shoot him on the spot? Would Frida have to watch?

The woman went up to the lift and pressed the button, which would evidently take them down to the garage.

Neither of them spoke. She seemed unmoved. She'd been given an assignment and she was on her way to completing it. There was

172

a chiming sound as the doors glided open. They got in and the woman pressed 'G' for garage. Viggo reminded himself to breathe. His mind was crystal clear. The only trace of the alcohol he had consumed was on his breath. He saw himself in the mirror in the lift. There was swelling around his eyes, deep lines between his nose and mouth, greyish skin, red eyes. The lift stopped with a jerk. Just as Viggo stepped out, his phone beeped. An alert from the *Expressen* news site.

Frida Malk Missing for Three Days – Police Working Against the Clock.

He clicked on to the news and saw that there was a picture of Frida's face. Viggo gasped. He could not take his eyes off the screen. Stared at it. The photo was taken at the latest end-of-school ceremony, when she was happy about getting to start high school. How did they know that she was missing? How did they get hold of the picture? His eyes filled with tears. He turned around, saw the lift doors closing. Thought about Estelle. If he disappeared now and Frida didn't come back, she would be alone with no idea what had happened to him. But he couldn't act in any other way, not when there was hope that he would get to see his daughter again.

Viggo noticed that he was standing in the middle of a parking garage. The young woman turned her head, looking for something. A van honked and she started walking toward it.

Viggo followed her.

34

'You sound strange, Per,' Charlotte said, pressing the phone harder against her ear. 'Has something happened? Is it Mia?'

She could hear that Per was doing something in the background; he seemed to be in motion.

'It's nothing. We'll talk about it later.'

Charlotte snorted. 'It's nothing but we'll talk about it later anyway?'

Per sighed deeply. There was a crackling sound in her ear when he exhaled.

'Like you and that criminal Tony then,' he replied, and it was her turn to sigh.

She was at home now. She had turned on all the lights in the apartment and was planning the move to their new house on The Island. Longed for it. She had started packing the essentials but the moving company could handle most of it. She didn't have time. She enjoyed taking a rest from the police station at the same time as her brain could not leave her job. She sat down on the couch, puffing up her Missoni pillows from NK and set her feet on the ottoman. Charlotte understood that Per was irritated. She had withheld important information from him. The glass of wine she had poured had reached room temperature and she took hold of it before she answered.

'Okay, I'll tell you.' She took a sip of the wine. 'I infiltrated his network as a nanny when I had just completed police training over twenty years ago. That was before he climbed up within the Syndicates. But I supplied the police with information about his routines, marriage, closest friends and so on. Tony went to prison thanks to the evidence I supplied the investigation with.'

Per did not say anything.

'Hello, are you there?' she asked.

'It sounds like a suicide mission,' he answered. 'Did he find out that you were a police officer?'

'No, we were able to keep my identity secret. After a year he moved to a different area and then we took the opportunity to pull me out with the excuse that I was going back to school. He doesn't know that I was the one who made sure that his thriving arms-smuggling was stopped.'

'But what the hell? Weren't you completely new? How could that be sanctioned by your superiors?'

'For just that reason – I'd never been seen as a police officer out in the field. No criminal could expose me because none of them had anything to do with me. I nagged to get the assignment, I knew that I would do it well, and I did.'

Charlotte brought the wine glass to her mouth. Took a sip.

'They deleted the little that was written about me on the net – at that time there was hardly an internet. I don't even know if he would recognize me if he saw me today.'

She could hear Per taking a sip too. Both of them were perhaps in need of something strong this evening.

'So you've infiltrated one of the worst criminal networks there is in Sweden. Why hadn't you told me that?'

'For my own safety. Tony is not a man you want to have after you. The fewer who know, the better. My boss has retired and the others who knew about the operation I trust. A handful of people in Stockholm.'

'Was that why you moved up here to Umeå, to get away from the Syndicates?'

Charlotte hesitated. 'No, the reason I moved here has to do with my personal life,' she said. 'But we'll discuss that another time.'

'What happens if you meet Tony in Umeå now? Kennet needs to know about this,' said Per.

'I know, I'm going to inform him.'

She didn't want to tell him about the call she had the other night, when no one said anything on the other end. It could have been anyone at all. A wrong number. Charlotte didn't intend to let any figments of her imagination put her off balance.

They were silent. Charlotte's fingers held on to the cord of the earphones. She leaned her head against the couch and thought about the fact that Tony was in Umeå. But she had a licensed weapon locked in the gun cabinet in the wardrobe.

'Shouldn't you tell me why you're feeling so low, Per?'

He started to say something but interrupted himself just as Charlotte got a news message on the phone screen. Frida Malk's picture had reached the press.

'What the hell?' she said out loud.

'I'll call you later, Charlotte. I have an incoming call from Kennet.'

Per hung up and she heard a beeping sound in her ear. Presumably Kennet had seen the same news.

She read the article. The police hadn't released Frida's identity, but there she was. Anyone could see who she was. The information must have come from somewhere else, not the police. She took another sip of wine and stood up. A few seconds later Per called back. He sounded out of breath.

'We have activity on Frida Malk's phone! Her friend Linn received a message from her on Snapchat – according to Kennet it's been traced to the I20 forest. It's turned off now but we have a place to search.'

'Maybe she's alive,' said Charlotte, setting the glass down so hard that wine splashed out on the table.

35

Viggo's hands were shaking; he had to clench his fists so as not to reveal himself. Every step on the concrete floor felt like a step closer to his own execution. All his senses were on high alert. If someone dropped a pin on the floor he would hear it. In his pocket he'd tried to call Ola Boman's phone in the hope that he could trace the call.

The ventilation system in the garage was humming and there was an odour of petrol. The girl crossed her arms as she walked and her exhalations revealed the cold in the air. Viggo felt nothing. *You don't feel cold when you're dead,* he thought.

The woman stopped behind a white van. Extended her hand to show that he should get in.

Viggo stood there. 'I'm not getting in without knowing who I'm meeting.'

His voice broke but his gaze did not leave the woman. She shrugged her shoulders and walked away. Left him in front of the doors at the back of the vehicle. One was open. He hesitated. His sweater was sticking to his back. He was just about to touch the handle when the door opened and someone pulled him into the van by force. Viggo screamed and tried to defend himself from the hold without success. His knees struck something. There was a flash before his eyes and he managed to think that maybe someone had shot him in the leg without him hearing the shot.

'Can you calm down, you asshole? It's just me!'

Viggo abruptly stopped resisting. He heard himself breathing, tried to keep up in his thoughts.

'Frida?' he replied while the outline of a man became clearer.

'No, just me,' the voice replied, and immediately he saw Abbe in one of the seats of the van. Viggo sat down beside him, his knee aching.

'Where is she?' he asked, feeling the adrenaline pumping in his veins.

'I don't know,' Abbe answered. 'Damn you stink of alcohol. Drink a little water, man,' Abbe said, handing him a bottle.

Viggo slapped away his hand so forcefully that the water spilled out, then he raised his hand toward the van door and struck it, struck and struck, against the ceiling, the wall, the seat, anywhere he could reach. He screamed out his frustration and fear. Abbe sat silently. Let him take his emotions out on the van. When his muscles were no longer able to carry on, he leaned forward and vomited.

'For Christ's sake,' said Abbe, opening the door and leaning his head out. Viggo left a stinking pool after him and then leaned his body against the back support. He breathed with his mouth open, smelled his own stinking breath.

'I need to talk with you,' said Abbe, closing the car door.

'Has Tony taken Frida?'

'No, he's not here because of you. He doesn't know that you're living here. Though maybe now he does know,' said Abbe, waving the phone that showed the article with Frida's picture.

Viggo's chest knotted up, bubbled over. He didn't know whether it was from relief or fear.

'So where the hell is she?'

'I don't know, but do you truly think I would let Tony take your daughter? Who the hell do you think I am?'

Abbe drank from the bottle that Viggo didn't want.

'One of Tony's henchmen,' Viggo stated. 'What are you doing in Umeå?' he continued before Abbe had time to respond to his comment.

'You'll find out soon, but I felt compelled to tell you that Tony isn't guilty of Frida's disappearance. I'll find out what I can, okay? Feel out our contacts a little. Our world is small and a missing young girl leads to talk even among us.'

Viggo didn't say anything, turned his head toward Abbe. The powerlessness took over every cell in his body. He did not want to do a single thing other than find Frida. Viggo took the water bottle from Abbe's hand, drank from it. 'So then why are you here?' he asked again.

'We're searching for a person who has taken over an extremely lucrative business operation in this part of the country. Something that Tony can't accept. By way of a rich snot-nosed kid in Stockholm we've managed to localize a pusher here in Umeå who seems to get drugs from the organization. His name was William something.'

'Was?'

'Yes.'

'Did you all kill this William? Has he done something with Frida?'

'Take it easy,' said Abbe. 'We brought in William, picked him up outside his apartment. He came in a taxi, without Frida.'

'So you have no idea if he took Frida or what he may have done with her?'

'When we took William we knew nothing that had to do with your daughter. I promise that we have nothing to do with her disappearance.'

Viggo nodded. He believed his old friend.

'So,' said Abbe, 'we talked with William and he gave us some names. The first turned out to be a dead end because the guy had jumped from a bridge. And we think he was only a customer. If he didn't resell on some internet site, of course.'

Viggo shook his head and shut his eyes tightly. 'Wait, wait,' he said, holding up his hand. 'Do you mean Anton, who jumped from the new bridge? He was a friend of Frida's, damn it. Why are you telling me this?'

'Because William whimpered another name too when I tried to question him. Frida Malk.'

Viggo looked at Abbe.

'William tried to buy his way out of a rather painful situation by offering bitcoins,' said Abbe, holding out his hand to Viggo. 'He said that he'd come across a large quantity and when I pressed him your daughter's name came up.'

Viggo closed his eyes even tighter. Frida had taken his bitcoins, of course. Why didn't he think of that? She was the only one who was with him when he was gambling. Who knew where he hid his passwords.

'Did William tell you how he got hold of my bitcoins?'

Abbe nodded. 'Yes, he said he knew a girl named Frida. That he could get more bitcoins through her because her father gambled a lot on the internet. Then I understood that this Frida was your Frida. Tony on the other hand didn't make the connection because he doesn't know that you're in Umeå.'

'Damn it!' Viggo said loudly, and his heart almost stopped beating when he realized that Frida had been blackmailed by that fucking idiot William.

'William exploited your daughter to get at your bitcoins.'

'Could he have killed Frida?' Viggo said, panting.

'I couldn't ask him flat out because Tony was there. But he talked about your daughter as if she was alive, that he could arrange more through her.'

Viggo's breathing was laboured, as if he'd run a hundred-metre race.

'We also got a third name. Hugo,' said Abbe. 'We suspect that he's the one who distributes large quantities of drugs up here. According to William, Hugo is smart as hell. Plays stupid, but he's anything but dumb when it comes to planning and executing drug deals.'

Viggo did not reply. *Hugo*. Why did that name sound familiar?

'If he's the guy we're looking for, then he sells drugs for millions. Tony is obviously furious. The Syndicates' sales haven't taken off in the north and he's had to lower the prices. The pushers are desperate.'

'Is his last name Larsson, this Hugo?' Viggo asked.

'Do you know who he is?'

Viggo stopped breathing. 'That was the name of the guy who drove Frida and Linn to the Nydala house. Maybe he has her.'

'We're keeping an eye on Hugo. Tony wants to get at his sales and when Tony knows all he needs to know, then we're picking up Hugo,' said Abbe, looking at his phone where new messages were constantly arriving.

'I have to tell this to the police,' said Viggo.

'You can't involve the police yet,' said Abbe, staring at him.

'But maybe he has Frida!' Viggo screamed. Saliva flew out of his mouth as he spoke.

'Why would Hugo have Frida? Why?'

Viggo shook his head. 'Maybe he's a rapist. Likes young girls? Maybe she saw Hugo do a deal in the house so he killed her . . . She would have put up resistance, Frida, she would have fought for her freedom, do you understand? Then maybe he . . .'

Viggo couldn't complete the sentence.

'Do you trust me?' said Abbe, putting his hand on Viggo's arm. 'Do you trust me?'

Viggo nodded, but could not meet Abbe's gaze.

'Can you give me a chance to take Hugo before you talk with the police? We're going to pick him up, I promise you, and he's going to tell me if he's done anything with your daughter. Trust me. We'll get it out of him faster than the police. Okay?'

Viggo nodded.

'I have to go. Tony is looking for me like a madman, but now you know that we haven't taken Frida and that Tony doesn't know that you're living here. Do what you want with that information, but never mention my name.'

'I want to be there when you take Hugo.'

Abbe shook his head. 'Not a chance. You'd kill him before we got anything useful out of him. But I promise to find out if he has your daughter.'

36

Linn had felt compelled to go out for a run – the only thing that could get her body to calm down. Kilometre after kilometre she tried to run away from herself. The pressure in her chest got lighter but her steps were still heavy. Like running with weights around your feet.

As she jogged on to the driveway, she saw an unmarked police car was parked outside the house. Now the police were sitting in her kitchen and her mother was smugly offering rolls and coffee.

Linn had slipped into the bathroom without saying anything, but it was time to face the new questions.

Linn spat down into the toilet, soundlessly, as she'd learned. She had emptied her stomach and even if the shame she felt was big, the relief was even bigger. A stranglehold that disappeared. The days that Frida had been gone just kept adding up. After the message she had received from Frida there had been silence. It was impossible to reach her.

She wiped away saliva from the edge of her mouth and flushed. Straightened up. Sweat was beading on her scalp; forcing the food out of your stomach was strenuous. Anyone who hadn't vomited on purpose wouldn't understand. She stood in front of the mirror and removed the ponytail that protected her hair, turned on the tap and cupped her hands to capture the water, rinse away the stench. When she was younger and a beginner she always brushed her teeth afterwards but now she no longer bothered to do that. When she got the courage to puke in the school toilets she started using throat lozenges. The little box that exposed other girls at the school.

Linn had told the police about the message from Frida and there was chaos. Frida's face on the front page of the newspaper. It was like getting a punch in the jaw from reality. She had to turn off her phone because everyone wanted to know more. Suddenly she was Umeå's most sought-after girl.

She had dreamed about it. Now she just wanted it to disappear.

She adjusted the tight exercise top that was damp from sweat, stuffed a Läkerol in her mouth and stepped out of the bathroom. She had met the police twice before – once in the Nydala house when Frida disappeared and again when she'd been missing for twenty-four hours. Then Linn had told herself that Frida was just with some guy. Now it was different. She was starting to run out of her own explanations for why Frida was gone.

The aroma of coffee met Linn as she came into the kitchen. Her mother was serving the black poison. Both police officers wanted milk and they each took a roll. Linn reached out, and her fingers met warm, baked dough that gave way at the light pressure. The roll would force her to go back to the bathroom in a while. She did that more often now that Frida was gone. She wanted to be *skinny*.

'Do you understand why we're here?' Per said, letting his roll sit untouched on the plate.

Linn nodded.

'Thanks for telling us about Frida's message so quickly. A search effort is being organized right now. But we need to supplement that with a few more questions. I also need your phone.'

Linn nodded again.

'Some new information has emerged about Frida,' Per continued.

She broke off a piece of cinnamon roll and saw her mother's dissatisfied look. Linn wondered whether the police had found Frida's drug stash, the pills she'd hidden for Anton before he died, and if they were going to ask her about that. Worry about that made her shift position on the chair and put the piece of roll back on the plate. She observed the police. Charlotte was sitting straight-backed, Per like a typical guy with his legs spread. It didn't look like they were going to accuse her of anything.

'Did Frida drink alcohol?' Per asked.

Linn hesitated. 'Yes, sometimes,' she said cautiously.

'Other drugs then?'

'No, never,' Linn replied without blinking.

Per straightened up and looked toward Linn's mother. Then at Linn.

'We're not here to accuse you of anything, but we do need more information about Frida to be able to get as complete a picture of her as possible. Do you understand that?'

'Okay,' said Linn, thinking that Per had sad eyes.

He took a sip of coffee but still left the roll untouched. Her mother would go crazy if neither of the police officers tasted her damn rolls.

'So now we're starting a major search effort at the 120 forest. Does that place mean anything to her?' Charlotte asked.

Linn met her green eyes. 'She and I went there sometimes, when there was a dog daycare there. But it's moved now.'

'What did you do there, at the dog daycare?'

'Looked at the dogs that got picked up in the afternoon.'

Charlotte wrote on her notepad. 'Did you talk with any of the dog owners when you were there?'

Linn thought before she replied. Tried to remember. 'No, don't think so. Just with the woman who ran the place. She was nice.'

Charlotte continued writing. 'Do you and Frida often talk about life, how you're feeling and your innermost thoughts?'

Linn's thoughts were whirling in her head. 'Yes, of course. She could be a little depressed sometimes but who isn't?' she said, laughing to joke it off.

'What do you mean by depressed? Can you explain?'

'Yes, like, she could get low. But lately she was happy, even if Anton's death hit her hard. She didn't think she would live to be more than twenty herself.'

Charlotte stopped writing on her notepad and turned her eyes to Linn. 'Do you know why she said that?'

'Nah, maybe because her dad is, like, pursued by some people.'

No one said anything. Linn explained.

'Frida told me once that her dad did something that forced them to move around a lot, but she didn't say what.'

Linn felt that she was betraying Frida's confidence; it gave her a stomach-ache. She looked down at the table and continued.

'Everything was, like, prohibited. She was, like, living in a prison . . . But she ignored the rules of course – you can't live without Instagram.'

Charlotte pointed at Linn's phone which Per had set back on the table.

'Open her Instagram, please.'

Linn did as she was told and went into Frida's account, *Nomansland*. Frida would kill Linn if she knew, but it became easier to breathe.

The policeman with the sad eyes took back the phone and disappeared into the hall to make a call.

Linn reached out her hand and stuffed the piece of roll in her mouth. Chewed slowly, trying to calm down her pulse that was making her heart pound so hard.

Charlotte picked up her roll and they chewed in silence. Her hair was shiny. Like Anja's. Linn felt an urge to become a police officer – it seemed cool. Maybe she should dye her hair dark?

'Is there anything else you'd like to tell us?' said Charlotte, and Linn glanced at her mother. Charlotte also turned to her and said loudly, so that it was heard out in the hall, 'Per, didn't you have some questions for Camilla? Can the two of you go into the living room so that we can do two things at once? Then we won't have to bother them longer than necessary.'

Per came back into the kitchen. 'Yes, of course. Can you follow me, Camilla?'

She stayed seated, casting an irritated look at Charlotte, but finally stood up. When she left the room Charlotte directed her attention to Linn again.

'Was there something you wanted to say?' Charlotte asked.

Linn pinched her lips together and tried to think of a good way to tell it without exposing Frida, that was important. She took a deep breath, looking at the living room. 'Frida used drugs,' she said quietly. 'Pretty often. She was always high lately, it seemed. Got them from a guy whose name is William.'

'We know that he sold drugs. Did Frida buy from him?' Charlotte asked.

Linn's cheeks got warm. She shook her head. 'He just gave them to her. How do you know who William is?'

'That's part of our job,' she answered.

'Do you also know that she hid a whole lot of drugs at home, in her dresser?'

Charlotte looked sincerely surprised. 'Where in her dresser?'

Linn sighed. Picked at her nails. 'In the left drawer, at the very back. But they're gone now.'

'Why are they gone now?'

'He took them.'

'Who?' asked Charlotte.

'Anton Ek, the guy who killed himself.'

Charlotte wrote on her pad. Seemed to think. 'As Frida's best friend, did you ever see her injure herself, on purpose that is?'

Linn shrugged her shoulders and stared down at the table. 'I never saw when she did that, but she has burns on her stomach and high up on one leg.'

Charlotte nodded. 'Do you know whether Frida received any form of threat or was being blackmailed, considering that she did drugs?'

Linn shook her head. 'No, nothing she told me. The only threat she talked about was what I said about her dad.'

Charlotte nodded at the same time as Linn's mother's voice came closer.

'Thanks for telling me,' said Charlotte, handing over a business card before Linn's mother came into the kitchen. 'Call me if you think of anything else, okay?'

Linn did not reply, but took the card and put it in her pocket.

'Well then, I guess that's all. We're done here, right?' said Charlotte, looking at Per.

'We had a break-in last weekend,' Linn said in a loud voice. She wanted to push away the thoughts of what a gossip she was.

'We reported that to the police,' her mother was quick to comment. 'Nothing was stolen. I think Linn came home and then the break-in was interrupted.'

Charlotte raised her eyebrows. 'You came home and someone was in the house?'

'Yes, someone slipped out through the patio door.'

'When was this?'

'The same night that Frida disappeared.'

'What time?'

Linn sighed. 'Around three, maybe, in the morning.'

'Did you see what the person looked like?'

She shook her head. 'Dark jacket, ski mask. Never saw his face and such, just a dark figure. Hard to describe.'

'Did anything seem different at home? Did it look as if this person was searching for something?'

Linn tried to remember. 'Not that I can think of. I went into my room and locked the door. I don't think anything was missing.'

Per was standing in the doorway. He pulled something under his arm and when Linn saw what it was she understood. A girl in her class had diabetes. Maybe that was why he looked like a sad dog.

'If you'll excuse us, my daughter has to do homework now and doesn't need to answer any more questions. I want you to leave.'

Linn's mother reached for the coffee cups. A clear order to the police that the coffee hour was over. Charlotte reached out her hand to Camilla's wrist and was just about to say something when Camilla got irritated.

'What are you doing?' she said, pulling away her hand.

'Sorry,' said Charlotte. 'But you have a very nice bracelet on – what lovely pastel colours. Where did you get it?'

'She got it from me. I make those sometimes,' said Linn.

'Aren't you a little old to be making plastic bracelets?' said Charlotte, but didn't take her eyes off her mother's wrist.

Linn's cheeks got warm. She actually was, but crafting was something she did when her brain was about to burn up.

'I have a whole pile here at home if you want one.'

'Were you missing any bracelets after the break-in?' Charlotte asked, and Linn didn't understand why that was relevant. No burglar would want her cheap bracelets.

'Well, I had seven left and they're all on my desk.'

Charlotte didn't say anything. But her pale face looked even whiter now. Almost grey.

37

Abbe watched as Hugo got into his car, an older model Volvo V70. He'd stopped at the Avion shopping centre and stayed there about fifteen minutes. The Clas Ohlson bag revealed where he'd shopped. Now he was driving toward the city centre and the Teg Bridge. Abbe had received orders from Tony to somehow get Hugo Larsson to the cabin – the hiding place that felt like a dark hole every time he stepped inside. Abbe longed for his own bed in Stockholm, or a hotel room with heat, shower and minibar. But none of them could be seen at places that might be guarded or have surveillance cameras.

In the cabin they would make sure that Hugo understood the seriousness of the situation. Did he want to live and give all the information he had to Tony, or be greedy and die? The problem for Abbe was how he could question Hugo about Frida without Tony noticing anything. He needed to have time on his own with the guy.

Abbe had called the contacts he trusted to find out more about Frida, but no one knew anything. The thought had struck him that Viggo's daughter herself had chosen to disappear, or committed suicide, but he couldn't bring himself to say that to his friend. A girl who'd been missing for three days would probably not be found alive. If someone had kidnapped Frida to sell her she would probably not be seen until she was used up and beaten to death by some sick bastard out in Europe. Or else it was a jealous guy who'd murdered her and hidden the body. It would take a long time to search through Umeå and the surrounding area. All alternatives were terrible for Viggo, but there was still one more and Abbe was now driving after him on the E4. Previously he'd followed Hugo a couple of times when he delivered newspapers, and also padded brown envelopes. It seemed as if the deliveries in Umeå for the furnishings company were done by hand, while what was sold in the rest of the country was sent when he worked at the mail distribution centre. Every local address was noted by Abbe, this time too. Hugo turned right at the roundabout and entered the I20 area. Abbe saw that the place was well-lit before he noticed all the police officers.

What the hell? They're searching for Frida here? he thought, getting stuck in a long line of cars a few vehicles behind Hugo. Many people were apparently curious. He put on his cap, pulling it down as far as he could without blocking his field of vision. *Damn.* It wasn't possible to turn around now, that would draw the attention of the police. The car rolled slowly past the barricades and through a gate. He knew that the old regiment was here and there was a school in the same area too. Why did they choose to search for Frida here, and what was Hugo doing here? *So maybe the girl is here.*

Hugo drove slowly and continued to the car park outside the school. He stopped the Volvo but stayed in it with the engine idling. Abbe parked a short distance away. A group of youths walked toward the police barricades, huddling to ward off the cold. He suspected that they were thinking the same thing he was. That the girl wouldn't be found out in the ice-cold, dark forest. Shielded by the twilight he observed the guy who perhaps knew where Frida was. Hugo, who passed completely under the radar with his narcotics sales. No one suspected him.

Hugo was a blank page.

Or a genius.

38

It was a miracle that Per was at work this morning. He lay awake looking at his sleeping wife for most of the night, patting her blonde hair which soon risked falling out. Several examinations were scheduled and surgery was planned. The doctors did not think that the cancer had spread to the lymph nodes, but more examinations would show whether that was true or not.

The cancer diagnosis had in some strange way made Mia calmer. Per was the one who was awake, drawing in the anxiety and letting it take over his mind.

He yawned and leaned against the counter in the break room. There was constant activity in the police building now. You could see no difference between day and night.

It felt as if someone had stuck cotton wool in his frontal lobe, preventing him from thinking clearly. He called it a brain fog. His eyelids were open but he couldn't take in what he was looking at, much less put together a constructive thought. Like an old drunk.

The coffeemaker bubbled as the last of the water seeped out. Per was staring at the drops that ran down the side of the carafe when Kennet interrupted his thoughts about cancer.

'How did the media get hold of this information?' he said, tossing the newspaper on the table.

Per looked at the front page and the picture of Frida that had shocked them all the night before.

The picture brought Per's mind to life; like an old computer from the 1990s his brain started to connect. With his index finger he pulled the newspaper toward him. Frida was smiling into the camera; this was a personal snapshot taken on a summer day. She had an ice-cream cone in one hand and a pink phone in the other. Her eyes were made-up and her teeth white.

Per turned the pages to the article itself.

Kennet sighed. 'The communications department claims that neither the name nor the picture came from them. Which I believe, because they haven't had any great insight into this case. My God, a preliminary investigation is confidential.'

'So how did they find out about it?' Per asked. 'Who's leaking pictures to the press?'

Per reached for a coffee cup in the cupboard. The police logo on the porcelain had faded.

'I don't know, but believe me, I'm going to find out.'

Per knew that his boss was well aware that you weren't allowed to enquire into sources, so that was probably an empty threat. The smell of coffee spread as Per poured it into the cup. He thought about Ola Boman – he must be going crazy that Frida's name and picture were out. For Witness Protection this was a nightmare. But for Frida herself, maybe it was good anyway. Tips from the general public should start streaming in and that was worth a lot.

Per went to the briefing room; it was almost six thirty in the morning and the darkness outside made the corridor dark as night. He met Tobbe Antonsson, who was just stepping into his office. Tobbe was head of the surveillance group. He was someone who advocated more openness between the departments. The problem was that everyone guarded their own turf, with hierarchy and competition for established goals. Tobbe had called a meeting simply to discuss the problem and Per agreed with him one hundred per cent.

A glow spread in the corridor when Tobbe turned the lights on in his office. Per stuck his head in, raised the coffee cup and was just about to say good morning when he stopped in mid-motion.

Had he seen right?

Per stepped further into Tobbe's office and looked at the picture that was on the desk.

There was nothing about where the picture was taken, but everyone in Umeå recognized the Norrland Opera House. The photograph showed two figures. One was Tony's closest man, Abbe Ali. But also in the picture, in the background, was another man who Per recognized and whom Abbe seemed to be observing. Hugo.

'Hi there,' said Tobbe, hanging up his jacket. 'To what do I owe the honour on this early Wednesday morning?'

Per indicated the picture. Cleared his throat. 'Why are you doing surveillance on Hugo Larsson and Abbe Ali?'

Tobbe's chair creaked as he sat down. He leaned forward to the desk. His eyes were ice-blue, like a wolf's, or like the hockey player Peter Forsberg, making Per avert his gaze.

'We're collaborating with the MOC unit and Abbe came to our attention when we were surveilling this guy.'

'So why are you surveilling Hugo Larsson?' asked Per.

'He's a mail carrier but we suspect that he delivers drugs when he passes out newspapers,' said Tobbe, taking a pause. 'We don't know why Abbe and the Syndicates are after Hugo, but you can guess that it has to do with drugs. Tonight my guys reported that Abbe is in an abandoned cabin in Vännäs. Look at this.'

Tobbe handed another picture to Per, who turned it over and saw an address written in pencil. Per's heart struck an extra beat. They needed to go there immediately if that was where Tony was.

'Damn, you and I must get better at cooperating. This is simply carelessness on our part,' said Per, unable to hold back his irritation.

'Believe me, I want nothing more. My plan was to explain all this at our briefing this morning. I know that you all are looking for Tony, but you have to sync with MOC when you go further with this in your investigation, so you don't bypass one another.'

Per wasn't really comfortable with the new acronyms, even if the MOC unit in particular had been created before the reorganization. When the country's narcotics departments ceased to exist, parts of the drug eradication programme ended up under the Major Organized Crime unit. A poor idea, in Per's mind; he'd always been of the opinion that the narcotics trade needed a separate section in order to be effective. In Umeå MOC collaborated with the surveillance unit.

'How did you happen to surveil Hugo? He's a mail carrier and works at an interior design company. Sure, he drove Frida and her friend to the house the night she disappeared, but otherwise there's nothing. He has no previous convictions whatsoever.'

'We know that large quantities of narcotics are sold from the Umeå area and MOC got a breakthrough in their investigation.'

Per was not satisfied with that answer. 'Yes, but what made you all focus on Hugo Larsson?'

'Lately these kinds of things have spread in Umeå. Several young people have ended up in hospital with the same substance in their blood.' Tobbe pointed to a picture of pills. 'These are two medications classified as narcotics which are extremely dangerous – Dolcontin and tramadol. We suspect that Hugo both sells and distributes.'

Per sighed audibly. 'Yes, those pills are part of our investigation too. Dolcontin is a morphine preparation that is rampant among our young people. We found something similar in Unni Olofsson's apartment. But what else do you know?'

'We got a tip via the website that Hugo Larsson is selling these drugs to young people. It was registered but as usual it took a while before anyone looked at it. Then it was assessed as sufficiently interesting and landed on our desk, and we took it further with MOC. But as I said, we've only just started our surveillance work on him.'

'Who turned in the tip?' Per asked.

Tobbe tapped his computer to life, brought the mouse over the desktop to find the right place on the screen.

'Let's see here . . . The police officer who received it made a note that the tipster was anonymous. But the IP address was traced because it concerned a felony. Let's see . . . Wait a moment . . . Here it says that the IP address goes to Kungsgatan 65A. A pharmacy chain. Must be the Utopia pharmacy.'

'Damn it! That's where Unni Olofsson worked,' Per said, hurrying toward the briefing room.

39

Linn sat with her phone in her hand; the police were done with it. They had traced which signal mast Frida was closest to when she sent the picture, and it was far from where she disappeared. Missing Persons would soon start their search at the I20 forest. It was Wednesday and four days had passed. All the crazy thoughts whirled around in her head but there was no one to talk to about them. It became clear how lonely Linn was now Frida was missing. She only had her, no one else. Sometimes she talked with Frida out loud as if she were there with her. She knew what answers Frida would give, so Linn answered herself with Frida's replies. Sometimes it felt like a tsunami of loss, as if she was drowning in it. Jogging became a struggle against it every time, the feeling of running away from what would be the end.

Linn should have gone to school but she could no longer bear to. So instead of fulfilling her school duties she was watching as the I20 area was cordoned off. There were police everywhere, along with people in yellow vests. So much activity but nonetheless a strange silence.

She was standing in the spot where she and Frida used to hang out when they didn't have anything to do, where the Elverket party space had once been. It had been replaced by a big, newly constructed office building. She found herself by the entrance, which was well lit but closed.

She looked over toward the sports hall, turned her gaze to be able to see the track and field arena with the football field covered with snow. Thought about all the times they'd made snow angels there. The record was forty-five, the entire football field was full of them. She smiled at the memory. Looked around and saw the big gravel field where the circus would set up during the summer. Now it would be a meeting point for Missing People.

The 120 was a place where many people exercised, including schools and a number of companies. But there was also a very large forest beyond that area. What was Frida doing here?

Linn looked toward the place where the dog daycare had been. It was also replaced by new construction. All that was left were parts of the white, rickety wooden fence. Both Frida and Linn dreamed about having a dog someday. She thought back on the times they came here after school and looked at the furry cuties. Mainly when it was warm out. Then they sat in the car park outside the white fence and enjoyed watching as the owners picked up their animals in the afternoon. Frida had gone into the building once, pretending to be a dog owner, just to see what it looked like. She'd come back with a big smile after meeting a woman who showed her around.

Miss you here she texted to Frida, along with a picture of the place where the dog daycare was before. She knew deep down that no answer would come back. But it was necessary to reach out, just in case. Linn refused to stop hoping.

It felt as if her body were electric; it crackled. Every morning Linn woke up free of the crackling, to realize a second later what reality looked like. That very moment, before she woke up completely and before reality hit her, was the best time of the day. Then her heart cramped.

There was a big commotion all over the city. Everyone was searching and had their own theories about what had happened to her friend. The newspapers showed pictures of Frida where she smiled into the camera. The police said that Frida was missing without a single trace. Not one surveillance camera had captured her and no one saw her leave the house in Nydala that night. What the hell was she doing in a forest? Linn couldn't make sense of it. The police had previously searched around Lake Nydala and now Missing People would help out. Linn ordered herself to go over to the meeting point, but her body ignored her. Her brain screamed but not her voice. She couldn't explain it. Instead she walked away from what was about to become a gathering place, toward the bicycle path.

The only positive thing about this mess was that her mother had stopped posting on Instagram. No faked pictures, no demands to be perfect, no scolding about her weight – just silence.

Linn pulled her knitted hat further down over her ears. For the first time this winter she'd put on coveralls. It was extremely cold out, but she didn't feel cold, and wiped away the dampness that ran from her nose. She was standing behind a parked car which was covered with fresh snow. She brought her index finger against the rear window and wrote *Frida* in the snow.

Linn had been cooperative and answered all the questions from the police, let every secret come out. What if Anton had told someone else that Frida had the drugs at her house, someone who wanted to get at them?

Linn turned around. The feeling was back. Someone was watching her. Her heart beat faster, she listened for steps, turned her head in every direction and realized that she was standing completely alone in a dark place.

She started running to where the people were gathering.

40

Charlotte looked at Per, who came into the briefing room with a gloomy expression. *What has happened?* she thought as Kicki asked the same question out loud. Per replied that they would soon find out. It was time to review the most recent events and update everyone who was working on the various investigations.

Charlotte had made herself tea and held her hands around the cup. She'd had a bad night. Tony's presence in the city had made her violate all protocols and put her gun in the drawer in the nightstand when she was sleeping. She had also asked Anja to stay in Stockholm for as long as Tony was in Umeå.

Per drew his hand through his thick hair, away from his forehead; a lock of hair fell down anyway and landed above one eye.

'So, we have quite a bit to review, good people,' he said, taking a place at the front by Unni's picture on the whiteboard. 'We have to bring in Hugo Larsson. I've just received information from Tobbe in Surveillance that he is selling large quantities of drugs. Tobbe told me that they became interested in Hugo after a tip came in via the website.'

'What do you mean, tip?' said Charlotte. This was new information to her.

'That he sells and distributes medications classified as narcotics for large amounts. MOC and Surveillance suspect that he's head of the operation. They know that he makes deliveries when he distributes the mail, they've just started unravelling the case, but . . .'

Per made a pause and everyone in the room sat completely quiet.

'The tip came in from a person we know about, Unni Olofsson. It was sent several weeks ago, from the pharmacy computer at a time when she was alone at work. So we think it came from her, but that needs to be confirmed.'

Charlotte put down the cup of tea and set both elbows on the table. She concentrated on listening to Per, who continued.

'Our focus concerning the murder of Unni will now be to find out what she knew about Hugo Larsson that made her tip off the police. This gives Hugo a motive to murder Unni Olofsson – maybe she threatened to expose him. William too, the pusher, perhaps threatened to kill Unni because she was asking questions that weren't appreciated. We have a witness from the university who told us that on one occasion William became aggressive toward Unni and that he supposedly screamed at her to stop interfering, otherwise he would kill her. Both William and Hugo sell drugs, so they may have murdered Unni together. We have two DNA matches from the murder scene after all.'

Charlotte raised her eyebrows. It felt like they were on the right track.

'In addition, it's not just the police who are keeping an eye on Hugo Larsson right now. Surveillance has noticed that Abbe Ali, Tony Israelsson's henchman, seems to be following him. Why would the Syndicates be interested in him if it's not drug-related?'

'Clearly that's what it's about,' said Charlotte, trying to collect her thoughts. 'We did talk with Hugo in connection with Frida's disappearance, because he drove the girls to the Nydala house.'

Charlotte thought about the brief conversation they'd had with Hugo, how willingly he cooperated with the police. He had an alibi for the time when Frida disappeared because he'd been at home with Camilla. She'd confirmed that.

'William sold drugs left and right,' said Kicki, standing up. Her bohemian sweater sat loosely on her body and the sturdy boots looked like a punk rocker's. 'Let's assume that he bought them from Hugo. In that case he must have annoyed Tony, who then killed William. The beating that preceded William's murder indicates that. Maybe Tony got out of William where he bought his drugs – that is, from Hugo – and for that reason now the Syndicates are following him,' said Kicki, sitting down again.

Charlotte was on the same line of thought as Kicki.

'And Frida's disappearance must in some way be linked to all this,' said Charlotte. 'She was dating William. We've also received new information from her friend Linn who told us that Frida hid a large quantity of drugs in her dresser for Anton Ek, the boy who recently committed suicide—'

'We didn't find any drugs in Frida's room,' Kicki interrupted.

Charlotte smiled at her. 'If you let me finish, I intended to say that admittedly we didn't find any drugs, but that only means that someone got there first and took them – a person who knew that they were there. Frida's disappearance may also be drug-related.'

'Does Hugo Larsson have access to their house?' said Kicki, making a rattling sound at the table as she moved her arm which was full of metal bracelets.

'We have to bring in Hugo Larsson for questioning concerning the murder of Unni,' Per stated. 'And we have to take a DNA sample from him. Contact the prosecutor, and find out where Hugo is, but sync that with MOC so they know what's happening and why. Also check with Carola about what's going on with William's DNA – if it matches either of the two traces we found at Unni's. I wouldn't be surprised if they did this together.'

204

Charlotte stood up and put her hands on her waist. But Per wasn't done.

'We have more to go over when it comes to Frida's disappearance. Viggo, Frida's dad, no longer believes that Tony kidnapped his daughter. He refuses to say why, but he called that in to Ola Boman at Witness Protection and was "a hundred per cent convinced".'

'But we can't simply dismiss him as a suspect. What if Viggo is under threat to say that?' said Kicki.

'I agree with Kicki there,' said Charlotte.

'Of course I agree too,' said Per, sounding irritated. 'Ola has had an interview with Viggo, who is in a protected residence. He made the assessment that Viggo was not under immediate threat from Tony. But we're still working broadly and aren't ruling anything out. In any event Tony and Abbe will be brought in for the murder of William. But we need to think more broadly in our investigation.'

Per sounded determined and got support in the room.

'We suspect that Tony is here in connection with the increasing drug sales that we've seen in Umeå. At the present time there is nothing to indicate that he has any idea that Viggo Malk and his family are living here.'

'So now we think that Hugo is the prime suspect in this tangle?' said Charlotte, taking a deep breath.

'He drove her to the house and he sells drugs that Frida frequently used. But we checked Hugo's alibi and what he said tallied.'

'What did he say?' Anna asked, looking unusually tired. No rosy cheeks, no workout clothes.

'That he went back to Camilla's immediately after he drove the girls to the house. So, about seven thirty p.m. We've had that confirmed by Camilla, and likewise by a witness who saw his mail truck outside the address.'

Per wrote the number four on the board above Frida's picture, four days gone, and turned to the group.

'We have a major effort right now at the I20 forest. What do we know about Frida's actions before she disappeared?'

Anna took the floor. 'We've gone through the surveillance cameras all over Umeå but haven't come up with anything. She isn't seen on any of them. Her phone hasn't been active since the day she disappeared, apart from the message she sent to Linn. Then it was connected temporarily and turned off just as quickly again. But that there has been activity on her phone gives us hope.'

'Unless someone else has her phone, of course,' said Charlotte, getting a nod of agreement from Anna, who continued.

'We know through questioning of individuals close to Frida that she was at home with her friend Linn Mattsson earlier in the evening. That the girls got a lift from Hugo Larsson to the house by Lake Nydala in his mail truck. He dropped them off at quarter past seven, then he drove home to Camilla's to work. Which has been confirmed by her, and also by witnesses who saw him go into the house at the same time. His car was parked there for two hours, then Hugo drove home. Which has also been confirmed by a woman who was out walking her dog when he came home and parked his truck.'

'But if he's our prime suspect in the murder of Unni, we can't simply dismiss him concerning Frida,' said Kicki.

'We're not doing that,' said Per. 'But right now we have nothing that indicates he's done anything with Frida.'

Charlotte reached for the cup of tea on the table, took a sip and then set it down. The tea had gone tepid.

'We know that Frida had some kind of relationship with William,' said Anna. 'Video material from the evening shows that they were necking pretty heavily at the party. Frida's friend Linn saw Frida in the house for the last time at about nine o'clock. That's our most recent sign of life from the girl, who at that point was extremely intoxicated and high on something. She then said to Linn that she was going to William's place with one of his buddies. Who that person was Linn didn't know, so there we have a gap and a question mark.'

'And the last sign of life from William was?' Kicki asked.

'A taxi driver drove him to his address,' said Per. 'Dropped him off at 1.56 a.m. Frida wasn't with him. Then he wasn't seen until his body was found at the university. We suspect that the perpetrator was waiting for him at home. That is, Tony Israelsson, or one of his men.'

'So we know that Frida wasn't with him when he disappeared,' said Anna, making a note on a paper.

'That's correct,' said Per. 'If she wasn't already at his place.'

'But where is she? Who has her?' Charlotte reached out to Frida's picture on the board. The smiling girl reminded her of Anja and she could not even imagine what Frida's parents were going through right now. Their actions on the evening in question were the first thing they'd checked, standard procedure, but that hadn't been flagged for anything suspicious either.

Per sighed audibly. The briefing had taken too long; his colleagues seemed restless and wanted to start working.

'Okay, listen up now. Here's the next step. We need to find out what Unni knew, other than what she tipped off the police about. Check with IT Forensics – they should be done with her computer at this point. We're planning an effort to bring in Hugo Larsson. We'll bring in every damned Syndicates member who's hiding up here. Surveillance knows where they are – they're in a cabin in Vännäs somewhere. And then we'll have to see what the search at 120 gives us.'

The group got ready to leave the room, but Kicki raised her hand.

'Yes?' said Per.

'Do you remember that William was found with a number combination of some type? It's to what's called a bitcoin wallet, or more precisely a private key, which allows someone to spend bitcoins from a certain wallet. This particular one is on a site called Blockchain and what we found on William was the password. It's very long, not something a normal person can keep in their head. We know that if you lose or forget your password, the bitcoins that are in that wallet are lost forever. So it doesn't work like an ordinary account at a bank where money can be traced. The value here was almost five hundred thousand kronor, so someone is probably sweating right now.'

'I understood approximately half of what you just said,' said Charlotte, and several others nodded in agreement. Including Per.

'So who does the wallet belong to?' he asked.

'That's still shrouded in darkness,' Kicki replied. 'We'll probably never know.'

'Aren't bitcoins used to buy things on the dark web?' Charlotte asked.

'Yes, among other things.'

'But shopping with alternative payment methods isn't illegal,' said Charlotte.

'No, but it is the case that this payment method attracts money laundering and other criminal activity because all the transactions occur completely anonymously. It's not possible to trace them to a certain person like the banks can.'

Kicki tapped her pen against the table while she spoke.

'I'm just tossing out a theory now, but our gambler Viggo here . . .' she said, aiming her pen toward Viggo's picture. 'A guy who plays poker on the internet ought to have a hell of a lot of bitcoins to play with. A buddy of mine plays poker on the dark web and only bitcoins are used there.'

Silence in the room.

'Check with Viggo if he's missing any of those . . . bitcoins,' said Per at last. 'And if those are Viggo's bitcoins that William got access to, what does that mean for the investigation?'

'That gives Viggo a motive to murder William,' said Kicki, and everyone stopped mid-motion.

'Money is always a motive,' said Per. 'But when William was murdered, Viggo was in our custody in a secret location.'

Kicki looked noticeably irritated about having her theory shot down.

'But it could mean that William pressured Frida to get at her father's wallet,' said Charlotte. 'Maybe Frida threatened to go to the police and tell? William may have killed her before he himself was murdered.'

Per looked at Charlotte and snapped his fingers. 'Good, that needs to be followed up,' he said, pointing at Anna who nodded.

'However, we don't have a body to support that,' she said.

'Exactly,' said Per. 'We searched through the house at Nydala and the surrounding area the day after she disappeared, but we were searching for Frida, not a murder scene. Take Forensics there and see if they can find anything.'

'But if William killed Frida in the house Saturday night, how did he manage to move the body without a single person having seen it?' Anna asked.

41

Charlotte's shoulders were held down by the heavy vest that would protect against any bullets in the event of a confrontation. Her scoliosis got worse when weight put pressure on her spine. It was always the same point that hurt the most; the doctor thought it was where the spine was most crooked, like a drawn-out S.

When the lift pinged and the doors opened she was met by a smell of concrete and rubber. The police building's garage. Two teams were on their way: team one would arrest Tony and Abbe in Vännäs, while she and Per made up team two and would bring in Hugo. They'd located him at a petrol station just north of the city. Assisting them were the SWAT team and the surveillance unit.

The MOC unit was not happy about the action against Tony, because they wanted to gather more evidence of his narcotics smuggling. But he was their only way forward in the investigation around the murders of Unni and William.

'Hope we get a quick answer on Hugo's DNA,' said Charlotte. 'If it matches what was found in the apartment then we've got him.'

Per nodded. 'Team one will soon be at the cabin in Vännäs,' he said, looking at his watch.

'I'm worried about the fact that we haven't found the place where William was murdered,' said Charlotte. 'Without that we can't tie either Abbe or Tony to the crime. No prosecutor is going to make an indictment without concrete evidence.'

'But we have to bring them in before the whole gang slips down to Stockholm again,' said Per.

'William may have been killed in the cabin,' said Charlotte, taking her gun from its holster. Stroked her hand across the smooth surface. Security. The anonymous call she got when she was at home with Anja revealed that Tony perhaps knew that his old nanny was a police officer, that he was already watching her. But he left no crumbs behind, he cleaned up; she ought to be dead now in such a scenario. Charlotte wanted to tell Per about the call but she was worried that then he would remove her from the investigation.

Per held up the car key. 'I'll drive.'

As they left the garage Charlotte saw that it was starting to get dark; the planning of the operation had taken longer than expected.

Charlotte put the earpiece in her ear, used her index finger to get it to sit comfortably.

'Is the SWAT team leaving the same time as us?' she asked Per. The name had actually been changed to the NRC unit but Charlotte usually referred to it by the old acronym because it was so ingrained.

Per shook his head. 'Their vehicle is rolling out now, but they're waiting until we're at the meeting point.'

She nodded. Thought about the fact that Tony would soon be in an interview room, which gave her goosebumps. The last time she saw Tony over twenty years ago she was standing in his kitchen carrying one of his children. She'd been living at his home. Seen all sides of him. The gentle side that the children and nanny experienced, but also the coarse side that his wife and companions lived with. Charlotte knew that he had a lack of impulse control, severe empathy deficit disorder and an inability to control his anger. She suspected there was untreated ADHD in the baggage.

'Why hasn't Surveillance been in touch? They ought to report status for both teams,' she said, leaning forward to get the phone out of her back pocket.

'They'll report to us when they're in place,' said Per.

Charlotte leaned back against the seat and unbuttoned her jacket. Per drove along the E12. The bright headlights gave good visibility and the lack of cars made it possible to press down on the accelerator. He seemed absorbed in other thoughts; he'd behaved strangely lately and they hadn't managed to finish the conversation about what was worrying him. Charlotte wanted to talk but new work-related matters constantly came up.

The further away from the city they went, the more trees surrounded them. Like a dense lane. There was plenty of game along this stretch. A traffic policeman she'd talked with told her that the biggest hazard with hitting a moose was that it would be pushed into the front seat, get stuck there and kick you to death with its hind legs.

The phone rang in Charlotte's pocket. She looked at the screen. Kennet.

'Yes, this is Charlotte.'

'Hi, sorry to disturb you now,' he said. 'The spreading of Frida's name and picture has given us a huge amount of tips from people who say they've seen her at various places. Everywhere from Paris to Flurkmark. We're investigating all tips.'

Charlotte laughed. 'Yes, it's both good and bad releasing the name and picture. Have you found anything interesting at I20?'

'No, but there's another matter the two of you need to know about.'

'Okay,' said Charlotte, looking straight ahead at the road. A van overtook them at high speed.

'Idiots,' said Per, slowing down.

'We've received a tip about a car which, according to the informant, is said to have been parked by I20 the morning after Frida disappeared,' said Kennet. 'Right where Missing People is starting its search now. The person noticed because of the time, which was five o'clock in the morning and the fact it was parked there for quite some time . . . and now when she was reading the newspaper she made the connection.'

Kennet paused and Charlotte saw the brake lights of the delivery van ahead of them. She asked Per to slow down even more.

'He almost seems to be drunk,' she said to Per while the boss continued to talk on the phone.

'The car, a Volvo, is used by Hugo Larsson. But it's registered in his mother's name, which is why we've missed finding out that he has access to it.'

'What?' she said so loudly that Per looked at her instead of the road.

'Yes, we suspect that Hugo was at the I20 forest the same night that Frida disappeared. We checked on the car and made contact with his mother. She's in a home and is half-blind. The staff laughed at me when I asked if she was often out driving her car.'

At the same moment Per screamed, 'What's that lunatic doing?'

Charlotte saw the back of the truck just before it crashed at high speed into the front of their car. The impact made her drop her phone. She saw how the landscape outside changed from trees to road, to trees again. Then the car was still.

42

Thursday, 28 January

Linn took a torch. Looked up at the sky and thought about her friend. It just felt sick that Frida would be out here somewhere, all alone. She'd thought about it all night. Linn swallowed what was stuck in her throat. She'd lied to get to be part of the search for Frida. Missing People had an age requirement of eighteen. *Shitty rule,* she thought. The man who gave her the torch handed her a yellow vest which she pulled over her head. He gave them strict orders not to use their phones or post anything on social media. Her mother was also supposed to take part in the search, she'd said, but she hadn't been in touch.

'You'll be part of search group five,' the guy from Missing People said, placing Linn next to two girls her own age.

They introduced themselves as Leonora and Saga. *Nice names,* thought Linn. She nodded and smiled at them. It felt as if all of Umeå was involved in the search for her friend. Frida had become national news and a sort of silent panic prevailed in the town. Parents kept their daughters at home awaiting an outcome and the media said that you should go out in pairs, never alone.

'Where else are they searching?' asked Saga, who had brought a headtorch with her, which she put on. It wouldn't be light yet for a few hours.

'Lake Nydala, Teg and here,' Leonora answered, turning on her torch.

The car park was full of shining dots that moved jerkily. Two dogs were part of the group and had vests put on them. Right across the street, where the circus would be in the summer, group three had started their search.

'How many of us do you think there are?' asked Linn.

'Must be thirty people in our group alone,' said Saga, turning her head so that her headtorch shone right at Linn.

Their feet made a crunching sound as they walked to the forest and further up toward the sports facility. Police cars were everywhere.

Linn's snowboots were ugly but good for plodding in snow. She pulled up the coveralls which sat loosely around her waist. She had weighed herself three times that morning and it turned out that she'd lost 3.4 kilos. She wanted to tell Frida that. And her mother.

'Have either of you ever met Frida?' Saga asked.

Linn focused on the bright spots from the torches. Searched with her gaze.

'I've never met her, but she's a classmate of my friend's little sister,' said Leonora.

'I heard that she used a lot of drugs,' Saga continued.

Linn pulled the scarf up over her chin.

'I've heard that too,' said Leonora.

'My mum's friend's cousin says that her dad is, like, a gambling addict and her mother's an alcoholic,' Saga countered.

Linn's cheeks went from cold to warm; she kept her eyes on her snowboots as the path turned into forest terrain.

'I'm sure it's her dad who killed her,' said Leonora, and Linn felt an explosion inside her.

'My God, you're talking a lot of shit! You don't even know her. You don't know what you're talking about and she's not dead!'

Linn let the words out without thinking. The girls looked at her with surprise.

'You knew her?' asked Saga.

'Know her, I *know* her,' said Linn. She thought about what the man from Missing People had said, that eighty per cent of those they searched for were found alive. Those were still good odds.

She got the light beam in her eyes when Saga looked at her. Linn started walking faster and ended up a few steps ahead of them. Tears were welling up in her eyes and she clenched her teeth. It was hard to breathe, her nostrils stuck together when she inhaled. The trees were still, the moon gave a faint glow and showed the outlines of the trunks. Snow that had fallen from the branches broke up the otherwise untouched fresh snow. As they came further into the forest the level surface behind was disturbed. Although the snowfall of the past few weeks was piled high, the snow was as light as powder and Linn had no problems moving ahead. Some in the group had poles that they poked into the snow where it was deepest.

The group in the forest called Frida's name, but Linn did not. If Frida was here it wasn't to camp, so why call out? The light from the torches moved around the trees and mixed with the snow. An owl was heard in the distance and the dogs sounded eager. Linn tried to concentrate on her own breathing. She was getting a little exercise anyway – she was starting to sweat from the exertion.

There was a snap.

Linn stopped mid-step with one leg in front of the other. It sounded like a tree would fall, but nothing happened. No one else seemed to react so she kept moving ahead. The beam of her torch jumped back and forth in time with her body movements. The further into the darkness they went, the harder it became for Linn to believe that they would find Frida here. Sometimes the snow was deeper than her boots and she felt grateful for her sturdy winter coveralls. She wanted to take off her hat, which made her scalp itch. But she kept it on. Instead she let her damp hands meet the cold air.

'Stop! I've found something!'

A distant person shouted right out in the forest and everyone in the line stopped abruptly. Linn's pulse went from laboured to racing.

43

Charlotte gasped for breath. She was lying down and sat up so quickly that she felt dizzy. Fluid stuck in her throat; she coughed repeatedly to open her airway. Leaned her body forward.

As her vision cleared it was met by green plastic that rustled when she moved. She raised her head and looked right into Tony's narrow eyes.

'Well, well, now you're awake,' he said, smiling. Charlotte's gaze was drawn to his yellow teeth. An empty bucket stood beside the cot. Tony had a gun resting on his knee – it looked like a Colt.

Her hand moved to her rib and the sudden pain made her wince. She took in air between her teeth to keep from screaming.

'Yes, you're probably going to feel that for a while,' he said, and Charlotte's other hand reached toward her hip and gun. Stupid, she realized mid-motion, to think that he would have let her keep her gun.

Grey concrete walls. A cot with a green plastic mattress. No windows. A heating element hummed by the door.

'Where am I?' she said between coughs.

'In my temporary room,' he answered, sitting down beside her on the cot. Tony's hand grazed Charlotte's temple. She pulled her head away but he took hold of her hair and forced it back.

'You're bleeding, but it's not dangerous,' he said, letting go.

One of Tony's minions stood in the doorway with his arms crossed. Looked at his watch. Gold Rolex. The memory came back. Forced its way into her awareness. The car crash.

'Where's my colleague?' she asked.

'No idea, you were the one I wanted. The other clown got to stay in the car.'

She supported herself against the cot and painfully straightened her back.

'Is he alive?' she asked.

'How should I know? But he didn't look healthy,' he said, laughing loudly.

'You know that the whole Swedish police force is going to search for me, don't you? You're not making it easy for yourself.'

She paused while she tried to find a sitting position that wasn't painful.

'Do you have any idea how much money your treachery cost me, my little nanny? You know, the cops are going to find you dead somewhere, I haven't really decided where yet. An overdose maybe . . . Or should I hang you?' He pointed at the ceiling where a rope was hanging from a hook. His voice was gentle and he cocked his head. 'I'm sure they're going to bring me in for questioning. But you know I'm not going to prison.'

'I don't know what you're talking about,' said Charlotte, meeting his gaze. She waited for the pain. Tony turned her head back with force. She saw herself reflected in his glasses and panic rushed over her.

Tony put his index finger against Charlotte's chin and forced her head backward until she could see the ceiling, and the rope that was hanging there with a loop.

She stared at it. Her heart was beating so hard that she thought it would jump out of her chest. Charlotte tried to press her head down, away from the rope. But Tony held it in place.

'I can see the headline: *Police Officer Found Hanged.*' Then he took a harder grip on her chin and brought her face to his own. He held up a syringe. 'Or perhaps: *Police Officer Dies From Overdose.* What do you think about that?' He released her chin. 'Yes . . . we have some plans for you. You don't think I'm completely stupid, do you?' Tony laughed.

'Did you kill William?' she asked.

Tony did not reply. He stood up and stuck the gun between his stomach and trousers. 'This is the way it is. You're not leaving here unharmed. That's the price you have to pay for fooling me. I'm tired of you, you rich whore.'

'Why did you murder William?' she asked, fixing her eyes on Tony. It seemed as if he'd gone from being crazed criminal to pure psychopath.

'Is this a fucking interrogation or what? You don't seem to understand that I'm the one who decides.' Tony's tongue licked his yellow teeth. 'I got good information from the boy but couldn't let him go – then he would have gone straight to you. He was scared and not particularly used to pain. Talked like a parrot as soon as I raised my fist.' Tony laughed at his own comment. 'The snot-nosed kid tried to buy his way out with bitcoins . . .' Tony's laugh echoed in the room again. 'But it was fun to play with him a little. Get him to believe that there was a way out. It made him more cooperative. By the way, you ought to be grateful that I killed him. He doled out drugs to young girls. Now he can't do that any longer, right?' Tony said, smiling.

'So, you would never sell drugs to teenagers?' Charlotte said.

Tony did not reply. He took a comb out of his jacket pocket. Smoothed his thin strands of hair before he put it back and continued. 'When we're done with you you're going to ask for more of this of your own free will.' He held up the syringe again. It was filled with a yellowish liquid. 'It's going to happen slowly, you understand. This is fun.'

He took hold of her arm. Charlotte stood up. Tried to pull her arm away, but Tony's fingers squeezed so hard that it felt like the bone would break.

'Wait!' she screamed.

Tony smiled. Waved to an associate who took a firm hold on her body. Charlotte felt the rubber band that Tony pulled around her upper arm so hard that the skin bulged.

She was hyperventilating. The associate kept holding on to her but his eyes wandered and he looked worried. He wasn't very old.

Tony stroked his index finger across the crook of her arm. Then he set the sharp needle against the skin. Charlotte opened her mouth. Did not scream. The skin gave way easily and Tony injected the liquid. Charlotte had no idea what she was getting. But it went straight into her blood.

44

Per pressed his index finger against the cast. A fracture in his left arm, severe headache and a wound on the forehead were what the doctor in front of him had treated. The odour of chemicals was intrusive. It was still dark outside and Wednesday had turned into Thursday. He had lost time by being at the hospital. More and more footsteps were heard outside the door. The doctor aimed a torch into Per's eye.

'You have damaged blood vessels but that's going to heal within a few days. Avoid contact lenses in the meantime,' he said, putting the light back in his chest pocket. A name tag revealed that the doctor's name was Karim.

What the doctor could not treat was all that was going on inside him. When Per thought about Charlotte he almost had a panic attack. He'd found out from Kennet that Tony had her. What was he doing with her now?

As the doctor backed the chair away Per got up from the bed.

'You have a mild concussion and need to rest,' the doctor said, looking up at Per. 'I'm prescribing a pain reliever for your arm. Do you have any questions?'

The doctor stood up too and was now facing Per, who shook his head and thanked him for his help. He opened the door and was about to go out to the corridor when Mia met him.

'Shame on you,' she said, wrapping her arms around his neck.

'Don't worry, I feel fine,' he said, placing his free arm across her back. 'But Charlotte is missing.'

Mia nodded and wiped away a tear that had worked its way down her cheek.

'Find her. Alive. Anja is devastated but she'll be taken care of in Stockholm. She wants to come up.'

He looked over at Kennet, who was talking with three uniformed police officers, and walked toward them.

'What else do we know?' he said, interrupting Kennet who was in the middle of a conversation with the police. He stretched his neck so the bandage from his shoulder wouldn't chafe his skin.

'What do you remember from the incident itself?' Kennet asked, pointing at a wooden bench in the corridor. Per eased his rear end down on the hard surface.

'It all went so damned fast. We were on our way to the meeting place to bring in Hugo. I didn't have time to react when the van backed into us – I thought it was slowing down. Charlotte was talking with you on the phone, then everything just exploded. I went in and out of consciousness, saw that someone took her but I was just so shaken up. Has anything new come out?'

'We know that they changed cars outside Hössjö,' Kennet said. 'A stolen one. We suspect that the attack was planned because Tony overtook you. We think they were after you from the time you left the station, and wanted to abduct Charlotte while you were alone and without reinforcements. It's an odd undertaking, backing into your car at full speed. Forcing someone off the road is more common. The car's camera images are still intact despite the powerful collision and we see clearly that it's Tony. He is standing far to the left and doesn't seem to realize that he's within the camera angle because his face is uncovered. Clumsy, but good for us. He is conversing with this man.'

Kennet showed a picture on his phone.

'Abbe Ali,' said Per. 'He's the one who showed great interest in Hugo Larsson. But wasn't he being surveilled? They were supposed to be brought in by the other team. What happened?'

'We'd got information that they were on their way to the cabin in Vännäs, where we were waiting with a full force. But something went wrong along the way; suddenly their plans changed and now they're missing again.'

Kennet looked at Per.

'We're going to find them,' said Kennet.

Per stood and tried to straighten up by pressing his shoulders back. His left side didn't really obey. Pain radiated from his left arm and he would be forced to take the pain reliever. He hugged Mia, who then left them so they could search for Charlotte.

'Do we have reinforcements?' Per asked, taking his coat from the wooden bench. He wouldn't start crying, he refused to give in to the fear. He tried to put on his coat with his right arm but Kennet had to help him.

'Yes, of course. The National Operations Department is both informed and connected, and the national response team is being flown up directly. I've been running amok over the whole police organization. Ola Boman is collaborating with them. I've also been informed about Charlotte's history with Tony. Why the hell didn't you tell me that?' said Kennet, raising his voice.

Per splayed his fingers, which were sticking out under the cast. They were itchy, and he sighed. The rest of his life he would regret not having said anything to his boss about Charlotte's history with Tony Israelsson. *My God, maybe that decision has killed her,* he thought, and the insight almost made him black out.

Per and Kennet started walking toward the exit. Freshly painted walls changed to faded ones; the renovation of the university hospital was taking a long time. Construction workers were as common a sight as nurses and doctors. Per walked as quickly as he was able through the corridor and out to the main entrance. When his pulse rose his arm throbbed.

'Then there was another thing,' said Kennet. 'While you've been in here we've made a find in the I20 forest.'

Per looked at his boss with anticipation. 'Is Frida alive?'

45

The forest was full of police officers. They set up blue and white plastic tape around the trees and cordoned off an area a little further away. Linn remained sitting where she had ended up in the snow; she had no strength in her legs to stand up. The torch in her hand rested against the snow. It created a shining hole in the whiteness. Other people who were part of the search were standing around her, all with their eyes toward big lamps and a white tent that was being set up, presumably to protect the spot. It had got lighter out but not enough. The hum from a generator penetrated the otherwise low sound level.

Saga patted her on the shoulder and Linn started. Wiped away a tear that ran down her cheek.

'It's not a body, it's something else,' she said in an attempt to reassure her.

'So, what is it then?' Linn asked.

'They aren't saying, just that it's not Frida.'

Linn reached out to Saga, got help in getting up. While Linn was sitting, snow had melted and worked its way inside her coveralls. She had goosebumps. She heard her mother's words about not getting wet and cold. As if Linn would care about that right now.

The nearest police officers were four trees away and talking with the guy in charge from Missing People.

'Where are you going?' asked Saga as Linn took the first step in the direction of the police.

'To talk with them.'

She wondered what she should ask – she had to find out what they'd found. Her left hand had a firm hold on the torch and her fingers were frozen stiff. She managed to turn it off and took the mittens out of her jacket pocket. The police barricade was more lit up than a Christmas tree. Someone shouted out in the forest.

'Per!'

Linn turned her head and saw the policeman with the sad eyes come plodding in the snow. He had a beanie on and one arm inside his jacket. She started walking toward him.

The tears welled up. The thought that Frida was perhaps out here alone, in the cold, made her hyperventilate. She struck her forehead. Hard. Linn was the worst friend you could have, just so worthless. And it was only now, as she plodded ahead in the forest and searched for Frida, that she realized that it had actually happened. That Frida was gone, for real. *What if she's been raped?* Her stomach cramped. Linn closed her eyes, sobbed, couldn't keep herself from vomiting and out it came. The white snow was soiled by a brownish beige mess. *Mother's goddam cinnamon rolls*, she thought. Sobbed again and spat out the last of it.

A policeman came up to her.

'Are you okay?' he asked, leaning forward to see her face. The light from a torch blinded her.

Linn straightened up. Wiped her mouth with the mitten. 'I have to speak with the police.'

'Who are you?'

'Linn Mattsson. Frida is my best friend and I might know where she is,' she lied.

'Okay, come with me,' said the policeman, indicating that she should move ahead.

'What have you found?'

'Unfortunately we can't tell you that,' he said.

As they approached the barricade he asked her to wait there by the snow piles they'd shovelled outside the tent. The sound from a helicopter was heard above the treetops. Linn looked up at the buzzing but was blinded and turned her eyes down again. It was like in a movie. White-suited men, the tent, the police officers.

Why did they go to that damn party? Why? If they'd stayed home none of this would have happened. Frida had pined for William, grieved Anton and been supported by Linn. Linn had always supported her.

When she saw the sad policeman come toward her she tried to smile, but it turned into something else. He looked beaten up, a bruise on his cheek and dried blood on his lip.

'Hi, Linn, my name is Per – I was at your house a couple of days ago. Do you remember that?'

He lifted up the plastic tape to be able to go under. She nodded in response.

'What is it you wanted to tell us?'

Linn took a deep breath and was trying to think of something good to say when there was crackling on Per's walkie-talkie. Loud. Per twisted a knob. The sound got quieter. He held it against his ear but Linn could still hear the voice on the other end.

'New find, we have a new find about forty metres into the forest from site one.'

46

Charlotte's arm was stretched out. She didn't know how many times she'd had a needle stuck in her arm. Everything was one big blob in her mind. Her skin was damp, her hair wet and her clothes sticky. As soon as she started to get control of her thoughts Tony came back with more dope. She no longer believed that she would get out of there alive. Things were moving too fast. They would never find her in time.

'So, my little nanny,' said Tony, pulling on the rubber band right above the crook of her arm while he continued talking.

Charlotte heard what he was saying but her brain was so disconnected that she couldn't take in the words. She turned her head to the wall, to keep from looking. The sweet odour from the raspberry gummies Tony was chewing nauseated her.

'The girl that everyone is writing about,' she heard Tony say through the fog. 'At first I didn't understand. But with a little research it turned out to be my old friend Viggo Malk's daughter.'

Tony laughed loudly as he took a fully loaded syringe from his buddy, another guy this time. Charlotte tried to fix her gaze on the man but her eyes wouldn't focus.

'I've been searching for Viggo – he betrayed me. Not as much as you, but enough. Now I'm going to pick up that bastard, thanks to the newspapers. So I'm here in Umeå to straighten out some business that has gone wrong, and then I get three birds with one stone. Someone up there likes me, you might say.' He ran his index finger over the crook of Charlotte's arm. 'I've tried to talk with you about where Viggo is, but you don't seem to know what's up or down.'

The laughter again.

'That's how it can go, but I have men who are going to find him. Now I have to leave you for a while, crocodile. When I come back I expect that you'll be dead or will do anything at all for a little more.' He touched his crotch. 'In the meantime you can entertain my under-stimulated little refugee.'

Charlotte felt how her eyelids closed. She didn't have the energy to say anything. Tony was just about to press in the needle when his phone rang, and the ringtone spared her for a moment.

Tony held the phone firmly between his shoulder and cheek. Something the person on the other end said seemed to make Tony upset. When he was done talking he turned to Charlotte and crouched down. His breath came close, the raspberry sweets mixed with something acrid. Tony brought his palm toward her eyes. In his hand were little blue pills. Her pulse rose. Dolcontin. If he gave them to her she would die, considering everything else she had in her system now.

The first clear thought she'd had in a long time. She would die.

'When I give you these,' Tony said with a scornful smile, 'then you can say a prayer and say thanks for a good time.'

He closed his fist and stood up. Patted the guy in the room on the shoulder and disappeared.

47

Kennet had gone with Per to the I20 forest. It wasn't customary for the district chief of police to be present on such occasions, but Kennet was no ordinary boss. He couldn't keep away from cases that affected him.

Per sat behind him on a snowmobile, holding his arm cast against his body. There was a stabbing pain with the slightest movement. Per thought it was silly to take the snowmobile the short distance up to where something had been found, but Forensics insisted that the snowmobile disturbed the area less than if you walked across a potential crime scene.

The morning sun penetrated through the crowns of the trees and there was no wind. Per sniffed to clear his runny nose. When the clouds no longer covered the sky the temperature dropped even lower. The mercury was at minus seventeen and the frostbite injury on his foot made itself known. Per took off the glasses he had to wear when he couldn't use contacts. Every time he breathed out there was steam on the glass.

'Let's go,' said Kennet and the engine raced when he pushed on the start button.

Per guided his free hand toward the handle on the side, and almost fell off when Kennet swerved around the trees. The media had got a separate barricade and Per could see several familiar journalists' faces over there.

The 120 area was much visited, both by students at the police academy and people exercising. But the further in among the trees Per went, the more he understood why they hadn't encountered anything earlier. Not even dog owners walked here during the winter. The fresh snow lay like a down blanket.

When Kennet stopped the snowmobile Per's feet were completely numb. The heavy boots no longer helped against the cold. He removed his helmet and got off.

'We'll have to walk the rest of the way, the terrain is difficult,' said Kennet, turning off the engine. Considering the activity in the forest, it was very quiet. A police officer waved at them to come over.

'Prepare yourselves,' she said, disappearing behind the tree again.

Per took a few deep breaths. Together with Kennet he rounded the tree and walked toward the discovery site. When they came closer to the people in yellow vests he saw that they were crying and consoling one another. They had been first on the scene but now they had to stand behind the barricade. Per thought about his two boys, Simon and Hannes, almost the same age as Frida. He clenched his teeth so hard that his jaw hurt. Then he rounded yet another tree, a spruce that would have made a perfect Christmas tree, and looked straight ahead. He heard Kennet panting before he himself saw her.

There she was.

Frida.

Surrounded by snow-covered spruce trees.

White from frost and snow.

Hollow gaze straight ahead.

48

Charlotte was wakened by a sound that cut deep into her ear canal. Screeching metal. At first she thought she was at home in her own bed, then reality struck her with full force. She opened her eyes. Closed them again just as quickly. The light was painful. Where did it come from? She squinted. Through the crack between her eyelashes she saw a red rope, stone, walls, someone's legs, athletic shoes. Everything was twirling but her mind became clearer. She tried to get up but her body put up resistance.

She raised her head a little from the bed. Then stopped. She turned her upper body to the side but one arm wouldn't follow along at first.

She felt no pain. No heart fighting in her chest. She was entirely calm, almost apathetic. She managed to reach out one arm and looked at it. Bare, needle marks in the crook of her arm, bruises.

The hum from the fluorescent light in the ceiling was familiar, but then she heard the metal sound again. The memory of the pills in Tony's hand came to her. Had she taken them? She couldn't remember. No, she couldn't have taken them – if she had, she would be dead now.

She saw someone moving in the room. She saw legs wearing jeans, slender thighs. Charlotte felt how dry her lips were. She tried to moisten them with her tongue but it was just as dry. Tight, chapped, impossible.

'Water,' she forced out in a hoarse voice.

The stranger came up to her. 'Quiet, you'll get water, but first you have to get out of here,' he whispered. Then he took hold of both her legs, right above the back of her knees. When he leaned forward to take hold of her upper body she saw it.

Pastel mermaids. The bracelet on the man's wrist. Similar to the one the man in Unni's apartment had on. Similar to the bracelets Linn made.

Her head fell back when he lifted her up from the bed. His face was covered by a scarf that reached all the way up to his eyes. He was wearing a cap.

'I'm taking you away from here, but it has to happen quickly,' the man said.

Charlotte forced herself to keep her head upright, she looked into his eyes.

There was something familiar about them.

49

Per's gaze was fixed on Frida's body. He couldn't move. Much less take air into his lungs.

She was held upright along the tree trunk by a rope that was tied around a thick branch a metre or two up in the tree. Her legs were slightly bent under the suspended upper body and her feet were in the snow with the ankles downward. Her knees were hanging a few centimetres from the ground. The blue rope cut into the skin on her throat.

'Why?' Kennet whispered, getting down on his knees in the snow.

Per finally managed to look away. 'She looks completely preserved,' he said quietly.

'The autopsy will show how long she's been dead. But the winter . . .' Kennet paused before he whispered the rest of the sentence. '. . . has frozen her.'

Per observed Frida again. Her shoulders and head were covered with snow. Black boots that didn't appear to be made for winter. She had no jacket on. Her long hair was tied back in a ponytail. White with frost. No corpse odour, no discoloration in the skin. Even her eyes were crystal clear, despite death.

'Could she have died from the hanging?' Per asked.

'We'll have to see what the autopsy shows.'

There was crackling from Kennet's walkie-talkie. He brought it to his mouth. Pressed the button and took a deep breath. 'Yes, we've found Frida Malk, deceased. Call for Forensics. And we must inform the next of kin as quickly as possible before the journalists over there figure out what has happened.'

A woman answered at the other end. 'I'll do that. But we have more information about the first location.' It crackled again. Per listened but his gaze was back on the young woman by the tree. 'A person has been standing here.' The apparatus emitted a clicking sound. 'We've secured evidence of what we believe is frozen semen on a scarf.'

Per turned his head to Kennet.

'What?' said Kennet.

'Wonder what happened to her,' said Per.

'We're living in a sick world, a goddamn sick world,' his boss replied.

Despite the activity around them, the forest was silent. Now she was no longer alone, Frida. She didn't need to hang here any longer – she would get to go away from here.

'The worst thing about this profession is reporting deaths, especially to parents,' said Per, wondering how Frida's parents would react. He was grateful that they didn't need to see their daughter the way she looked now.

The rays of the sun broke through between the trees behind them, meeting Frida's body and making the frost on her glisten like crystals.

Like a snow angel.

50

Viggo and Estelle were in the hotel room. They had learned several hours ago that their daughter had been found dead in a forest. They hadn't let go of each other since they got the news. They were lying on the floor, her back pressed against his chest. Sometimes she shook uncontrollably, sometimes it was his body that gave way to forces he'd never experienced before. He wondered if they would ever be able to stand up again. The police had sent a minister but he quickly understood that neither of them wanted him there, much less to formulate words for a man whose god was a swine. Viggo's nose and eyes were running. The carpet gave off a synthetic smell that mixed with the scent of Estelle's shampoo. He bored his face into his wife's light hair.

The police had started a homicide investigation. The body was sent for autopsy and a prosecutor had arraigned a suspect. Who that was they weren't told. Estelle held him hard, pulled him even closer.

'This is your fault,' she whispered.

Viggo's heart was as if paralyzed, nothing she said could affect him. 'I know.'

'Someone who works with Tony must have murdered her. No one else has a motive,' she said in a gentle voice, sniffing snot back into her nose.

Every time he closed his eyes he saw his daughter in front of him. It felt like the image was exploding over and over again and it made him refuse to close his eyes.

'There's something I have to tell you,' said Viggo.

Estelle released her hold on him, sat halfway up and supported herself with her hands against the floor. Viggo sat up across from her, and took her hands. They were ice cold and trembling slightly.

'I found pills in Frida's room – drugs she'd hidden in her dresser.'

He waited for an outburst, but Estelle was quite calm.

'What?' she said. 'What do you mean?' She stared at him.

'Frida used drugs, I think.'

'When did you find them?' she asked.

'A few weeks ago, before she disappeared. I took them.'

'What did you do with them? You threw them away, right?'

Viggo took a deep breath. Shook his head. 'I gave them to a woman who's a pharmacist, because they looked like medicine – some of them, in any case.'

Estelle nodded but didn't seem to really take in what he was saying. No follow-up questions came so he squeezed her hands again. Sought her gaze.

'I've been unfaithful,' he said, taking a deep breath. 'With her, the pharmacist.'

'What?' she said vaguely.

Viggo sought eye contact. 'Sorry, I don't know what I . . .'

Estelle looked into his eyes. Vacant gaze. Silence.

'Say something,' was all he could get out.

'What should I say?' she said quietly. 'Why are you telling me this now?'

Viggo shook his head, didn't know how he should answer.

'How long have you been seeing each other?'

'On and off for maybe . . . a year and a half or so.'

She turned her eyes away from him and stared right in front of her. Shook her shoulders. 'It doesn't matter any more. You've been unfaithful, I'm a drunk and our daughter was evidently a druggie. Frida is dead. Nothing matters any more.'

Viggo had no response. He felt the same thing.

'Do you love her?' asked Estelle.

Viggo shook his head but thought about her question. He hadn't loved Unni, but she made him feel good. Gave him affirmation when Estelle disappeared in her drinking. Maybe he had loved her a little, but not like he loved Estelle.

'No, I didn't . . . but she was murdered too.'

Estelle gasped. 'What are you saying?'

'The "Bathtub Murder". That was her.'

Estelle's mouth opened, her eyes widened.

Viggo let go of Estelle's hands. 'What if Unni . . . Yes, sorry, her name is . . . that was her name. What if she also died because of me?' He buried his face in his palms.

'What do you mean?' asked Estelle.

'Those pills in Frida's room. Unni promised to find out where they came from. There were . . .'

Viggo got up, feeling dizzy. Estelle remained seated and looked at him.

'There were so many . . .'

'How many?'

'A couple of hundred that were in a shoebox in her dresser.'

His wife's eyes became like black holes. 'Why the hell didn't you tell me, or at least the police?' She raised her voice. 'That may be why Frida was killed!'

'I wanted to protect Frida from the police! From rumours! From suspicions!' He choked up. 'I just wanted to protect her,' he whispered. 'Find out who pushed to her and put the bastard in jail.'

Estelle got up on her feet, placed herself so close that he could smell her shampoo again. Her palms were pressed against his damp cheeks. Her mouth grazed his.

'Why haven't you told me this until now? Now when she was found dead. Why, Viggo? I don't understand.'

Her touch was gentle but the words were hard. Her forehead met his chin. Stopped there.

'I didn't connect Unni's murder with the pills or with Frida's disappearance. I didn't even know that Unni was dead until now. And Abbe promised that it wasn't Tony who had taken Frida and—'

'Wait now,' Estelle interrupted him. 'Have you seen Abbe Ali?'

Viggo nodded. 'He looked me up. He said the Syndicates had nothing to do with Frida and I believe him. If Tony had known that we're living in Umeå I would've been dead by now. I trust Abbe.'

His knees met the floor and his wife meekly followed him down.

Viggo felt the warmth from her breath and she let the tears come without wiping them away.

'I'm going to tell the police that Unni had drugs at home that came from Frida,' he said.

'She's dead now, so it no longer matters,' Estelle whispered. 'You failed to protect her, Viggo. We both failed.'

Viggo was tired, as if he'd played poker for several days in a row. His eyes were burning. His soul was worn out. Would they get through this? He didn't know.

'I want to move – to Norway,' said Estelle, lying down on the floor again. Stared up at the ceiling. Cried. Viggo did the same. The ceiling was white.

'Like we should have done from the beginning, if we'd just listened to the police,' she said, letting her fingers be laced with his. 'And we'll take Frida's ashes with. I'm not leaving her here.'

Viggo turned to her, looked at her tears, which were running down on to the floor. Thought about the mission he'd received from Abbe.

51

Charlotte looked out through the windscreen. When the engine was turned off she knew that they were at Umeå University Hospital. The man who had driven her there opened the car door for her. His head and face were still covered by a hat and scarf. She'd been unconscious at times and the memories of the drive there were blurred. Once she'd woken up and been certain that they were in a garage.

'Can you walk?' he said, and she nodded. She didn't feel as dizzy and the shaking in her legs had subsided. She took his hand, looked at the bracelet around his wrist again. They were standing by the emergency room and she would need to take a few steps to reach the entrance. The air met her skin like needles; all she had on her upper body was a thin blouse, and she was barefoot.

Outside the emergency room it was otherwise calm – only an elderly woman with a stroller stared at them.

'You'll have to manage yourself now,' the man said, closing the car door behind her.

She nodded. Released his hand. 'Thanks, whoever you are,' she said, taking the first step toward the entrance. She did not feel the ground beneath her.

'We'll probably meet again soon,' the man said, going around to the driver's side and getting in. As the car pulled away she looked at the number plate. Blinked to be able to see better but the car disappeared too quickly.

There are probably surveillance cameras here, she thought. The entrance doors opened and she was let into the warmth.

Slowly Charlotte walked into the emergency room and after only a few steps a nurse came rushing to her. Placed her arm as support under hers. Judging by her expression Charlotte must have looked like she was dying.

'What has happened to you, honey?'

Charlotte focused her gaze on her bare feet, the painted toenails. She felt a tear release from her eye down along her cheek.

Soon she was lying down. Gaze directed at the ceiling, following the fluorescent light. A doctor took hold of Charlotte's arm and traced the needle marks with his index finger.

'What have you taken? Do you know, Charlotte?' he asked.

'You know who I am,' she replied, shaking her head.

'We're working with the police and you're a bit of a local celebrity here in town,' said the doctor, smiling at her.

'I don't know what I have in my body,' Charlotte said. 'Don't know how long I've been gone but a man rescued me. Can you call the police? We have to check your surveillance cameras.'

'You've been missing for over twenty-four hours,' he said, then asked a young woman in a green outfit about samples to be taken. At the same time her clothes came off and she was connected to devices. More needles were stuck into her wrist. *Fluid,* she thought. The thirst she'd felt was gone but she could still not moisten her lips. She had a private room and it was full of activity in there. The male doctor looked young.

'We've notified your family and your colleagues about where you are, so they're on their way. But now we need to examine you,' he said, leaning over her with a little torch. Asked her to look left,

243

then right. The light made her eyes sting, and the torch clicked when he turned it off.

'It was Tony Israelsson who kidnapped me. I must speak with my colleague. They have to find him, otherwise he'll kidnap Anja,' she said, resisting the doctor's attempts to take samples.

'Can you say your personal identity number?' he continued. 'Do you know where you are?'

Charlotte answered his questions. She closed her eyes, forcing away the memories from the place where she'd been held. She was out of danger now. But not Anja.

A woman set a tray with a glass of orange juice and a sandwich on the table beside her. Charlotte ran her hands through her dry hair.

'Has Frida been found?' she asked the male nurse.

'You'll have to discuss that with your colleagues,' he said, slipping out.

Charlotte sat up halfway in the bed and let her head meet the soft pillow. Her eyelids felt extremely heavy. She couldn't sleep yet, according to the doctor. But she closed her eyes.

The nurse came back, leaving the door ajar and Charlotte was forced to open her eyes again.

'I forgot to say that your colleagues who are on their way are going to put a guard outside your room. We have police around the whole hospital area, so the person who did this won't get at you in here.'

The nurse was trying to calm her but didn't really succeed.

'Anja, my daughter. I have to borrow a phone so I can call her. May I borrow yours?'

'Of course, here,' he said, giving her his phone.

Anja answered after one ring.

'Hello?' Charlotte heard.

'Hi, it's Mum.'

244

Anja started to cry. 'Mum, are you okay? Have they found you?'

'Yes, honey. I'm at the hospital in Umeå. Shaken up but unharmed. You have to promise me to do as the police say, okay? You're going to get protection – you're in danger too. Promise me that you won't go out and that you'll obey the police.'

'Why am I in danger?' Anja sounded sincerely scared.

'I can't explain everything now, darling, but I'll be in touch again soon and—' she started to say, but Anja interrupted her.

'I want to come up to Umeå. I'm going crazy sitting here wondering what's happening with you.'

Charlotte didn't know how she should respond. As long as Tony was out there it didn't matter where Anja was – she was in danger both in Stockholm and here.

'Let me talk with my colleagues and we'll see. Love you,' she said and they ended the call.

She looked at the plastic bracelet she had around her wrist and remembered the bracelet on the man who rescued her. She closed her eyes. Saw his eyes before her. The bracelet. The eyes. She had seen him before. The jacket with the Armani logo was also familiar. Like a neighbour you saw every day but still didn't really notice.

Then it struck her. She had reacted to the design, that a hoodlum had such discreet, good taste. Abbe Ali had that jacket on in the photograph Per put up in the briefing room. The one that was taken outside the Norrland Opera, when he was watching Hugo Larsson.

52

Per flushed the toilet at the police station and looked at himself in the bathroom mirror. His face had clear, sharp lines. Under his eyes the skin was swollen and the sides of his mouth hung down. He looked angry, even though the phone call from Charlotte had been an enormous relief.

Mia was at yet another appointment but the investigation prevented him from being with her. Per ran his hands through his hair and then put them under the tap. The cancer hadn't spread to the lymph nodes, but they didn't really know what it would look like in the breast until they opened it up. Per had to call the father of one of Simon's teammates and ask if they could pick up and drop off his son at hockey practice. Their lives would look like this for some time – revolving around treatments and how Mia felt – and his job didn't make it all any less complicated.

Per reached for a paper towel but the holder was empty. He dried his hands on his trousers. When his phone rang he was torn out of his musings. He recognized the number but couldn't place who it was.

'Yes, this is Per Berg, Umeå police,' he answered.

'Hi, this is Tomas Ek again, Anton's father.'

'Hi, Tomas. How are you both doing?'

'We take it one day at a time. When I last spoke with you, you couldn't say anything about the murder of Unni Olofsson because of the ongoing investigation. Can you now?'

Per looked up at the ceiling. He couldn't. Above all not to Tomas Ek, who had no connection to the crime victim.

'Sorry, I can't say anything concerning the investigation. We haven't found anything yet that indicates that—'

Tomas interrupted him. 'We requested our son's call log to find out who he had contact with. Anton's mother and I don't seem to know half of what he was up to. But it's there in black and white. He and Unni had a lot of contact.'

Per pressed the phone closer to his ear. 'What do you mean by *a lot of* contact?'

'Anton talked with Unni several times a week. He even called her at night, presumably when . . .' Tomas paused. '. . . when the anxiety was the toughest for him. I went to the pharmacy where she worked. A man told me that Anton was often there when she was working. The staff thought it was her son or relative because they seemed to be so close. Can you understand how that feels as a dad? That my son went to someone else for help. And then he took his own life.'

'No, I can't, I . . .' Per fell silent. He didn't know what he should say. 'Do you know what they talked about?' he asked instead.

Tomas was sobbing on the other end.

'No, but a woman at the pharmacy told me that Unni often hugged Anton when he was there. We hugged him at home too but he mostly pushed us away at the end. His OCD only got worse and there were more arguments at home. But why did a stranger get close, and not us?'

Per lowered his shoulders, looked down in the sink. He sympathized with the man he was talking to. Tomas was trying to understand why his son had killed himself. And he was doing his own investigation because he wasn't getting information from the police.

'Sometimes it's easier to talk with someone who's not family,' said Per. 'Young people often seek other people's views of things, values other than those they're fed at home.'

'Maybe so,' said Tomas, but didn't sound convinced.

'We've gone through Unni's call log, but haven't traced any number to Anton. Whose name is on his account?'

'His godmother in Gothenburg – my wife's old classmate who gave him the phone as a Christmas present. She pays his phone bills.'

Damn, thought Per. They'd missed that.

53

Charlotte was sitting on the hospital bed fully clothed. She hadn't been discharged yet but she'd asked for the doctor to come. Even though Kennet ordered her to sleep, rest and stay where she was, she was in a hurry to get back to the station.

She didn't know where she'd been held captive. But when she closed her eyes she could see Tony. The sneer. She felt the needle that was pressed into her skin. She'd found out that it was heroin they'd given her. It would take a while for her body to process it. She felt nauseated and she'd vomited. But the sweating was the worst, and the pressure across her chest that she would have to live with until they captured Tony. He and Abbe had gone to ground.

The house in Vännäs was abandoned of course but there were clear signs that several people had been staying there recently. They understood that this was where William had been murdered. Evidence from the killing was still in the cellar. Why he'd been dumped at the university was still unclear, but they suspected that it was a warning to anyone who knew anything. Tony liked that sort of thing.

Charlotte looked at her phone. The screen was filled with a picture of her and Anja, and her eyes teared up. What would have happened with Anja if Tony had killed Charlotte?

Anja would have been scarred for life. Forced into a life with only Carl, who had no idea how you talked with a teenage girl on her way to becoming an adult, much less someone who'd been subjected to such trauma as she had. Charlotte suspected that he would have tried to change her into a copy of himself. Charlotte struggled instead to give Anja a chance to love herself for who she was. Tried to convince her that she shouldn't define herself based on the family she grew up in. That her value as a human being wasn't based on that.

The phone rang and the photo of Anja and her changed into a picture of Per.

'Hi,' he said. 'I just wanted to hear how you're doing.'

'On my way in. I can't just lie here. Can't sleep, can't rest, I've got to come back.'

'You do know that the crash was only a day and a half ago? That's not enough rest. Kennet is never going to approve you going back to work. Especially not with this case.'

'I know, but I'm coming in anyway. Who knows Tony best? Exactly. I know how he thinks. You need me in the investigation.'

'I just got a call from Tomas Ek,' said Per.

'What did he want?'

'Unni Olofsson was helping Anton with his drug dependency. She was there for him and tried to help. Tomas told me that they had frequent contact and that he often visited her at the pharmacy.'

'Tomas told you that? How did we miss that?'

'I just spoke with the staff at the pharmacy and they confirmed what Tomas said.'

Charlotte pressed the phone closer to her ear.

'With what happened to you we couldn't bring in Hugo Larsson as planned, but they arrested him today. He is arraigned, on suspicion of the murder of Unni Olofsson,' said Per.

'Has he been questioned?' asked Charlotte.

'No, I'm going to question him now.'

'I'm coming in,' said Charlotte just as the doctor entered the room. 'Kennet can chain me to the desk if he wants, but I must be there in some way. It's my investigation too.'

'Okay, but you can't sit in at the interview. And I'm warning Kennet so he doesn't lash out as soon as he sees you.'

Charlotte laughed. 'I'm just going to convince my doctor to release me. See you soon,' she said, smiling at the doctor, who didn't smile back at her. Instead he put his hands on his hips to signal how inappropriate her behaviour was.

'And where are you going?' he asked as she stood up.

'To solve a murder,' said Charlotte, heading for the door.

54

Per took long strides across the 'pay gap', over to the bosses' offices. Kennet would be furious when he heard that Charlotte was on her way in. Per looked at the clock: it was just past two. Mia had a doctor's appointment this afternoon but refused to let him go with her. She could manage by herself, she said. That didn't feel right, but it gave him the chance to focus on the investigation. Now he was forced to prepare himself before questioning Hugo. He leaned against Kennet's doorframe and cleared his throat. Peeked in and saw that the boss sat absorbed in paperwork.

'Hi, Per, come in.'

Per took a step inside, took off his glasses. 'Listen, Charlotte wants to come in for a while,' he said.

Kennet looked up. 'Not a chance. She hasn't been discharged yet, has she? Besides, she shouldn't be working with the case given her connection to Tony, you know that.'

'She's probably being discharged now. But listen, I think she needs something to distract her and no one knows Tony better than her. She's needed more than ever. Charlotte knows how he thinks and knows his weaknesses. I'll take responsibility for her.'

'Per, she still has drugs in her system.'

'She can stay inside, sit at her desk. Is that okay?'

Kennet sighed and leaned back in the chair. 'You told me that Charlotte's first words when she called from the hospital were that Abbe rescued her. Why did he do that, do you think?'

'That we'll find out when we arrest him. I'm also going to question Hugo Larsson shortly.'

'Good,' said Kennet. 'To think that we could arrest him without any drama. He didn't seem at all prepared that we would be on his trail.'

'We'll have to see what he says in the interview. More and more I think that the semen on the scarf we found in the vicinity of Frida's body is his,' said Per, following his boss to the briefing. 'Who would otherwise leave such clear evidence at a crime scene? It's completely absurd.'

Ola Boman was the first person Per saw as he stepped into the room. All the chairs were occupied, and Kicki was standing by the wall. Per took a couple of steps toward them.

'It's been an eventful day, as you all know. Frida Malk's body is at autopsy. Before we receive the draft report about what happened, we're starting a preliminary investigation of homicide. I'll come back to that. But I've spoken with Charlotte, who gave us useful information about her time with Tony . . .' He paused before he continued. 'Charlotte confirms what Viggo told us. That Tony didn't seem at all aware of who Frida Malk was until the newspapers published her name. Then he connected them. On the other hand, Tony bragged to Charlotte that he killed William, and we've found the place where William was murdered – the cabin in Vännäs Tony moved to when we started chasing him. So there our suspicions were correct.'

Per looked out over his colleagues. 'Now Tony knows that Viggo Malk is living in Umeå, so Witness Protection has moved them again to another town. Charlotte and her daughter Anja must also be protected. So priority one for National Operations is to find Tony.'

Kennet cleared his throat to get a word in.

'This brings us to Hugo Larsson,' said Kennet.

'Yes,' Per agreed. 'We suspect that Hugo is the one selling large quantities of drugs here in Västerbotten. Surveillance has been keeping an eye on him for a while and they know with certainty that he delivers packages with narcotics and other drugs when he delivers the mail. They placed an order via the dark web and had it delivered by Hugo. We've set up monitoring at the mail distribution centre to find out if he has help from inside. Extremely handy to have access to that when you're selling stuff on the internet. He has never needed to go to a post office to mail the packages, he sends them during his shifts at the mail hub.'

'But how can he be connected to the murder of Frida?' asked Kicki.

Per went closer to the whiteboard with the picture of a smiling Frida. 'Hugo Larsson's mother owns an older model Volvo. But she is almost blind and never drives it. Hugo, on the other hand, does. That Volvo was parked by the 120 forest the same night that Frida disappeared – that's not news to any of you. But now we've also found a couple of strands of hair in the back of that car.'

Everyone in the group nodded. Everything indicated that Hugo Larsson was the perpetrator.

'Do we know if those are Frida's?' asked one of the investigators in the group.

'Soon,' said Per and continued. 'Now we've found out from Viggo that he discovered a large quantity of pills in Frida's room a few weeks before she disappeared. And here it gets really interesting.'

He turned to the other whiteboard. 'Viggo had an affair with our murdered Unni,' he said, pointing at her picture.

Kicki stopped moving the spoon around in her cup of tea. 'What is that you're saying?' she asked.

'He wanted to confess it to his wife first so we only got the information just now. He also told us that he took the drugs from Frida's room with him and gave them to Unni. Viggo asked her to find out what they were. And Unni managed to link the drugs that Frida had at home with Anton. Maybe she asked him flat out about them, because she knew that he used drugs. So our theory is that Anton told Unni that he bought drugs from William, who in turn bought them from Hugo Larsson. This theory is strengthened by the fact that Unni submitted a tip to the police about Hugo.'

'I'll be damned,' said Ola, and Per continued.

'According to the students at the university, Unni asked a lot of questions and tried to find out who was supplying drugs to the young people in town. Here William's name has come up, so we think that it's Hugo who supplied him with the drugs he sold. For a while we were working with the theory that Hugo and William killed Unni together because she was on their trail. But the strands of hair that were on the tape around Unni's arms weren't William's.'

'So whose were they?' asked Anna, who had been unusually quiet during the review.

'That we don't know yet, but right now we are proceeding with the theory that Hugo felt pressured by Unni's little investigation and simply silenced her. He had a strong motive to kill Unni because she was on his trail. We hope to find a DNA match in her apartment.'

'But why did Hugo kill Frida?' asked Anna.

'The evidence we found in the vicinity of the body is suggestive of a sexual motive. We'll know more when the autopsy is done. But it should be Hugo's semen and scarf we found at the crime scene. It wasn't a match for William.'

'Should we rule out that her death has anything to do with the fact that she's Viggo's daughter?' asked Kicki. 'She did have quite a few drugs at home – could there somehow be a connection?'

'We're not ruling anything out,' said Per, looking out over his group. They'd been working around the clock for a week, and the lack of sleep was starting to take its toll. He had asked them to go home and rest for a couple of hours, but a dead young woman made them ignore his request.

'We'll get Hugo to talk now,' said Per, pulling up the sleeves of his sweater. 'Then we'll need to talk with Camilla Mattsson too. She's the mother of Linn Mattsson, Frida's best friend. She runs an interior design company and Hugo is employed hourly by her as a kind of jack-of-all-trades – from what we understand he's the one who packages goods and ships everything that's sold on the internet. She should know a few things about who he is and how he moves. She may know much more than she lets on. According to Camilla, Hugo was with her the night that Frida disappeared. Maybe she's given Hugo a false alibi? Maybe she's protecting him for some reason. Make contact with the prosecutor and see to it that she's brought in for questioning.'

Per's phone rang. The forensic medicine unit. They were done with Frida's autopsy and had a preliminary report. He put the woman on speaker phone so that everyone could hear.

'We've taken a saliva sample from Hugo Larsson and as you all know there were two places at the I20 forest where evidence was found. One was Frida Malk's body. At the other, where we found semen a short distance from her body, we've got a confirmed DNA hit back.'

'That was fast,' Anna interjected.

'It's an important case,' said the medical examiner. 'The semen not far from Frida's body belongs to Hugo Larsson.'

'And the strand of hair in the Volvo?' asked Per.

'Incomplete data – we need more time, but considering the other evidence, it couldn't be anything other than Frida's.'

'That bastard,' said Per.

'Wait, there's more,' said the woman. 'It was also his bodily fluids that were on Unni Olofsson's body.'

Per's jaw was clenched. 'We have him,' he stated, and left the briefing room.

55

Linn was standing in her room. She'd called in sick from school. She had to do that herself because she couldn't get hold of her mother. The last time she'd seen her was when she came home from the 120 forest after they found Frida. Camilla had hugged Linn and cried with her. Caressed her back, wiped away her tears, but hadn't said a word. Just been there. Consoling. Linn had taken a pill and slept for thirteen hours. When she woke up her mother was gone. She hadn't seen Hugo either.

Linn's phone was starting to get overheated from all the messages and calls. Being best friends with someone who was murdered – nationally known Frida – apparently made her interesting. Even the school's most popular girl gang had invited her to go to the movies that evening.

She saw herself in the mirror, noticed the dark lines under her eyes. She had two pimples on her chin that she hadn't covered with make-up and her hair was straight, wispy. The desire to dress up was gone. Even the urge to vomit. On the bed was a bag with new clothes. Her mother had bought them for her. Presumably as consolation.

Normally she would have called Frida now. They would have tried on the clothes together. Laughed, argued about who was the thinnest, and Frida would have wanted to borrow the clothes from her. Linn bent over, picked up one of the garments from the bag and tore off the price tag. A blouse from Ida Sjöstedt. She pulled off her sweater and looked in the mirror. Her bra was too big now her breasts no longer filled it out. Linn pushed up the cup. Damn, she didn't want to have small breasts. Her collarbone stuck out, that was good. She held her breath at the same time as she pulled in her stomach, moved her hands across it. She could easily see and feel her ribs. Linn placed herself in profile, bent her neck back so that her hair came even closer to the small of her back. Breathed out.

She put on the new blouse and guided the strands of hair toward her face. Made a pouty expression and inspected herself. With accustomed movements she took out her make-up bag and transformed herself into someone who could be seen outside. She picked up her phone and took a serious selfie, placed a shimmering filter over it. Wrote: *RIP Frida.*

She posted it on Instagram but immediately got a bad feeling that started in her head and ended up in her stomach. She looked at the picture – there were already several likes. Linn bit on the nail of her index finger, tore off a piece with her teeth. Damn, should she delete the post? The picture of her was perfect, she didn't want to take it down, but still . . . Maybe it was strange? She held her thumb over the screen. Should she delete? She got more likes, sat down on the bed and saw how popular she was. The post got to stay.

As she was on her way out to the movies with the girl gang, once again her phone chimed. A newsflash. She had started following *Västerbottens-Kuriren* after Frida disappeared.

Person Held on Suspicion of the Murder of Frida Malk.

The picture showed a man whose face was blurred, but Linn recognized him all the same.

Her legs started shaking below her and she sat down on a chair in the hall. Looked at the picture. Brought her hand to her mouth and called Camilla. Voicemail.

It must be wrong. *They must have arrested the wrong person*, she thought, and read the article.

Did Hugo kill Frida? If so, why?

Linn ran into the kitchen where her mother usually was. Everything was like normal: clinically clean. Linn leaned against the kitchen counter. The house was silent.

She tried calling again. Still just voicemail. Where in the world was she? Linn was used to her being gone for long periods, but it was always possible to get hold of her. She stared down at the kitchen floor and thought about Hugo. Handsome Hugo who wouldn't harm a fly. Why did the police think he had killed Frida?

What if her mother had caught Hugo and he'd killed her too? Linn ran out into the hall, grabbed her handbag and started searching for the little white card she got from the police.

Anja's mother. I have to call her.

56

Per sat down across from Hugo and his attorney. Hugo was eating a cheese sandwich and Per observed him. The dark, curly hair – a little like Jon Snow in *Game of Thrones*. The sad-looking eyes, perfectly formed eyebrows. The lips were full, symmetrical and framed by light beard stubble. His skin was pale, as if he'd lived his life in constant darkness. *Winter is coming*, thought Per, and realized that for some reason he didn't want this guy to be guilty. Maybe because he gave a kind impression. Uncertain, gentle. An unusual murderer. But everything pointed to Hugo. They'd reviewed the preliminary autopsy report, and the DNA results connected him both to Unni's and Frida's crime scenes. Besides, Frida's phone had been found at his home.

Per rattled off the formalities before the interview, but Hugo hardly appeared to be listening.

In the search of his apartment they'd found hundreds of porno films, all with extremely odd sexual acts. The women in the films were older, Unni's age. His place was reminiscent of a 1980s bachelor pad. Black leather couch, marble table, hundreds of CDs, plastic flowers. On the other hand there was nothing in the apartment that indicated drug selling. He must have run that from another location.

Hugo Larsson had left school with low grades and did not go on to further education. He was twenty-seven years old and also worked as a mail carrier and distributed morning newspapers. For the past year he'd also been a jack-of-all-trades at Camilla Mattsson's interior design business, which mainly sold over the internet. No prior convictions, and now suspected of two murders and felony narcotics crimes.

Hugo seemed unreasonably calm sitting there in the interrogation room.

'Do you know why you're here, Hugo? Besides the suspicion of felony narcotics crimes?' Per asked.

Hugo stopped chewing, set down what remained of the sandwich on the table. 'Maybe.'

His mild intellectual disabilities made him easy to read. Per set out a picture of Unni. A living, smiling Unni. He wanted to see how Hugo reacted to the image.

Hugo leaned forward. His greasy index finger left butter on the folder where he touched it.

'Do you recognize this woman?' asked Per.

Hugo looked at the picture. 'Nah, what's her name?'

He said that much too quickly for Per to believe him.

'Her name is Unni Olofsson. So, you haven't seen her before?'

Hugo poked his other index finger in his mouth and loosened something that had got stuck between his teeth. 'No, why would I?'

'If you haven't seen her before, can you explain how your DNA, in the form of urine and semen, ended up on her dead body?'

Per gave Hugo's attorney a copy of the report from Forensics about Unni's corpse. Hugo and the attorney whispered with each other. When they were done, Hugo looked at Per but did not answer, only shrugged his shoulders and looked at the picture. His lips pouted under the beard stubble.

Per leaned toward him. 'Tell me about the day when Unni was murdered. Were you happy, sad or angry about anything?'

'Don't know, how should I know?' he said in a gentle voice.

Per leaned back. According to Hugo's hospital patient record, a knot on his umbilical cord had caused oxygen deficiency during delivery, which probably explained his odd behaviour. He had needed extra support in school, coped with work but there were difficulties with feeling and reflecting. Hugo managed his everyday life on his own and outwardly there didn't seem to be anything mean about him. He gave the impression of being nice, which others also testified to.

'Did you urinate on Unni, Hugo?'

'No.'

'So how did your urine end up on her body?'

'Don't know.'

'Tell me, how did Unni end up in the bathtub?'

'Don't know.'

'If my client says he doesn't know, then he doesn't know,' the attorney interjected.

Per sighed, and leaned forward again. He looked at Hugo and forced himself to look kind.

'We have enough evidence to lock you up for a long time. Can you explain how your DNA ended up on Unni's body?'

Hugo crossed his arms over his stomach. Talked with his attorney.

'Golden shower,' he said confidently. 'The clothes were different than in this picture. You couldn't see her breasts when I found her in the bathtub.'

Per tried to look unmoved but he was shocked by the reply. Hugo admitted that he'd been at the crime scene.

Per hesitated. 'Was Unni alive when you came to the apartment?'

'No.'

'Was she dead then?'

'Yes.'

'Who was with you?'

'Up in the apartment?' asked Hugo, looking confused.

'Yes, there were two of you – we know that from the evidence we've collected,' said Per.

Hugo looked at his attorney, his gaze wandering. 'I went up alone. She was dead when I got there, I said that.'

'Was the door to her apartment open or closed when you got there?'

'Uh . . . it was closed – the door, that is, but not locked.'

'What business did you have with Unni? Why were you there?'

Hugo sat silently.

Per continued with the gentle tone. Avoided being assertive. 'How did you find out that Unni tipped off the police about your drug deals?'

Hugo opened his mouth, staring at Per. 'Huh?' he said.

'Unni exposed your rather profitable operation. How did you find out that she was on your trail?'

'I didn't kill her. She was dead when I got there, was just going to . . .'

'So, who killed her then?'

'Well, she found pills, lots of them, and she went around and snooped a lot. Talked with people about me. But I . . .' He shifted his sitting position on the chair. 'I was just going to get the drugs and . . .'

'And what then, Hugo?'

'But I didn't kill her. You have to believe me.'

'Why should we believe you, Hugo? Your DNA was found on her. That can't be explained away. But you can tell us who the other perpetrator is. Because if that person killed Unni and you cooperate, if you tell us exactly what happened, then maybe we can arrange a lighter sentence.'

Hugo collapsed. He wouldn't get out of this and he knew it.

'I was just there to pick up the drugs.'

'Why was it important to pick up the drugs?'

Hugo's cheeks flared up. 'They were evidence, but I was just going to pick them up and not . . .'

'So Unni caught you and you killed her?' asked Per.

'No. You're not listening.'

'You didn't like that she was snooping?'

Hugo didn't say anything.

'If you weren't the one who killed Unni, you should tell us who did,' Per continued. 'Because all the evidence points to you.'

The attorney whispered something in Hugo's ear.

'I deny the accusation. I didn't kill her.'

Hugo pinched himself on the arm, which was full of similar marks. His gaze said everything. He was scared.

Per took out the next picture, of a smiling Frida full of life.

'You seem to have a rather broad interest regarding women.'

Hugo wrinkled his nose. Over and over again.

'This is Frida Malk, she was found hanged in the forest. Maybe you've heard about that?'

Hugo did not reply and Per continued.

'We've confiscated your mother's car, and do you know what we found?' Per took out the report of the findings in the car. 'Evidence.'

Hugo turned his eyes away when Per looked at him. 'Yes,' he said. 'And? I drove her and Linn to a party.'

'In the boot? How did a strand of hair from Frida end up in the boot? And how did her phone end up in your apartment?'

Hugo pinched his arm again. He stared at the photo of the young girl who smiled into the camera. Then he opened his mouth to say something, but closed it again.

'Tell me what you did after you dropped off the girls at the Nydala house.'

'You've already asked that and got an answer,' said Hugo.

'Yes, but now we know that Frida for some reason has been in your boot and her mobile phone was found at your home. How do you explain that?'

Hugo turned to his attorney, who said, 'I need to talk with my client privately.'

'In a moment,' said Per. 'Your mother's car was parked by the crime scene the same night that Frida disappeared. You can't wriggle out of this, Hugo. Tell me what happened. What did you do after the girls went into the house?'

Hugo sat silently. Looked down at his hands.

Per took off his glasses and massaged the bridge of his nose. 'About forty metres from the place where Frida was found, we found a scarf. From there you could see Frida easily.'

Hugo looked carefully at the picture of Frida.

'Your semen was found on that scarf,' said Per. 'How do you explain that?'

Hugo kept his eyes on the picture and let his finger glide along Frida's cheek. As if he was consoling her.

'We have sufficient evidence to charge you with the murders of both Unni Olofsson and Frida Malk.'

Then came the reaction. Hugo quickly stood up.

'I didn't kill her, damn it!'

He screamed out the words, saliva flew out of his mouth and his curls fell down over his forehead. His gaze was dark, his lips moist.

'Sit down,' said Per.

Hugo did as he was told. Just as quickly as he'd flared up in anger, he calmed down again. His back was bent and his eyes sad as his gaze wandered between the tabletop and Per.

'I didn't kill her, neither of them,' he said firmly.

'But you do know who murdered them?'

Hugo shook his head.

'How is it that your DNA was found at both crime scenes?'

'I don't know.'

'Come on now, Hugo, tell me what happened to Frida.'

His gaze wandered again. 'I got her from William.'

'Excuse me, what did you say?'

Hugo pinched himself aggressively on the arm. 'Yes, he didn't want her any more so he said I could take her. In the house that evening.'

Per felt the sweat pooling under his shirt. 'Tell me about that evening, Hugo. How did Frida end up in your car?'

Hugo looked at his attorney. Whispered again and after a moment of hesitation Hugo opened his mouth.

'I was waiting outside, not far away. William told me to take her. She got into my car voluntarily because she thought I was going to drive her to William's place. But I didn't do anything with her.'

Hugo's forehead was shiny, the pale cheeks looked warm.

'What do you mean that you got her from William?' asked Per.

Hugo stared down at his arm. 'He didn't want her any more, I said that. I didn't sleep with her either. She's not my type. But she had really gone, like, strange, so I drove her to . . .'

'Where did you drive her?' asked Per.

Hugo seemed to want to disappear.

'Where did you drive her, Hugo?'

He shrugged his shoulders. 'I didn't drive her home because she was drunk or something and I didn't want to leave her like that with her parents. So I drove her to Linn's house.'

'What are you saying?' Per said, shocked.

'I left Frida in Linn's room, sleeping like a pig. Thought that she could sleep off the high there.'

Hugo took a bite of what was left of the sandwich. Looked at his attorney, who nodded in agreement. Per tried to understand, put the threads together.

'So you left her at home with Linn. Were Camilla or Linn at home then?'

Hugo chewed and talked at the same time. 'No one was home then, when I left her in Linn's bed.'

Per bit his tongue so as not to scream at him. 'Do you have a key to Camilla and Linn's house?'

'Yes,' he said.

'What kind of relationship do you and Camilla have?'

Hugo looked at him and smiled for the first time. 'A beautiful relationship.'

Per dropped the subject for the moment. 'So you left Frida on Linn's bed. What happened then?'

'I drove home.'

'In previous interviews you stated that you drove to Camilla's after you dropped off the girls, which she has also confirmed. Were you lying then or are you lying now?'

Hugo met Per's gaze. 'I never lie. I was with Camilla a while but then William called, so I drove back, but just to pick up Frida.'

'So Camilla gave you a false alibi—?'

'My client can't know what Camilla has said or not said,' the attorney interrupted. 'Pure speculation.'

Hugo shrugged his shoulders.

'Did Camilla or Linn know that you left her there?'

'They weren't home then, but I called Camilla and told her that I'd done that.'

'So Camilla has known the whole time that Frida was with you the night she died?'

'Yes.'

'What happened with Frida, Hugo?'

'She . . .'

'She what?' Per asked.

'She died.'

Hugo's shoulders collapsed. The next moment there was a knock on the door.

Per cast an irritated glance in that direction, but when he saw Charlotte's stern expression and her index finger indicated that he should come out, he paused the interview. She wouldn't have disturbed him if it wasn't important.

'We have to find Camilla, she's been lying to us the whole time,' Per said to Charlotte once he'd come out in the corridor. 'What's so important that I couldn't finish the interview?'

'It's actually Camilla this concerns. Linn called. She says that Camilla is gone. She has apparently not been at home for a full twenty-four hours and can't be reached.'

'Damn it! Then she may have realized that Hugo would talk and she split for that reason,' said Per, ramming his good hand on the wall. 'We have to find her – and now!'

57

Linn ran to the toilet. The nausea came on so quickly that she barely made it in time. Because her stomach was empty, only the bile she spat out ended up in the basin. There was a big difference between deliberately forcing up the contents of her stomach and what happened now. Her stomach was cramping by itself. Not having control over that was awful. More or less like her reality. Hugo was suspected of the murder of her best friend and her mother was missing. Besides, Linn knew that someone was watching her. She felt it every time she went out. Probably the same person who'd been in their house the night Frida disappeared. When she reached out her hand to flush she saw that it was shaking.

Charlotte was on her way. Linn took the phone out of her back pocket. The screen was full of Snapchat messages from the girls who wondered why she didn't show up at the cinema.

Linn went into her room, opened the wardrobe where her clothes were hanging perfectly. Every hanger was the same, the distance between them exactly the same. Her mother was manic. Linn pulled up the desk chair. Placed one foot on the cushion and heaved herself up to the top of the wardrobe. At the very top there was a vent, where she'd hidden things from her mother since she was little. To start with it was sweets, then diet pills. With an accustomed movement she took out the little bag. Thought about

Frida. Jumped down from the chair and sat on the bed. She was just about to take a pill when she heard steps in the hall. Linn set aside the bag and ran out.

'Camilla?!' she shouted.

No answer.

Linn stopped in the middle of the hall. Snow on the doormat revealed that someone had come in. She stopped breathing.

'Hugo?'

The sound came from the kitchen. Linn stared in that direction and took a step forward. Two steps. When a person appeared in the doorway she screamed right out. But she remained standing there.

'Easy, easy. I don't mean you any harm,' the man said, holding up both hands to show that he wasn't going to do anything.

Linn stared at him. She knew who it was but couldn't get a word out.

'I'm your dad.'

The man she had a picture of on her computer.

Dad, she thought.

'Dad?' she said.

He took a step in her direction. She responded by backing up a step.

'What are you doing here?' she asked.

'I need to talk with you, but first I have to find out where your mother is.'

Her dad came a step closer. Linn stood still.

'I don't know, she hasn't been home since yesterday. What's happening? What are you doing here?'

Her father reached out his arm. She pulled back out of pure reflex and he lowered it again. His movements were gentle, but his gaze hard.

When the front door opened behind her she saw that his eyes opened wide.

'Police!'

Linn turned to the female voice, saw Charlotte storm in with gun drawn.

'Down on the floor and hands over your head!' said Charlotte in a firm voice.

Linn screamed at her. 'That's my dad, stop!'

Charlotte looked at her with surprise. 'Abbe Ali is your father?' she said.

Linn nodded. She'd got a name for her father. *Abbe Ali*.

Charlotte lowered her gun a little. Abbe stood quite still, let the police search through his clothes. Then they took out handcuffs and forced him to put his hands behind his back, told him to get down on the floor.

'What are you doing here?' said Linn, letting all the emotions come.

'I've been here the whole time. But at a distance,' said Abbe, and his dark eyes met hers.

Linn laughed. Someone had been watching her, just as she thought. But it was her dad.

The police called other officers and Linn watched as her home was invaded by them. Abbe still sat calmly on the floor.

'Why haven't you contacted me?' she asked, getting down on her knees on the floor in front of Abbe.

'Your mother didn't want that, and I live a rather . . . different life, and didn't want to get you mixed up in that.'

Charlotte tried to get her attention. 'Linn, where's your mother? If you know, you have to tell us.'

'I don't know. Camilla hasn't been in touch for a really long time.'

Linn wanted to ask her father a lot of things, but nothing came out.

'I've kept away to protect you,' said Abbe. 'Your father is not a good person. I harm other people.'

Linn didn't know what to say. The man in front of her didn't seem particularly dangerous. Charlotte crouched next to her.

'Are you okay?' she asked.

'Yes, but where's Camilla?'

'We're wondering that too,' said Charlotte, standing up.

Abbe was led out of the door and Linn watched as a lot of police officers completely took over her home.

58

Per sat down across from Hugo for the second time that day. The raid at Camilla's house hadn't made them any the wiser. Per had asked his team to search the house thoroughly – especially Linn's room, where Frida had supposedly died, according to Hugo. But nothing revealed *how* she died. Or if she had really died there. They found a few drugs but nothing else that stuck out. In the garage there were boxes of interior design products that Camilla sold online. But nothing that set off alarms about anything strange. Apart from what they'd found out today, that Abbe Ali was Linn's father. He hadn't seen that coming. They found no computer in the house besides Linn's, and according to Linn, Camilla always had her laptop with her.

This time Charlotte was also present at the interview. She had thrown herself into work again and Kennet was as angry as a wasp. She was tired but there were only two alternatives for her as long as Tony was at large: let Ola Boman and Witness Protection take care of her, or be at the police station and work in the meantime. Kennet had given in; he understood that she was valuable for the investigation.

Per's heart was beating faster than usual. *Stress,* he thought, and resisted the impulse to feel his chest. He continued where the interview had ended before.

'Hugo, you said that Frida died at Camilla's house. Can you tell us more about how she died?'

Hugo shook his head slightly.

His attorney had been given a long time with his client. The prosecutor would file a murder charge and ask for life imprisonment. Hugo had been advised to cooperate for a chance at a somewhat shorter prison sentence. The evidence was overwhelming.

'Camilla called me,' he said. 'She said that Frida was lifeless in the bed, so I went there again. She was like dead, Camilla said.'

'Like dead? Was she dead or not?'

'She was dead when I arrived, but I know that she was alive when I left her.'

'How do you know that? Did you feel her pulse?'

Hugo didn't move. He was looking at Per but somehow not. As if Per wasn't sitting there.

'Nah, she was breathing. Heard her breathing.'

Per looked at Charlotte, who sat quietly observing Hugo.

'What happened when you came back to Camilla's?'

'She was crazy. Screamed and howled. Said that Frida was dead, that she died in her sleep, of an overdose or something.'

Per and Charlotte looked at each other. Camilla had been lying to them through the whole investigation. She had lied to her own daughter, who lost her best friend. Frida could have been saved.

'So Camilla Mattsson saw Frida Malk dead in her house?' said Charlotte. She leaned forward and was barely a centimetre from Hugo's face. 'Why didn't you call for an ambulance, or us?'

'It was an accident. No one killed her. She died in her sleep. It was the drugs,' said Hugo.

'So why not call for help? Instead you stage a hanging in the forest. What is it you're hiding?' said Charlotte.

'You know, she was lying on her back with her arms out at her sides when I came back, kinda like Jesus on the cross, but she wasn't lying that way when I left her. I think Camilla tried to save her. Or I know that she did. She must have done that.' Hugo started biting a fingernail. One of his legs was shaking under the table.

Per analysed what Hugo was telling them. Offhand, it felt as if what he was saying could be true. Neither of them had any motive to kill Frida; she didn't seem to have any great knowledge of the drug business.

'According to the autopsy report she had a fatal cocktail of drugs in her system,' said Per, pounding his good hand on the table. 'If you'd taken Frida to a hospital, perhaps she would have survived!'

Then the attorney spoke up. He'd been unusually quiet during the interview, but this was the limit for him too. 'You're harassing my client! These are pure speculations. Shape up.'

Hugo sat quietly, still biting on his finger. He looked up at Per. 'Sorry,' he whispered. 'That wasn't the idea, everything happened so fast.'

Frida had no signs of livor mortis, thought Per – she'd been preserved by the cold. So she must have been hung up in the cold forest shortly after she died, or else she had really died there.

'Why didn't you call an ambulance? What is it you're hiding?' said Per angrily.

Hugo shrugged his shoulders.

'Why didn't you call the police?' Per repeated.

Hugo looked at his attorney. Sought support. 'I didn't kill her,' he said at last.

Charlotte pointed at the photograph of the scarf, the DNA evidence that Hugo had been at the 120 forest. Hugo understood without her having to ask the question.

'I didn't do anything with Frida. She was Linn's friend and she was so young. I don't like young girls,' he said, and his eyes did not move an inch from Charlotte's.

'So how did your semen end up there?' she asked.

He shrugged his shoulders. 'Don't know.'

Charlotte leaned forward again and hissed at him. 'If it happened as you maintain, you're still going to be charged with contributing to another person's death and tampering with a corpse. Why did you take Frida's phone?'

Hugo looked at her under the fringe that had fallen down over his forehead. 'I had to go and get it after we'd been in the forest . . . It was still at Camilla's house.'

Charlotte thought. 'So you were the one who was in the house when Linn came home that night? When she thought there was a burglar, it was actually you who slipped out through the patio door?'

He stared at his fingers, nodded.

'Where was Camilla then?'

'In the car not far from the house. I had to run in and get it and then Linn came home. I didn't know what I should do, so I went out the patio door.'

'Were you the one who sent the message to Linn from the 120 forest?' asked Per. 'From Frida's phone?'

Hugo's eyes met Per's with a mournful expression. 'You know, she'd been in the forest a long time and you never found her. Didn't want her to hang there any longer . . .'

'Why did the two of you hang her up there to start with?'

'It was Camilla . . . She . . . I felt sorry for Frida. I didn't want her to hang there. I thought that you should find out where she was. So she could come home.'

Hugo brought his hand up to his eye, wiping away the moisture. Per tried to understand Hugo. He'd first put Frida in the back of the car, then drove her out to the forest and tied her up to a tree, arranged a hanging. An action that suggested a callousness you seldom encountered. How could he have done all that, to then feel sorry for Frida and want her to be found?

'Where is Camilla?' he asked, and Hugo opened his eyes wide.

'What do you mean? At home, I suppose?'

'No, she hasn't been seen for some time and we're looking for her.'

'She has nothing to do with this! I . . . It's my fault that Frida is dead. I left her in Linn's room.'

'But then she was found tied up to a tree in the forest,' said Per sharply. 'The two of you were in on that together.'

Hugo shrugged his shoulders.

Per fell silent. Inspected the man across from him. For some reason Hugo wanted to protect Camilla.

'She was found deep in the forest. How were you able to get her there?' Per asked, thinking about the snowmobile they'd ridden to where the body was found.

Hugo looked down at the table. 'We set her on a toboggan and pulled.'

'Did you ever stop and think that what you were doing was wrong – wrong as hell? You must have felt something, because then you helped us find her. Or what? What were you feeling out there in the forest?'

It seemed as if Hugo was thinking about how he should reply. 'It was cold and it was snowing a lot,' he said at last.

Per thought that could explain the lack of tracks in the snow. Half a metre of snow had fallen after Frida disappeared.

'You tried to make it look like a suicide,' said Charlotte. 'Help me understand why you wanted to make it look like a suicide if the two of you didn't kill Frida.'

Hugo remained silent.

Per sighed audibly, not concerned that his disappointment was heard in the whole room. They could charge Hugo with the murder

278

of Unni, contributing to another person's death and tampering with a corpse for having moved Frida's body. Not to mention felony narcotics crimes. They had sufficient evidence, but something was off. Hugo admitted that he had moved Frida and tied her up in the forest, but not that he'd left obvious evidence not far away. Why didn't he admit that? He didn't deny that his DNA was on Unni.

'Unni then? Tell us about her,' said Charlotte.

Hugo stared ahead with a vacant expression. He blinked slowly. 'I didn't kill her either.'

He met Per's gaze and looked tired. Per suddenly became worried that Hugo was telling the truth. That it actually wasn't the perpetrator who was sitting in front of him.

'Tell us who it was,' said Charlotte.

Hugo raised his shoulders. Sighed. 'You're doing bad police work,' he said.

'So help us do it better then,' said Per. 'Make us wiser.'

He snorted. 'I went into her apartment and, like I said, the door was unlocked. So I go in and then she's lying there dead on the bathroom floor.'

'Earlier in the interview you said that you went to Unni's to retrieve drugs. Why?'

'They were evidence and . . . well . . . she needed to know her place – stop snooping, like.'

'What do you mean by "knowing her place"?'

'She should just be scared, not die, that is.'

'So how does Unni end up dead in the bathtub?'

Hugo looked with a hollow-eyed expression at Unni's pictures. Hesitated before he answered. 'I put her there.'

'Tell us what you saw when you went into her apartment.'

Hugo sat quietly for a moment. Appeared to be thinking. 'There was a little blood in one place . . . like on the doorframe or whatever it was and when I went into the bathroom she was lying dead on the floor. By the bathtub.'

'Why did you move her to the bathtub?'

'Otherwise I couldn't clean. There was blood on the floor.'

'Why would you clean?'

Hugo pinched himself on the arm. 'Because I should. It was messy, blood and that.'

'Did someone tell you to clean, Hugo?'

'No, no one.'

Per looked at him. It was as clear as a blue summer sky that Hugo was lying. Someone had told him to clean up. But clearing away evidence and cleaning up were not two different things for Hugo. If someone told him to clean up, he probably interpreted that literally. For that reason he'd wiped away the blood on the floor, not removed evidence. He had cleaned.

'Who told you to clean?'

'No one.'

'But you urinated in the bathtub, on Unni – why did you do that?'

Hugo raised his eyebrows, looked surprised. 'I didn't pee outside the bathtub, I know that. I never miss.'

Per didn't know how he should comment on that, so he let it be.

'Was it Camilla who told you to clean, Hugo? If that's the case, you must tell us that now.'

'She has nothing to do with this,' Hugo said in a loud voice.

'Did you touch Unni's body in any way other than moving her?'

'No, or yes – her sweater . . . nothing else.'

'How did you touch the sweater?'

'Pulled it up a little to see her tits. But I just looked, didn't touch her.'

'Why did you do that?'

'Just curious, wanted to see them. Wouldn't you have been?' he asked Per, as if it were obvious.

'Did you call anyone?' Per asked, ignoring Hugo's question.

'Nah.'

'Why not?'

Hugo shrugged his shoulders.

'Who murdered Unni Olofsson? You know who it is, but you're protecting that person.'

'It's not my business to get involved in.'

'Did you see anyone else in the apartment at that time?'

'No.'

'You take the time to pee and masturbate on her, but don't call the police? That makes no sense to me.'

'I . . .' Hugo looked briefly at his attorney before he answered. 'You know, I didn't kill her. But . . . the other things I did on her. On Unni. But not on her,' he said, pointing at the photograph of Frida. Hugo leaned back in the chair.

Per inspected him. Why did he admit to the evidence he left at Unni's, but denied the semen that was found by Frida's body? There was no logic in that.

59

Abbe saw how the police car he was sitting in turned and drove toward a gate that opened. He'd been sitting in the car for a long time outside Camilla and Linn's house while they searched the place. Waited. When the police were done they drove him to the police station and he'd been told that he would be taken for booking. His daughter had been put in the care of a female police officer who drove her away. Their eyes had met through the car windows. Her life would never be the same.

Now as the car was rolling into the police station, the tyres squealed against the concrete floor. A uniformed police officer opened the door and asked him to get out. He did as he was told, was taken hold of by rubber gloves and led to a metal door, which then opened. A mechanical sound. Behind it was a wooden bench with rounded corners that seemed to be part of the wall. His rear met the hard wood. The light from the ceiling was sharp, like at a hospital. He knew that it was time to end this now and he needed to do it before more people died.

Two policemen were on their way to him and their equipment rattled in time with their steps. Abbe was asked to stand up. He'd done this before – not in Umeå, but he knew what was expected. DNA samples would be taken, there would be a physical examination, change of clothing and then he'd be put into a cell before questioning.

Abbe stopped the policeman with the rubber gloves who took his phone out of his pocket.

'Under "G" is a name I want a responsible police officer to call.'

Behind Plexiglas a policeman was sitting at a desk. He looked up from the keyboard. 'Which name under G?'

'There's a policeman in Stockholm, his name is Sigge Gant. Or, rather, that's not his real name but that's what he's called on his phone.'

'So what is his real name?' the policeman asked.

'I know that his first name is Klas, but I never got his last name.'

Abbe watched how the man's fingers moved over the keyboard.

'So, they have to call Sigge Gant.'

'Why is it so important?'

'You're going to understand but I can't say more. Just do it, please.'

'Duly noted,' said the policeman. Abbe saw how they stuffed his phone into a plastic bag.

He let himself be led toward the medical examiner on duty; a swab would be twirled around in his mouth and put in yet another resealable bag. His clothes would be taken off for inspection and analysis.

Abbe was on the police register for a few minor things but nothing serious, not like Tony. And Abbe did not intend to take the blame for the murder of William. Tony shot him because he didn't want to leave any loose threads. It was thanks to the information from William that Hugo had become of interest to the Syndicates.

Abbe had felt secure with his daughter being friends with Viggo's daughter. He'd watched Linn many times, unnoticed and at a distance. End-of-school ceremonies, birthdays – he'd shared a lot with her without her knowing it. Every time Viggo's daughter had been there in one way or another. What Abbe had missed was the drugs.

That Tony ended William's life with a shot to the forehead was unplanned and extremely twisted. A pure execution that simply screamed the Syndicates. They could just as well have put an ad in the newspaper. The placement of the body at the university had been a way to try to confuse the police. A drug sale that went wrong. It had worked out so-so.

Abbe was inspected, photographed and examined. When they were done with him he ended up between two police officers in a corridor. He followed a white line on the floor. On his feet he had white tube socks and a pair of slippers. He wasn't taken to a cell, but instead straight to the interview room. Abbe needed to be sharp, clear. It smelled of chlorine mixed with detergent, as if the floor had recently been scrubbed.

They met several police officers in the corridor. There truly did not appear to be a shortage of police in Umeå.

Abbe was led to interview room number eight. In there he was met by two police officers he recognized, together with someone who claimed to be Abbe's attorney. He would replace him as soon as he could. Abbe inspected Charlotte as he sat down. The woman whose life he'd saved. Tony would have killed her if Abbe hadn't got her out of there. To think that the police never found her. Even though she was right under their feet when they searched the cabin in Vännäs, in the bomb shelter under the cellar. Abbe would tell them that now. He would tell them everything.

60

Charlotte looked at Abbe. Maybe now she would find out why he had stood up to Tony and rescued a police officer. But it wasn't uncontroversial for her to be allowed in the interview room, because Abbe had participated in her kidnapping. She and Per had argued about it but finally he gave in under the condition that she didn't get involved in the questioning. She had promised that.

Per had called the number Abbe requested, to the man he called Sigge Gant, and it turned out that Abbe was a registered source. He was listed in the police department's internal register of particular informants, squealers and other secret sources of information. A dangerous list to be on if you worked with Tony. In Charlotte's world Abbe had been a criminal type with no empathy, but what she had experienced recently made her a little doubtful.

Per appeared to be waiting until Abbe was through with his attorney, but then he got right to the point.

'Why did you rescue my colleague from Tony?'

Abbe laughed cautiously; he seemed surprised. 'He would have killed her otherwise.'

Charlotte looked at Abbe's wrist. The bracelet with mermaids had of course been put in a plastic bag.

'You drove her first to a garage. Why not dire< hospital?'

'I had to make sure no one was following. Couldn't take the risk of driving straight to the hospital. So she . . . or you, had to sleep off the drugs for a while,' he said, looking at Charlotte. 'You weren't risking your life as long as you didn't get more shit in you.'

'But why? You were taking a big risk.'

Abbe appeared to ponder, as if he himself didn't know why he'd rescued her. 'The noose is tightening, you understand. Tony is about to lose it.'

'What do you mean?' Per asked.

'All the shit that happened when we came up here. Tony was here to straighten out his affairs and then we run into Charlotte. He goes crazy and wants revenge. But what the hell, I couldn't watch while he murdered a police officer. At the same time the girl disappears. We thought that you all were after us because a dead guy had showed up in a snowdrift – we didn't understand that you thought we'd taken the girl. Do you get it? It got crazy confusing.'

'Why were you in Unni Olofsson's apartment?'

Abbe looked at Per. Charlotte's cheeks were warm, there were rings of sweat under her arms. She thought about the drugs Tony had forced into her.

'There was starting to be a lot of talk about that woman within the Syndicates. That she was going around asking questions about the same thing we wanted information about. There was a rumour that she'd been murdered. Incredibly stupid woman, she had no idea what she was getting herself into. When I went to her place I realized that, sure enough, her apartment is a crime scene but the Syndicates want the information that she apparently was murdered for. Who sold the drugs and made lots of money. Although you all had gone over everything with a fine-tooth comb. Who was she?'

She was someone who knew too much about Hugo Larsson, thought Charlotte. *And she was murdered for that.* But she didn't say anything.

'Forgive me for treating you roughly there in the hall, but I couldn't be a suspect for that murder,' said Abbe, looking at Charlotte.

'But why are you choosing to sit here with us now?' Per asked. 'Because that's probably not due to either pure luck or good police work. You've escaped for a long time with Tony. You're smart, Abbe.'

'I want out,' said Abbe, as if that were obvious. 'I want to get away from that shitty world. It's only a matter of time before Tony realizes my double-dealing. Then I'm done anyway.'

'You're a protected source, Abbe. Tony will never know.'

But Charlotte knew that wasn't really true. Those were nice words on paper but it didn't always work that way in practice.

Abbe shrugged his shoulders. 'Quite a few of Tony's business deals have gone to hell lately. Guess why? It's just a matter of time before he connects me with the cops.'

'Tell us about Camilla,' said Per.

Abbe took a deep breath. He would be the most hunted man in the underworld. The one who sang. 'Before she moved to Umeå she worked as a stripper at Tony's club. That was where we got to know each other. When she got pregnant she moved here and started up her interior design business, which is going well from what I understand. A little too good – Tony wanted part of the cake, as they say.'

Charlotte heard how Abbe's legs moved under the table, noted how his forehead was damp at the hairline.

'In what way does he want a part of the cake? What do you mean?' asked Per.

'He wants to take it over – all of it.'

'Why is that? What would he do with an interior design business? Does he want to launder money through it?'

'Tony has had his eye on it for a while, and then we managed to find out the extent of the business by following that stupid guy, Hugo.'

'Hugo Larsson?' Charlotte interjected. The words came spontaneously and she got an irritated look from Per. *One more time and you're out*, he seemed to be wordlessly saying to her. Abbe didn't seem to notice anything but instead continued talking.

'We didn't manage to pick him up because Tony suddenly wanted to get you first. But Tony intended to use him.'

'In what way would you use Hugo?'

'Through a little creative convincing – he would take Camilla's daughter and move her to the cabin in Vännäs.'

'Your daughter?' said Per.

'Yep, my daughter. That was Tony's idea of course.'

'Do tell.'

'To start with we thought that Hugo was the boss, but we realized pretty soon that it's Camilla who runs it. Tony's plan then became to use Linn as extortion to take over everything. Camilla would be forced to reveal everything about deliveries, times, contacts – yes, everything. Otherwise Linn would die. Everything was going to hell.'

'Camilla's interior design company, tell us about that,' said Per.

'You don't seem to understand the extent of Camilla's operation. It's a drug cartel that extends over all of Europe. She has literally walked over dead bodies to be where she is today. She uses the interior design company to launder the money.'

Charlotte tried to take in what Abbe had said. So Camilla was behind the enormous spread of drugs in the county. But it was considerably bigger than that. How could she have worked completely under the radar? No one suspected her or disbelieved the success story she had painted around herself. Charlotte thought about the interview with Hugo, how he'd tried to protect her. Camilla was the one who'd wanted to get Frida's body out of the way. And she had the strongest motive to want Unni dead.

'If you protect my daughter, I'll give you Tony,' said Abbe, interrupting Charlotte's thoughts.

Just then the door opened. Anna looked in and interrupted the interview. Asked them to come out.

'Yes, what is it?' said Charlotte.

'A woman with Camilla's description has been pulled into a car at Västerslätt. The witness reports having seen a masked man force her into a van.'

'Tony has her,' Charlotte declared.

61

Linn had broken down and cried on a policewoman's shoulder, and asked to be able to speak with her dad. That would have to wait, they said, but then suddenly they changed their minds. Now she was waiting in a room at the police station, not allowed to leave it without a guard.

Linn got up from the chair when Abbe was let into the bare visitors' room. The green sweatshirt looked nice on him. She didn't know what to do with her hands so she laced her fingers together, waited for him to act. Did he want to hug her? Shake hands? Should she call him Dad or Abbe? Adrenaline came in a rush, like taking a pill. Her nerves softened as soon as their eyes met. Her dad smiled broadly, reached out his arms to her. Linn took a few steps forward, her cheek touched his sweatshirt. She put her arms around his waist. It didn't feel like she was hugging a father, more like an acquaintance.

'Do you know how long I've waited for this?' he said, holding her tight. With his hand he stroked her hair. His voice was dark and calm.

She let go of his waist and looked up at him, at his eyes and his slightly bent nose. She had inherited his nose.

'Sit down,' he said, and without taking her eyes off him she sat in the soft armchair. A pitcher of water stood on a round table between them. Abbe sat down too. He smiled but soon turned serious.

'I'm sorry about what happened to your friend,' he said, taking her hand. Inspected it as if it were something valuable. 'I don't know what will happen with me now, I'm not an okay person. I've done a lot of bad things. But I've also cooperated with the police for many years and hope that can help me.'

'Are you a policeman or something?' Linn asked, and her heart jumped.

'No, but I've helped them with a lot of things, given them information about criminals and such.'

Linn looked at him knowingly. 'Like the guy in the Johan Falk movies?' she asked.

He laughed and nodded. 'More or less like that, yes. We're called informants.'

Linn stretched her back. Her father was truly like Frank Wagner. Linn thought about Frida, how much she wanted to tell Frida that her dad was a hero who worked with the police.

His dark eyes sought hers. 'There are things about your mother that you're going to hear. These aren't nice things.'

Linn raised her eyebrows. 'What kind of things?'

He moved out as far as possible on the chair and leaned toward Linn.

'Your mother runs an illegal operation. In addition to that, she uses her interior design company to launder money – drug money.'

'What?' Linn shook her head. Her mother devoted all her waking hours to the business. 'What do you mean, launder money? Drugs? What do you mean?'

'Simplified, I can say that Camilla brings medicines classified as narcotics into the country – large shipments – and resells them on the internet, and to guys like William. She's made good money on that. With that money she started the company and through fake invoices makes it look like the money has come in through legal sales.'

'Do the police know this?'

Abbe nodded.

Mum's a drug pusher, thought Linn. It wasn't possible to take in. All the Instagram pictures, were they just so that no one would suspect who she really was?

'What's going to happen to her?'

'She'll probably be charged as a suspect in narcotics crimes and fraud.'

Linn's shoulders collapsed. She could barely manage to keep herself upright. How had she missed this? The drugs that she and Frida took came from her own mother.

'Do you think Hugo killed Frida? The police won't tell me anything.'

'I don't know. Sorry, Linn.'

Her armpits were damp and her sweater stuck to her skin. She sniffed to clear her nose, but it kept running.

'What will happen to me now?' she whispered.

'Hopefully you can live with your aunt, if they find her suitable, until you're an adult.'

'Can I live with you when you're released?'

'We'll have to see. I'm going to live the rest of my life hunted by the Syndicates. I'll never be entirely free and I don't know what will happen to me now.'

'But if they find out that I'm your daughter . . . then they'll search for me,' said Linn, her body turning cold from the insight.

'We have to continue to keep our relationship secret. That way you can live without a threat hanging over your head.'

Linn's heart dropped right down into her stomach. 'So we can't see each other any more?'

'Unfortunately not.'

62

Per took a few determined steps toward the car with Charlotte close behind him. They had to interrupt the questioning of Abbe to provide information about Camilla and Tony. The MOC, Surveillance, National Operations – they were all involved in the suspected kidnapping. Abbe was the responsibility of Witness Protection now and Ola Boman had been given the task of keeping Abbe alive until Stockholm took over.

Charlotte's recently purchased, comfortable boots from Stinaa.J made her steps in the garage soundless. No more uncomfortable designer shoes.

She reached out her hand with the car key and pressed the button. The familiar beep sounded at the same time as the car's headlights blinked.

'I'll drive,' said Per, taking the key out of her hand. 'You may still have drugs in your body.'

'Come off it, you can't drive with one arm,' said Charlotte, taking back the key.

Per shook his head but got into the passenger seat.

'Do we know exactly where they are?' she asked.

'We'll know that soon,' he said as the garage filled with colleagues on their way out on the same mission.

Per held on to the handle above the side window. The sirens on the police car roared in his ears as they left the garage. They came out on the street and every pothole was painfully felt in his arm, which was still in a sling. The city landscape around them became blurred details. Car chases were uncommon up here in Umeå but Charlotte knew what she was doing and did not skimp on the horsepower. According to witnesses, the car at Västerslätt had driven toward Rödäng so Charlotte headed in that direction.

'Must say that it was a stupid move by Tony to kidnap Camilla in broad daylight with other people around. What was he thinking?' Per asked with his gaze on the snow-covered road.

'I agree, but he's probably desperate and angry. And he doesn't know that we've found out that he wants to get at Camilla. Have we requested a helicopter?'

'It should be on its way,' said Per, taking out the protective vest.

'Which way should we go now?' she asked on the police radio. It crackled.

'The vehicle is driving along Sockenvägen not far from Backen,' the emergency response centre said. 'Registration JVK 455. A black minivan. Reported stolen last night. We have a car that has taken up the chase.'

'Do we know for sure that it's Camilla and Tony?' Charlotte asked Per, taking her eyes off the road for a moment. She put on the indicator before overtaking.

Per tensed every muscle in his body. *Damn how she drives,* he thought. If it hadn't been for the flashing lights there would have been angry honking.

'The description of the woman matches Camilla,' said Per. 'And her car is still at the place where she was kidnapped. It's her. The question is whether Tony has taken her himself or if it's one of his underlings.'

'It's Tony. He wants to take over Camilla's whole operation – he won't leave that mission to anyone else,' said Charlotte, pressing the accelerator.

'You do know that we have a winter road law, right?' said Per at last, breathing out when they were done overtaking and the oncoming cars had moved to the side.

'Sure, sure, I know how to do this. Don't worry.'

Per looked at his colleague. Tried to see if she was stable. The kidnapping must have left its mark on her but she pushed aside the emotions like a snowplough did with snow.

'What does Tony think will happen now?' she asked. They were driving toward the Backen area, leaving clouds of snow behind them.

'Whatever he does he'll go to prison. The kidnapping has attracted too much attention,' said Per just as the buzz from the sky made him look up. The police helicopter.

'Maybe he wants to get at Camilla's network, regardless of what that entails,' Per continued, 'and regardless of whether he risks going to jail for it?'

He removed the sling. Needed to free his arm. It hurt so damned much. The carelessness would delay the healing process. He thought about Mia – he needed to call her. The mobilization would attract journalists and she would have to see everything on TV. The radio crackled again.

'We've stopped the vehicle on the bridge just after Killingholmen. The bridge is cordoned off from both directions so he's stuck there now.'

'Okay, good,' said Per on the communications radio. 'Call in a negotiator.'

Charlotte sat quietly; the engine was in overdrive and at every curve the back tyres slipped a little. When they came up to the bridge they could see the stolen minivan out there, idling. They couldn't see inside – the back doors were closed and four police cars blocked off the entrance to the bridge. The police van and response team blocked the view. Charlotte turned off the ignition; Per got out before the engine fell silent. The cold made his nostrils stick together. Blinking blue lights could be seen far away on the other side of the bridge. Tony was truly caught. Charlotte placed herself beside Per. Her breathing was calm.

'I'm not sure that Camilla is still alive,' said Charlotte, looking out over the snow-covered bridge. 'But we need her to find out why Frida and Unni died. She must be brought to account for that.'

The sun was high in the sky; the view was also clear for the police in the helicopter that was buzzing above them. Per thought about Camilla. A seemingly ordinary mother who ran one of Sweden's most successful narcotics cartels.

'Camilla must understand that it's over,' said Per. 'We have her, thanks to Tony, which is ironic.'

The response commander turned to them.

'We haven't been able to establish communication with anyone in the van. We're waiting on the negotiator,' he said, indicating that they should follow him.

Charlotte raised the blue and white plastic tape so that Per could pass. She stopped behind a dark-clothed man from the armed response team.

'Can you neutralize the kidnapper?' Per asked.

'Answer, no,' said the man. 'But we have people on the way to the adjoining area.'

Per understood this meant that sharpshooters were coming. He looked around – spruces and birch trees. The bridge went straight out from the forest and met trees on the other side too.

The branches of the spruce trees were bent under the weight from the snow. The water below was frozen and covered with snow. The sky was blue, like a summer's day. If the situation had been different he would have appreciated the beauty. He looked at Charlotte.

'What's happening in there?' she asked, still calm.

All they saw was the back of the van. The rear lights revealed that Tony had his foot on the brake.

'Listen, threat of violence is my guess,' said Per, turning to her again. Her earrings glistened as the sun's rays made a direct hit. He thought about Frida in the forest. Looked back at the car with Camilla in it.

The exhaust from the pipe disappeared. The rear lights went out. No one said anything. The nature around the bridge was silent, the snow helping to dampen all sounds. Per looked at the police negotiator who had arrived and was now in the process of setting up a centre for communication.

'Tony isn't going to talk with any negotiator,' said Charlotte. 'He's the one in control. Soon it will all be over.'

Charlotte knew Tony, she was the only police officer on the bridge who actually knew who he was and how he thought. It was a strange situation. The van was there. Easy to storm, completely unprotected. But it could all soon degenerate and, despite everything, it was a hostage situation. Per thought about Anton, who had jumped from this very bridge.

One back door of the vehicle flew open with such force that it echoed across the landscape. The armed response team made their way closer to the van. Tony had no way out.

'Cover me. I can go out on the bridge and try to talk with him,' said Charlotte to the response commander, putting her gun in the holster.

Per swore and was forced to follow, together with the response commander. Slowly they approached; still no movement from inside the open back door. It wasn't possible to see inside. She stopped a couple of metres from the vehicle. Per was forced to use his injured arm when he took out his gun. The response commander took light hold of his jacket, pulling him back a few steps.

'Not too close with the gun,' he said.

Per watched Charlotte's back as she stood so close to the vehicle that she could reach the open door if she took a few steps forward. She had a protective vest on but Tony could easily shoot her where she stood. Per listened for the sound, the one that revealed a gun ready to fire. The click. He stared at her, his legs almost buckled. She was too close. This was going to hell. The response commander looked frustrated; Charlotte's place was behind him, not in front.

'Damn you,' Per whispered just as the other back door opened.

Per saw a pair of bound hands that stuck out first, then Camilla was pushed forward. She was placed farthest out on the edge and stood with knees bent. Tony was still wearing a mask and had one arm around her waist; in the other hand he held the gun that was pressed against Camilla's temple. He was using her as a living shield. When Camilla set her foot down on the ground her legs buckled and she would have fallen if Tony hadn't held on to her.

'Tony, you can't get yourself out of this situation. Release Camilla,' said Charlotte. 'You have nowhere to go.' Charlotte had both her arms in the air.

Per looked at the response commander, who pointed toward his ear, showing that he was talking with his colleagues. Charlotte would take shit for this. She was breaching all protocols. Forcing everyone to follow her.

Camilla stood quite still and looked right at Charlotte. They could see the steam from her breath. The wind took hold of her hair, which played around her face. Her red coat fluttered lightly in the wind. Tony took off the ski mask.

'This bitch is going to die!'

Per gasped.

Charlotte took two steps back.

'Tomas?'

63

Linn stayed behind in the room after her dad left her. She didn't know when or if they would meet again. A policeman was already waiting to drive him to Stockholm. Linn still had his scent in her nostrils from the hug she got.

She was supposed to see someone from social services who would take care of her. She didn't understand why, but her aunt would come, just as her dad had said. Linn got up from the arm-chair and went to the window. Saw her figure reflected in the glass. It felt like she'd aged. The life she'd lived with Frida was like another time, even though barely a week had passed since she disappeared. Now she would move in with her aunt, go to a new school, try to make friends. Fit in. Become someone else.

There was a vibration in her back pocket. Linn sighed and took out the phone. Anja had sent a Snap.

> *How u doing? Really sorry about Frida. I'm in Umeå now if u want to talk? But we have to call, I can't leave my guard.*

Linn looked at the door. Didn't know if she could leave the police station either. Her heart felt lighter. She already had a friend in Stockholm where her aunt lived. Anja.

Thanks. At the police station. Be in touch soon.

Linn wondered where Camilla was and called again. Same voicemail as always. What was she doing? Linn thought about all the Instagram pictures Camilla had taken over the years. All the demands that everything should be perfect. So the whole time she was a simple criminal.

Linn remained standing in front of the window in the room where she'd just seen her dad. She looked at the health centre, which was right across the street. Cars came and went. An elderly woman got into a taxi. Linn had googled Tony Israelsson. Seen his face. Like a grandfather. He didn't look a bit dangerous. He could have been married to the old woman who just got into the taxi down there.

What if Tony found out that Abbe had a daughter with Camilla? The realisation that Tony could actually find out who she was hurt. Was this the way her life would look like now? Like Frida's? She would be forced to stay hidden.

When the phone vibrated again she started. She thought about her mum. Linn wanted to tell her that she wasn't angry. Disappointed, but not angry. She picked up the phone and stared at the newsflash from *Västerbottens-Kuriren*.

Hostage Drama on the West Beltway Bridge!

Linn put her hand over her mouth when she saw the blurry pictures, taken from a distance. Linn stared at her mother's coat. She went back to the chair and sat down. Sat on something.

What the hell? she thought, feeling with her hand. Nothing in the chair. She reached for the back pocket of her jeans. Something poked out. She stuck her hand in and removed it. A slip of paper folded so tightly that it felt like a stone. Her dad must have put it there when they hugged. She unfolded the Post-it note. Read it.

> *When you're 18 you can use this account, which will help you start a new life. The money is yours. If anything happens to me, make contact with Viggo Malk. You can trust him. I'll be in touch when it's safe. Love you. – Abbe*

Linn set down the note and picked up her phone. Her hands were shaking. She read again about what was happening at the bridge. Rushed out of the room, looking for a police officer to talk with.

64

Charlotte looked out over the bridge. She forced her breathing to settle down after realizing who had kidnapped Camilla.

'Tomas,' she said again, although louder this time.

Anton's dad.

Tomas's hair pointed in all directions. His eyes stared. He threw the ski mask on the ground.

'She doesn't deserve to live – no one does who sells drugs to our children,' he said. 'Do you know how many young people die from drugs? Do you?'

Tomas pressed the gun even harder against Camilla's cheek.

'Tomas, we're here to help you. I understand that—'

'You think you're smart,' he interrupted. 'You're so fucking bad at your job. Do you know that she killed Unni too?'

He forced Camilla toward the edge of the bridge.

'If you release Camilla then you can tell us,' said Charlotte. 'Let her go – she'll be arrested. You've lost your son and any prosecutor will see that as an extenuating circumstance. But for that to happen, Camilla can't die.'

'Check your email – what I'm saying is true. Anton saw her strangle Unni, the only person who wanted to help our son.'

Tomas's hand with the gun was shaking. That worried Charlotte.

'Anton was there when it happened – he heard everything. Camilla is a murderer who sells drugs to our children!'

He's desperate, Charlotte thought. *And he's so tense that the gun might go off by mistake.* She noted every strained muscle in Tomas's face. Wanted to read his next move before he himself knew what he would do.

'Tomas. Take the gun away from her head,' said Charlotte.

'She's not going to get away.' Tomas dragged Camilla the remaining distance to the bridge railing. Her eyes were wide open. 'It doesn't matter that you've cordoned off the bridge. My goal was to come here with her. She's going to die the same way Anton died.'

Charlotte sought his gaze. It was starting to wander between her and the railing.

'Tomas. Put down the gun.'

With a quick movement Tomas aimed the gun at Charlotte instead, who instinctively backed up.

'What the hell?' Per panted behind her, just as a shot was heard. The echo made the birds scatter across the sky. The response commander had given orders to neutralize Tomas.

Tomas's body turned; he lost hold of Camilla, who landed on top of him. She got up on all fours.

'Hell's bells,' said Per, and Charlotte ran straight to Tomas at the same time as the response force. Then she changed her mind and turned instead toward Camilla, aiming the gun at her. Tomas was lying on the ground with his face in the snow.

Ambulance sirens wailed in her ears. The helicopter whirred at a low altitude. Charlotte and Per stood beside each other with their guns each aimed at a perpetrator. Charlotte lowered her arms when their colleagues took over. It was starting to get dark. The streetlights on the bridge came on.

'How did he know about Camilla? We had just understood how it all fitted together,' she said to Per.

'He said something about an email,' said Per, taking out his phone.

Charlotte placed herself beside him while he opened his inbox. There he saw an email from Tomas, sent a few minutes ago. He must have done it while he was in the car. It had gone out to the police and to Swedish news media.

'What the hell? It's a suicide note from Anton,' said Per.

Charlotte took out her own phone and opened the email on it. She crouched down. Read.

'My God,' she said out loud to herself as her finger moved across the screen.

'So it's true,' said Per. 'Anton was at Unni's place when she was murdered. He saw everything, exactly like Tomas said.'

Charlotte looked quickly away to Camilla, saw how she was being put in an ambulance, guarded by their colleagues.

'Then it was Camilla,' she said, getting up. 'It was Camilla who strangled Unni, not Hugo. And those are her strands of hair on the tape.'

65

Charlotte looked down at her boots as she passed through the automatic doors at the hospital. The warmth enveloped her like a caress. She thought about Tony, about where he might be. No effort on their part had led to an arrest. Abbe had tipped them off about a farm outside Mariefred, which was being searched right now. Their colleagues in Stockholm suspected that he had fled abroad. National Operations was turning over every stone in their search.

'Hello, do you hear me?' said Per.

Charlotte nodded. 'Sorry, my thoughts were elsewhere.'

They walked through the corridor from the main entrance. The hospital was starting to feel like home.

'Anna has talked with Anton's mother. Tomas evidently found the boy's suicide note under a pile of mail and newspapers. She thinks that Anton put it there so that they would find it, but that they simply missed it in all the chaos. Think if we'd had that letter a week ago – we would have saved so much time.'

'Anton's suicide note was gruesomely detailed,' said Charlotte. 'You wonder what he must have felt when he hid in the cupboard and saw Unni being strangled.'

'It wasn't the murder of Unni that was the reason for his suicide,' said Per, glancing at the glucose reading on the phone. 'It was because he couldn't bear to live any longer. But he wanted everyone to find out what he'd seen.'

Charlotte clenched her jaw. 'But what made Tomas act like he did today? It's unusual for people who aren't criminals to take such risks.'

'According to his wife, something burst inside him when he read the letter and afterwards he behaved differently. Not so strange that he didn't foresee the police response. But a professional criminal would have. Tomas is simply a grieving father trying to get justice.'

'Who was capable of stealing a van, anyway,' said Charlotte, taking off her jacket, making sure that no one at the hospital saw her gun. 'They are taking DNA and fingerprints from Camilla now, right? It ought to match the strand of hair. We'll see for sure when the results come from Forensics.'

They passed the cafeteria and the kiosk. It was a quiet day at the hospital.

'Yes, it was damn lucky that the hair follicle was there,' said Per. 'Otherwise it would have been considerably more complicated to test. Now it ought to go quicker.'

Charlotte nodded. 'Kennet is being flooded with calls from journalists who want to have the note confirmed. Why did Tomas send all the material to the media?'

'He probably didn't want Anton's suicide to become just one of many, and he did say in the email that he was afraid that Camilla would get off. He doesn't trust the legal system.'

The lift pinged, and they made room for two doctors who nodded at them. Charlotte pressed the lift button.

'Tomas is in surgery now,' said Per. 'We'll get to ask him when he wakes up. The shot was well aimed, just hitting his knee.'

'Yes, I'm glad that Tomas survived. I can understand what he did. What he and his wife have gone through is devastating. The tipping point into madness is razor thin for someone grieving.'

They stepped into the ward where Camilla was being taken care of.

'It's said that all of us are potential murderers, if the situation demands it,' said Per.

Camilla would be taken to the police station as soon as she was discharged, but Per and Charlotte wanted to question her immediately.

They greeted a policeman who was standing by her open door.

Camilla had a bandage on her forehead; according to witnesses, Tomas struck her before he forced her into the vehicle. Now she was sitting handcuffed in bed. She didn't seem to have been badly injured. Charlotte sat down on a chair in the corner, Per remained standing. He showed clearly that he would record the conversation with his phone by setting it on her bedside table. She looked at them with a gaze that didn't reveal what she was feeling.

'Why did you kill Unni?' Charlotte asked, leaning forward. She intended to get right to the point.

Camilla brushed something away from her leg. Forced herself to look unmoved.

'I'm not saying anything without my attorney,' she said, glaring at Charlotte. 'You ought to understand that.'

Charlotte leaned back in the chair. Took off her hat. Her head ached. 'Do you understand what you're putting your daughter through?' she asked.

Camilla laughed. 'Everything I've done is for her. So that she'd have a good life and not have to grow up like me, in misery, with no money for food and be forced to do things that aren't healthy.'

'Many people live in poverty without killing people,' said Charlotte.

'Listen, you fucking upper-class bitch, what do you know about being poor and having to degrade yourself every day to put food on the table? I've created a successful company all by myself, with no help from anyone. My daughter is living a good life thanks to that, so the guilt-tripping won't work.'

'So selling drugs was to help Linn?' said Charlotte, and the scorn in her voice made Camilla's eyes blacken.

Per took a step toward the bed. 'Your own daughter has taken the drugs you've sold, did you know that?' he asked.

'Linn doesn't use drugs.'

'She admitted it herself to us, so yes, she does. Your drugs.'

Camilla turned her head away.

'There was a strand of hair in Unni's apartment that we hadn't been able to match with anyone. Now we've taken DNA samples from you, it will turn out to be yours, right?'

Camilla laughed at them. 'You can't prove a thing. I'll be out in a few hours. I've never met anyone named Unni. I don't even know who she is.'

'What we're going to prove is that you strangled Unni because she threatened to expose you and your operation. But you messed up and sent Hugo to retrieve the drugs and clean up. What you meant for him to clean away was the evidence, but Hugo took it literally and only cleared away what he thought was messy – the blood on the floor. But, in any event, Hugo isn't like everyone else, and he got distracted by a little staging and left evidence behind. Which he was probably also honest enough to tell you. Is there anything we're missing?'

Camilla barely seemed to be listening.

'Hugo Larsson has thrown you to the wolves,' said Per.

Camilla laughed. 'Hugo, the boy. His testimony hardly counts. He's not all there and you know it.'

'I wouldn't say that,' said Per. 'His answers are honest. But he's afraid of you. Or else he's in love. We'll find that out. So Hugo's testimony, DNA evidence – which presumably will back up what he's saying – and a witness to the murder. Maybe it's time to cooperate?'

Camilla picked at her cuticle.

'You have no alibi for any of the crimes, except your accomplice, and you're the only one in the whole city who had a motive to kill Unni,' said Per.

Camilla took a breath, shook her head and looked away.

Charlotte sensed some embarrassment in Camilla, who wouldn't look them in the eyes.

'We know that you had a tough upbringing. You had no choice other than to do what you did to put food on the table. Your time at Tony's can't have been easy for a young woman,' she said, and meant every word.

Camilla pursed her lips. The skin on her throat turned red.

'But I believe, honestly, that you don't want your own daughter to use the drugs you sell. Unni wouldn't either. She wasn't out to harm you, she was out to rescue young people,' said Charlotte.

Camilla turned her face to her. No trace of regret as far as Charlotte could see.

'Somewhere inside you there is a mother who protects her daughter. Don't you feel regret that you murdered someone who actually cared about Linn?'

Camilla's eyes darkened. 'Unni came up to me in town, just like that, and told me everything she knew. Said that she would go to the police.'

'Tell us what happened,' said Charlotte.

'I went over to talk sense with her. But she was completely unreasonable. Screamed that I was vile. Then things turned dark

310

for me,' said Camilla. 'I barely remember what happened. She fell backwards, struck her head on the bathtub. It was an accident. Do you hear that? It was an accident,' she said, emphasizing the final word.

'So you stuck a knife in her and strangled her by accident? Come on, Camilla,' said Charlotte.

Camilla straightened up. 'I brought the knife to frighten her into obedience, not to kill her. I panicked when she fell and struck her head – she was so damn angry.' Camilla laughed at her own comment. 'Unni told me to stop selling, otherwise she would go to the police.'

'A wiser alternative than murder,' said Per.

'Just like that? You're a cop, you know it doesn't work that way. Once you're in you can never get out. It's just keep going or die. The deliveries keep coming and I'm good at running the operation. Really good. There are many people who make a lot of money – are they simply going to accept that I retire? There isn't exactly a union to turn to.'

A woman came into the room, out of breath. She introduced herself as Camilla's attorney. She looked angry.

'You have no right to question my client in my absence.'

'Yes, she's an adult,' said Per.

'It's cool, it was an accident,' said Camilla, leaning backward in the elevated bed.

'Tell us what happened with Frida Malk, your daughter's best friend.'

'You seem good at your job, make a theory. Entertain me. You've talked with Hugo so you probably already know what he did. You can't accuse me of that.'

Charlotte pointed at her. 'We think that Frida died of an overdose in Linn's bed the night between Saturday and Sunday. You find her and panic – you don't want to end up in a police investigation or have us snooping around in your home. So instead of calling for help you take her out in the forest with the intention of making it look like a suicide.'

'That was Hugo's fault, not mine. He left her in Linn's room. She was dead when I found her.'

'She was your daughter's best friend. How are you going to explain to Linn that you didn't call for an ambulance?' said Charlotte.

'It was Hugo,' Camilla persisted. 'His semen is in the forest close to the place where Frida was found.'

She fell silent.

'How do you know that Hugo's semen was found near Frida's body?' Per asked calmly. 'We haven't told that to anyone.'

Charlotte was grateful that they recorded the interview because the attorney told her client to stop talking.

'You and Hugo drove Frida's body out in the woods to make it look like a suicide,' said Per. 'You didn't want the attention of the police for several reasons. Your illegal operation, but also because you had already murdered an innocent woman. So you let a seventeen-year-old girl die of an overdose.'

Per looked at Camilla to see if he got any reaction. None.

Charlotte continued. 'After that you planted Hugo's semen at the scene, to make him a suspect. You knew that he left traces of it at Unni's and in that way we could connect the deaths if needed.'

'These are wild theories without substance or evidence,' said Camilla's attorney, but Charlotte's phone interrupted the protests. On the screen she saw that it was Kicki who was calling, so she excused herself and went out in the corridor.

'Hi, Kicki.' Charlotte pressed the phone against her ear.

'Hi. Yes, we confiscated Camilla Mattsson's computer in the vehicle on the bridge.'

'Good. Have you found anything?'

'It wasn't easy to open it because it was encrypted, but everything is here.'

'Everything?' Charlotte asked, casting a quick glance at Camilla's room. Assured herself that she couldn't hear.

'Everything is here, and I mean *everything*. This is the computer that Tony wanted to get. If you have it, you have the operation.'

'What do you mean?'

She heard clicking sounds from Kicki's end.

'Here is information on suppliers, manufacturers in France, date and time for planned deliveries, previous deliveries, also account numbers and information about where she has placed all the money . . . Yes, simply all you need to completely take over or sabotage.'

Charlotte bent her neck back, looked at the fluorescent lights.

'How did Camilla get the pills through Customs?' she asked Kicki. 'Can you see that?'

'Not yet, but we see that the trucks have taken the classic route over the Öresund Bridge. My guess is that she paid some gang for information about when Customs control has been unmanned on the Swedish side.'

'So Camilla's operation is active internationally, like Abbe told us?' said Charlotte.

'Yes, what she's done requires a great deal of planning and criminal contacts outside Sweden she can trust.'

Charlotte looked toward the room where Camilla was.

'That must have cost a lot,' she said before Kicki continued.

'The deliveries have been sent along with her ordinary, legal purchases through the company. The truck must simply have made an extra stop on the way where the load has been repacked.'

Charlotte laughed, couldn't help but be impressed by the logistics. A single mum who became known for her entrepreneurship had fooled everyone.

She ended the call with Kicki and went back to Camilla, who was talking with her attorney. Per observed them.

'We know how your transports of drugs have been brought into the country – we know everything,' said Charlotte, placing herself in front of the bed where Camilla was sitting.

'You think you know so damned much, you have no idea,' she said, moving down to the edge of the bed, closer to Charlotte. Stretched her back, brought her hands over her hair. Her face was pale but her eyes looked like two black holes. When she gripped the edge of the bed with both hands and tried to get up, Charlotte backed away out of pure instinct. The energy coming off her was hateful, like a furious animal.

'Do you have any idea where Tony Israelsson is? Do you?' Camilla hissed. 'I know that he wanted to kill you and if you think you've got away, you need to think again.'

Charlotte's heart struck double beats. It was like plunging into ice-cold water.

Camilla smiled, leaning forward over the edge of the bed. 'You're going to have to pay a high price – much higher than me,' she said, sitting down again. 'That's the way Tony works.'

66

Charlotte picked up the storage box that was labelled 'Kitchen' and unfolded the flaps. Anja was on the top floor in their new house and Charlotte could hear her arranging furniture up there. Their everyday life had changed. Tony was still at large and a threat hung over them. Protection sat outside in a car and was a constant presence. Just like her gun. In the midst of it all, she and Anja were trying to live as usual. Per was on his way to help with the move so she wanted to get out the wine glasses. It was Friday evening after all. Even Kicki had offered to help, but that was the limit for Charlotte. Having her here would feel like letting in a spy.

The light from the ceiling was sharp, and she was going toward the wall switch to turn down the brightness when the doorbell rang. Charlotte looked at the box on the kitchen island; beside it her personal gun was lying quite openly. Before they moved in she had replaced the front door with a more secure one and installed alarms.

'Hi! Come into the chaos!' she said to Per.

Simon and Hannes gave her a quick hug before they ran into the house. They each had a hockey stick with them.

'Yes, sorry, but they refused to leave the house without the sticks. They got a pair of new, super-expensive ones they'd been dreaming about and now they take them everywhere. We've created hockey monsters and are going bankrupt,' Mia said, embracing her.

'How are you feeling?' Charlotte asked.

Mia took off her jacket. 'It's okay, well into the treatment,' she said, adjusting her blouse. Charlotte thought about her long blonde hair, if it would fall out, but didn't ask.

'My God, how nice,' Per exclaimed. 'Yes, we're going to enjoy it here, aren't we, Mia?'

He hugged his wife. Charlotte noticed that both of them had a pair of indoor shoes with them. Per took out a pair of summer slippers and Mia a pair in the ballerina style. Charlotte smiled at that. It was nice of them but they didn't need to adapt to her habits. It was just that type of obligation that she disliked about Stockholm.

'Yes, make yourselves at home,' she said, going back to the box on the island. She hid the gun in a kitchen drawer that was still empty and took the wine glasses out of the box. She looked around. Where had the movers put her wine bottles?

The boys ran up the stairs and Charlotte watched them as they disappeared toward the top floor. Per came back from the hall and held up two bottles of red wine.

'We thought that maybe you haven't had time to get the necessities,' he said, laughing.

Charlotte thanked him and sighed. 'Then we just need a corkscrew,' she said, and started searching through the moving boxes. But Per took one out of his back pocket.

'I came prepared.'

'Truly,' she agreed.

Mia walked around and looked, and when she disappeared into another room Per came closer to Charlotte.

'Nothing new about Tony?' he asked, holding out his glass.

'No, he seems to have gone to ground.'

'How long do you think you'll be able to live like this?'

'No idea, but what choice do I have?'

'I talked with Kennet today. They see a noticeable reduction of narcotics in the county. So in any event we've achieved something good by exposing Camilla and Hugo.'

'Maybe,' said Charlotte, bringing the wine glass to her lips. 'Although it doesn't seem to be the case that the demand will go down simply because those two are gone. Presumably the Syndicates will take over.'

Per sighed. Nodded.

'That will have to be our colleagues in Stockholm's headache,' she said.

'Linn is going to live with her aunt down there, right? Who is she?' Per asked.

'I think so, apparently she's a nurse and has fared better in life than Camilla. But you wonder how Linn is going to handle that. You saw what attention Anton's note got in the press.'

'It's truly awful for Linn,' Per continued. 'All that's being written about her mother.'

'Yes, it's terrible. It will be interesting to see how the psychiatric investigation turns out. If it will be prison or hospitalization.'

'She's an ice-cold murderer,' said Per.

'The positive thing in all this darkness is that Anton's suicide note stirred a debate on how young people with mental illness don't get help.'

'Yes, in any event the enormous media coverage has made the politicians wake up – they're forced to debate and make changes. That was probably what Tomas wanted to achieve.'

Charlotte nodded. Placed herself in front of the drawer with the gun. She wanted to carry it on her person but that wasn't possible with children in the house. That went against all regulations.

'What will happen with Abbe Ali?' she asked.

'Don't really know. I hope we can protect him but that will probably be hard.'

The phone rang again and Charlotte sighed just as Anja came down from upstairs.

'Yes, this is Charlotte von Klint.'

'Carl here, am I disturbing you?'

You always disturb me, she thought, but answered no to her ex-husband.

'I want to congratulate you on the new house in Umeå. What number property is it since you left me? The fourth?'

Anja came up beside her, sniffing at the wine in the glass. Charlotte demonstratively moved it away.

'To what do I owe this honour?' she asked sarcastically.

'Anja told me that she's thinking about studying at Umeå University,' said Carl, and she knew exactly where the conversation was going. 'Over my dead body!'

'If you'll listen to me then—'

'Now you should listen to me. She's going to study at Lundsberg, as tradition dictates. I'm surprised, Charlotte, don't you want the best for your daughter?'

Charlotte took a few steps out into the hall. She wasn't prepared for the artillery that came from the man she had divorced four years earlier. She was still processing his betrayal.

'Of course I do,' she said.

'You should—'

'I can't talk about it now, you can call me tomorrow.'

'I called simply to tell you that Anja is never going to move up to Umeå,' he said and hung up on her.

The air went out of Charlotte. Would she ever be free from Carl?

The doorbell rang. She raised her eyebrows. Thought about Tony but dismissed the thought. She was protected.

'Are you expecting more help?' Per asked in surprise.

'No,' she said, and her heels echoed as she quickly walked over to the door. Looked at the screen that showed who was standing outside.

Ola Boman.

She adjusted her hair before she pushed down the door handle. The cold air that met her made the hairs stand up on her arms.

'Sorry to disturb you, but something has happened,' he said, leaning toward her. He had a bag from the state liquor store with him. *Nice,* thought Charlotte and let herself be embraced, taking in his scent in her nostrils.

'Per and Mia are here, but you're welcome of course. Come in,' she said. She waited for him to take off his jacket and then followed him into the kitchen.

As Ola stepped into the room she saw that Per lit up.

'Hey there, so you're here . . . How nice,' Per said, and was quick to pour wine for his colleague. Ola stopped him and held up the liquor store bag.

'I brought a little old-fashioned beer with me,' he said, laughing.

Beer, thought Charlotte. *You've got a lot to learn about me.*

'Yes . . . something has happened that I wanted to discuss with Charlotte, but it's good of course that you're here too.'

'I see, that's nice. What about?' said Per. 'What has happened?'

Charlotte moved closer to Ola. She was afraid of Tony and what he might do. It wore down her energy to constantly be prepared to fight.

'We haven't tracked down Tony Israelsson yet,' said Ola. 'But on a tip from Abbe we've searched the farm outside Mariefred that was his hiding place. The media are probably going to dub it the 'house of terror' or something like that because there were three bodies that are right now being taken in for identification. From what we can see, he has bigger problems than taking revenge on you.'

Charlotte did not let herself be calmed. Camilla's words were still present in her mind. She laughed to appear unaffected and was just about to raise her wine glass when Per's phone rang. He moved away. She looked at him, then at Ola who seemed to be looking for something in the tableware drawers, which were still empty.

'Do you have anything to open a beer bottle with?' he said, pointing at the bag he brought with him. She was just about to interrupt him when he opened the drawer with the gun. He turned around, raised his eyebrows and looked at her. She knew very well that it wasn't okay but didn't say anything. He placed a towel over the gun and closed the drawer. Charlotte's cheeks got warm and she took a sip of wine, relieved when Per came back after his call.

'That was IT Forensics. They confiscated Camilla's computer at the arrest on the bridge, where she had all the information about her operation. The one Tony wanted to get at.'

Charlotte nodded.

'IT Forensics told me that someone has emptied all the accounts that were linked to Camilla's operation – they're zeroed out.'

'When did this happen?' asked Charlotte.

'That's being investigated right now. But I hope it's not Tony who's got access to the accounts,' said Per.

Charlotte looked at Per.

'Could Linn have got access to the information on the computer?' he asked.

Charlotte shook her head. 'No, not without help, at least. And she doesn't seem to have had a clue about what her mother was doing. How much money did Camilla have in her accounts?'

Per leaned against the kitchen island. 'We don't know yet – enough to be able to live a good life. But that was criminal money that had to be laundered somehow.'

Charlotte raised her wine glass. 'Maybe through poker playing,' she said. She didn't know, of course, but she had her suspicions. It was not unlikely that Abbe had somehow managed to get access to the accounts, and he and Viggo were close friends.

'I want us to raise our glasses for Unni Olofsson, who sacrificed her life to expose the network that injured our children. Cheers for Superwoman Olofsson,' said Per.

'Yes, her murder and Frida's death meant that we could put Camilla and Hugo away,' Charlotte added.

Charlotte looked at Per and Mia, then at Ola. He smiled at her.

She took a sip of wine. Ola drank straight from the bottle, and for the first time she experienced beer drinking as something attractive. She was just about to set down the wine glass when they heard one of the large windows on the top floor shattering. The sound cut through the house and Mia shrieked. Before Charlotte had time to react Ola pressed her down on the floor behind the kitchen island. She tore out of his grip and threw herself toward the drawer, seizing the gun.

Tony is here, it's time, she thought.

Mia stared at her from where she was crouching and screamed for her children, who didn't respond.

'Anja!' Charlotte heard the panic in her own voice.

'Here!' Anja called from the hall.

'Damn,' said Per, taking the gun out of her hand; he got up and ran crouching to the stairs. Charlotte waited for the second shot. Prepared herself for it. Noted every sound. It was silent from the top floor where the boys were.

Charlotte followed him, staying right behind Per as he took the stairs two at a time. Would the shot hit her head or her back?

Her thoughts went in all directions. The boys were nowhere to be seen. No blood. Per called to them. No answer. The hockey sticks were on the floor. She stepped over them before they turned to Anja's room.

There they sat, the boys. On the bed, pressed against the wall. Terror in their eyes.

'Sorry, we were just trying to make a shot. It wasn't the plan that the puck would go so far . . .'

'I was the one who shot, Dad,' said Hannes.

'No, it was me,' said Simon. 'Not Hannes.'

Charlotte's legs gave way; she let her back meet the wall and slid down on to the floor in relief, and to be a little comical. She watched as Per went up and hugged them.

'It doesn't matter, boys,' said Charlotte, taking deep breaths to calm her heart rate. Laughed. It felt as if an electric shock had passed through her body.

'So what have we learned from this?' said Per, tousling Simon's blond hair.

'Not to make slap shots indoors.'

'Exactly,' said Per, laughing. He looked at Charlotte and shook his head. 'My God, I was quite sure it was a bullet that broke the window,' said Per.

'All of us probably were,' said Charlotte, getting up from the floor at the same time as the colleagues who'd been sitting in the car outside also stepped into Anja's room.

'Send the invoice for the broken window to me,' said Per.

'Not a chance,' said Charlotte. 'Simon can pay me back when he's a hockey pro, because, apparently, he can really shoot pucks,' she said, taking her gun back from Per.

ABOUT THE AUTHOR

Photo © 2021, Kajsa Göransson

Anki Edvinsson is a familiar face to many Swedes from her former career as a television host, journalist and weather forecaster. Edvinsson more or less grew up at a police station, spending her time with her father and his police colleagues. Her older brother also made a career within the police force.

Edvinsson moved from Stockholm to Umeå in the north of Sweden, where her husband grew up, and joined the local news team. Following her dream to become an author, she signed up for a writing course and began writing the crime novel that later became her debut. After eight years in the town and with valuable insights from her years as a reporter, the setting of the book of course became Umeå.

Curious to get to know her characters and explore the causes of crime – what makes a person choose that path? Who becomes a murderer? – she is studying for a bachelor's degree in criminology at Umeå University.

The Snow Angel is her first book to be published in English.

ABOUT THE TRANSLATOR

Paul Norlen previously translated *A Darker Sky* by Mari Jungstedt and Ruben Eliassen and *Hell Is Open* by Gard Sveen for Amazon Crossing. He lives in Seattle.

Follow the Author on Amazon

If you enjoyed this book, follow Anki Edvinsson on Amazon to be notified when the author releases a new book!
To do this, please follow these instructions:

Desktop:

1) Search for the author's name on Amazon or in the Amazon App.
2) Click on the author's name to arrive on their Amazon page.
3) Click the 'Follow' button.

Mobile and Tablet:

1) Search for the author's name on Amazon or in the Amazon App.
2) Click on one of the author's books.
3) Click on the author's name to arrive on their Amazon page.
4) Click the 'Follow' button.

Kindle eReader and Kindle App:

If you enjoyed this book on a Kindle eReader or in the Kindle App, you will find the author 'Follow' button after the last page.